DECEIVING DARKNESS

THE SHADOW DEMONS SAGA, BOOK 10

SARRA CANNON

Cover by Ravven

Get new release updates and exclusive content when you sign up for my mailing list.

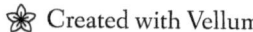 Created with Vellum

For our sweet little one that was lost.
And for the hope of a rainbow to come.

ONLY TIME WOULD TELL

HARPER

What should have been a night of victory and celebration had left me with an eerie feeling of dread in the pit of my stomach. The kind of feeling you get when you wake up from a dream terrified, even though you can't quite remember what it was about.

Two priestesses of the Order of Shadows were dead, I was finally home, and my dear friends in Cypress were free. I should have been on top of the world, dancing with the others in the throne room, but instead, I sat on the steps leading down to the dungeons, trying to figure out what had me so on edge.

"It was too easy," I whispered to myself.

Today, we had released four emerald gates—one in each US time zone to hit them at exactly three in the afternoon—and each one had been too easy.

Unlike the rituals we'd performed to free the sapphire gates, we'd met with zero resistance. Not from the witches of the town, which wasn't as much of a surprise since we'd started with our allies, but also not from any of the other gates.

With the sapphire rituals, we'd met larger and larger armies at each gate as the Order attempted to stop us from setting witches and demons free.

In the end, we'd still freed them all, but we'd lost many demons and witches along the way.

We'd expected the same today.

Even in our ally towns like Cypress, there were still witches who didn't want their demons set free. They were addicted to power, and they didn't want to lose even a single drop.

We'd expected at least some resistance from those witches.

Instead, they had all seemed to disappear. Anyone who'd openly opposed the freeing of the gates had left town in the night and simply walked away.

No one came to fight.

It should have been a relief, but it scared me.

The Order knew their emerald priestess was dead. They knew I had the master stone, which meant I had the ability to free the gates.

They also knew I was home. Jackson and I had fought some of the amethyst priestess's cat-like witches back in the past, so she had to know they were unsuccessful. And the ruby priestess had known almost as soon as I'd returned to the castle.

Was that why I was feeling worried tonight?

I stared down the steep stone steps toward the entrance to the dungeons.

The ruby priestess had suddenly appeared at the gates of the domed city this morning, claiming to make good on a promise she'd made to me that if I somehow managed to make it home, she would join my side in this fight.

And I'd just let her in.

Had I made a huge mistake? What kind of foolish person lets one of their greatest enemies into her home?

And for that matter, what kind of foolish witch shows up to her enemy's house and allows herself to be placed in the dungeons?

Something more was going on with her, and I itched to know what it was.

Jackson wanted to wait until morning to talk with the priestess. He said a full night in the dungeons alone would do her some good, but I wasn't sure I could wait.

The distant hum of music and the sound of steps dancing against the stone floor overhead called to me. Jackson and some of the residents of the city had wanted to throw a small party to celebrate my return, and of course, I had wanted to celebrate the fact that Eloise—a woman who had been like a mother to me—was finally free.

Yet, here I was. So not in the mood for celebrating.

There was still a very long battle ahead of us, and the weight of that knowledge was heavy on my shoulders. I placed a hand on my chest as my heart thrummed against it, and I closed my eyes, wishing my father was still alive. He was the true ruler of this kingdom, and he would have known what to do in a situation like this.

I took a deep breath and stood, my mind made up.

I headed down the steps, my green and white silk gown whispering behind me as it slid over stone. The moment I pushed through the doors to the lower dungeons, Gregory scrambled to his feet, his eyes wide with terror.

He gave a quick bow and cleared his throat.

"Princess," he said. "I wasn't expecting to see you down here."

I glanced toward the cell where we'd left the ruby priestess. I could just see the edge of her red skirt pooling on the floor.

"Is something wrong?" I asked.

"No, you just surprised me," he said. "I only sat down for a moment."

I smiled. Was that what had him so nervous all of sudden? He was afraid I'd be angry with him for sitting down? Maybe he'd accidentally fallen asleep, and I had scared the crap out of him.

He'd been on duty down here all day, insisting that guarding the ruby priestess was too important to entrust to anyone else.

"Why don't you take a break?" I said. "Go up and get a piece of cake or something to drink. Come back down in half an hour, or better yet, send another one of the guards down. You've been down here too long without taking some time for yourself."

"I'm fine. Truly," he said, darting a nervous glance toward the occupied cell. "I wouldn't dare trust such an important job to anyone else."

I shook my head. That had to have been at least the tenth time he'd said those words today.

"I'm ordering you to take a break, then," I said. "Send Easton down in a few minutes and don't come back until morning."

His eyes widened again, and he wiped a bead of sweat off his forehead. I'd never seen him like this. Maybe asking him to guard the ruby priestess had been a terrible idea after what he'd been through at the hands of her sister, Priestess Winter.

"Princess, I'm—"

"Gregory, don't make me ask you again," I said in a harsher tone.

I didn't like having to order anyone around, but I certainly didn't appreciate the way he'd been acting today. If he couldn't pull himself together, I'd have him taken off guard duty for the next month.

Maybe send him to Tahiti or someplace warm where he could take a damn vacation. I couldn't very well have my guard captain turning into a nervous cat who jumped at the slightest noise.

He opened his mouth to speak again but seemed to stop himself. He gave another low bow and disappeared around the corner.

"Sounds like you're having quite the party upstairs," Magda Thorn, ruby priestess of the Order of Shadows, said from her cell.

I wiped my sweaty palms against the front of my dress and stepped forward. "I'm surprised you can tell that from all the way down here," I said. "I can just barely hear a hint of it."

"I have very good hearing," she said, a slow smile spreading across her still-red lips. She hardly looked like a woman who had been sitting in a damp cell for the better part of a day.

"Why are you really here, Magda? If I may call you Magda."

"Such an old-fashioned name now," she said, adjusting her weight on the small stool. "Of course, I've gone by many names over the years. Whenever my oldest daughter would become pregnant for the first time, I would always have such fun choosing my next name. Not everyone gets a chance to reinvent themselves, you know."

I winced at the mention of the horrible things the priestesses did to their own daughters and granddaughters. When their oldest child would have three daughters of her own, the priestess would consume the soul of that oldest child and assume her identity in order to conceal the truth of their stolen immortality.

"A terrible practice, of course," Magda said. "But a necessary one. It's amazing the distasteful things you can get used to doing when you have no other choice."

"There is always a choice," I said, pulling a stool from the corner so that I could sit.

Magda laughed. "You do still have so much to learn."

"That's why I'm here now," I said. "You promised to give me information that could help us in this war."

"When I heard the music, I was afraid you would leave me in here all night without coming to say hello," she said. She seemed to notice my dress for the first time, and an appreciative smile spread across her face. "And don't you look pretty. An interesting choice of color. Celebrating the release of the Cypress gate, I imagine? And maybe a few others?"

I swallowed. So, they did know.

It was no secret that Cypress was our closest ally from the emerald gates. I'd tried to keep the information hidden to avoid making Eloise and her daughters a target, but somehow, the Order had found out, anyway.

"Funny how no one came to stop us," I said. "Do you want to tell me why?"

"It's not that complicated," she said with a shrug, as if I should have already figured it out myself. "We couldn't stop you from releasing the sapphire gates, and we lost too many of our own in the process. It's not the best use of our efforts right now. Besides, the more of our warriors who see just how strong you are and how free they could be someday, the more resistance we get inside our own covens."

I tried to hide a smile, but I hoped she was right about that. The witches who opposed us usually did it because they liked having the power of their demons inside them. But I also knew that a lot of the women taken into the Order had no idea what they were really doing until it was too late.

Most of them didn't find out about the demon part of it until the night of their initiation, and by then, the choice to back out had already passed them by.

If given the choice now, I hoped a lot of them would choose freedom, even if it meant giving up some of the power they'd come to love.

"So, what's a better use of your efforts, as you put it?" I asked.

"Harper, before I tell you anything, I want to make something very clear," she said, leaning forward slightly. "I'm not simply helping you out of the goodness of my heart."

I stared at her. The thought of this woman in front of me having any goodness in her heart was ridiculous. Good people didn't eat their daughter's soul or force demons into the naked bodies of eighteen-year-old girls against their will.

But I decided to at least try to keep things civil between us, rather than point that out to her.

"So, I'll ask you again. Why are you here?"

"I want to help you win this war without losing my own head in the process,' she said.

"It's not your head I want," I said.

Her eyes widened slightly, and she smiled, touching a hand to her chest. "Of course. I'd like to keep my heart, too, if you don't mind."

I raised an eyebrow. "Does that mean you actually have it with you?"

She sighed. "Yes, unfortunately that is a secret my dear sister Hazel did not share with me or any of our other sisters," she said. "Hazel was into all kinds of experiments with her magic, and I still have no idea how she managed to remove the master stone from her own chest and place it in that of one of her false daughters. The rest of us have poured over her journals to find any mention of how she did it, but she never wrote about the process that we know of, and of course, now she's gone. So, I'm afraid that secret died with her."

I released a relieved sigh. I hoped she was telling the truth about that, because I really didn't want to have to figure out where to find the hearts of the remaining priestesses in order to put an end to them all.

"That means you brought your heart—the master stone I need to free all the ruby gates—to a city where you would have no power," I said. "What made you so sure I wouldn't simply take the stone from your chest and end it right there the moment I let you into the city?"

"Because you're not that kind of person," she said. "It's one thing to take a life in battle, but I have come to you as a potential ally. And I'm more valuable to you as an ally."

"We'll see about that," I said under my breath.

"There are many things I know that you do not," Magda said. "If, for example, you knew where to find my sisters, Gladys and Alexandra, you would have already gone to attack them. Or am I wrong about this?"

I looked into her eyes and smiled. "And here I thought I was the one questioning you."

The ruby priestess threw her head back and laughed. "I knew I liked you," she said. "You have passion and fire and wit. In another lifetime, we could have been friends, I think."

I didn't respond to that. I couldn't ever imagine being friends with someone who had done the things she'd done.

"Come on, Harper. What do you say? I want to live," she said. Her eyes locked on mine with a mix of desperation and fear that surprised me. "I know I have done things you consider terrible in order to maintain my life and my youth for all these years, but I've gotten rather used to being here. I'm not quite ready to go, and I certainly don't want to die the way my two sisters did."

I paused to figure out how to respond to her.

I needed her help, even though I wasn't even sure I could trust whatever it was she planned to tell me. But I couldn't free the ruby gates and the thousands of innocent demons tied to them without killing her.

Without this woman dead, the war could not be won.

I didn't want to spend the next few years just trying to find one of her sisters, either, while more demons died every day. And I wasn't the kind of person who could make a promise I didn't intend to keep just to get ahead, no matter what was on the line.

"Before you make your decision, I will tell you this." She straightened and brought a trembling hand to her neck. It was the first sign she'd shown of being truly scared. "I think there may be a way to free the ruby gates without taking my heart. My connection to the Order would be severed and all the demons and witches in my coven would be free. I wouldn't live forever, of course, but I'm just at the beginning of a cycle now and this glamour is young. I would have at least forty years, I hope. That's all I'm asking."

My mouth fell open slightly, and I had to catch my breath.

"How?" I asked, moving to the edge of my seat. "How is that possible?"

"I can't give you all of that information yet," she said, her expression more serious than I'd ever seen it. "Not until I have your promise to do everything you can to spare my life. There are things about the Order of Shadows you couldn't even imagine to be true, and if I spill our secrets to you, there will be no turning back for me. Ever."

"You said there may be a way to free all the gates at once without killing you. You don't know for sure?" I asked.

My heart was practically beating out of my chest. Was she lying to me? Was this all some elaborate trap? Or were there truly secrets so deep we hadn't even considered them?

"Let's say it's a calculated guess," she said, a hint of a smile playing at her lips. "I won't lie and say it will be an easy path for you, but you will find out the truth of the Order one way or another, dear. If you survive until the end."

"A calculated guess? One you're willing to risk everything for?" I asked. "Tell me why, when you could try to fight with your sisters and possibly live forever?"

She grew quiet and leaned forward, her voice almost a whisper.

"Have you ever really wondered what the purpose of all this is?" she asked. "The recruiting and the demons. The constant cycle. Why would we do it?"

I shrugged. "That's easy," I said. "For power."

"And why do you think we want so much power?" she

asked. "In the past hundred and some-odd years, have we tried to take over the world? Steal the presidency? Change laws or become supreme rulers of all things? What's our end game? Have you ever even considered it?"

I studied her face, trying to figure out just what kind of game she was playing with me here.

"Why does it matter what your end game is?" I asked.

She raised an eyebrow and straightened. "Oh, it matters a great deal, child. It matters more than anything," she said.

"Okay, so what is it you're trying to accomplish?" I asked. "What is it you want to do with all this power?"

She leaned forward again, nodding. "That's exactly the kind of thing you need to be thinking about," she said. "It all goes so much deeper than you have dreamed. The consequences of losing this game are much bigger than you think."

Of course. She was definitely playing games now.

But something in her words had struck a chord inside me.

What did the Order want? Was there really more to it than just an endless cycle of initiations?

"So, tell me your personal end game," I said.

"I will help you unlock all the Order's secrets, but first, you have to agree to my terms, Harper. In exchange for what I know, you promise to do everything in your power to keep me alive. That's all I'm asking."

I stood and paced back and forth in front of the row of cells, my nerves making it impossible to sit still.

Could there really be a way to end the Order and free everyone without even having to kill each priestess? We could save years.

We could save so many lives.

Or I could lead everyone I care about into a trap designed to kill us all.

This was too big of a decision to make on my own, but I was pretty sure I already knew what Jackson would say. And probably most of the others.

None of the priestesses could be trusted.

And yet, she had come here knowing full well that I could have taken her heart from her chest the second she stepped through the entrance to the domed city. She wanted to live. I could see it in her eyes.

And she was afraid of something—or someone—else, far more than she was afraid of me. I could sense it.

So, the real question was whether I could truly trust myself.

"I don't mean to rush you, dear, but the clock is ticking," she said, her voice echoing against stone. "Some of what I have come to tell you is quite time sensitive, which is why I was glad to see you tonight rather than tomorrow morning, when it might be too late for people who matter to you a great deal."

My breath caught in my chest, and I closed my eyes, swallowing a lump of fear that formed in my throat.

Be smart, Harper. She's just trying to force you to promise.

The voice in my head was logical, but what if the priestess was telling the truth? What if I waited until morning and tried to argue my point with my friends while someone out there was dying? Aerden? Lea? My own sister, Angela?

I would never forgive myself.

Oh my god, what should I do?

I forced my feet to move again, thinking through it one more time.

All I had to promise was that I would do what I could to

save her life. If I did my best and still failed, it wasn't a betrayal. And if she lied to me, the deal was off, anyway.

Before I could change my mind, I walked toward the cell and locked eyes with one of my greatest enemies. Or possibly one of my most valuable allies.

Only time would tell.

"As long as every word you say to me proves true, I promise to do everything I can to save your life," I said. "But lie to me, and I will rip that ruby stone from your chest so fast, you'll wish you never showed up on my doorstep."

I pulled up the stool and sat down again, straightening my shoulders.

"Now, tell me what you know."

BUTTERFLIES

LEA

I stared at my reflection in the full-length mirror, looking for some outward sign of change.

A new wrinkle. A maturity in my eyes that matched the lessons my heart had learned. Even a single grey hair would have at least been evidence of something.

I looked exactly the same as when I woke up yesterday morning, but everything had changed since then. My entire world had been completely turned upside down. Everything I believed about myself, about love, about promises and loyalty. It had all changed.

Every time I closed my eyes, I could still see the bright light of a golem standing there in front of me as it brought the Stone Guardian—Kael—to his knees.

A golem Aerden had somehow conjured out of thin air.

Out of love for me.

How in the hell had he even done that?

I reached out to steady myself against the back of a nearby chair.

As the daughter of the king, I had seen just about every kind of power known to demonkind displayed on the battle-field and the training grounds. When I trained with the Resistance for all those years, I saw demons from nearly every corner of the kingdom fight and share their unique abilities.

But never once had I known a demon who could conjure such a large, powerful being made of pure light.

Not even the King's Guard had been able to touch the diamond Stone Guardian last night in the arena. He had swept them aside as if they were nothing more than flies buzzing around his head.

Even my own conjured arrows had failed to hurt him in any way.

And yet, the golem had taken Kael down in a single blow allowing Aerden a chance to split his diamond heart in two.

That golem had been the most powerful being I'd ever seen in my life, and to know that it had come from the same part of Aerden that loved me all this time in secret...

I turned away from the mirror, shaking my head.

How was I supposed to deal with all of this? How was I supposed to feel?

For one thing, I was furious at Aerden for lying to me. At Jackson for going along with Aerden's lie all these years and letting me believe I'd done something wrong.

That I'd lost his love, because I wasn't worthy of it.

I wanted to hold onto that anger and that pain, because it was familiar. Those were emotions I was used to, and they made me feel strong. In control.

But there was something else, too.

Something harder to define.

I brought a trembling hand to my lips, my stomach fluttering in a way I hadn't felt in decades as I remembered the way Aerden had kissed me.

Or had I kissed him?

I closed my eyes, lost for a moment in the memory of that kiss. Wondering what it might feel like to kiss him again.

A tear fell down my cheek, and I wiped it away so hard, I left a red mark streaked across my face.

No.

I was definitely furious. Too furious to start daydreaming about kisses from a liar. I would not go back to being that mushy princess who believed in happily-ever-afters.

Not after all these years of pain and heartache.

If he had told me the truth from the beginning, maybe things could have been different between us. Maybe we could have found a way to be together, despite the traditions and the promises that had been made.

But it was too late for that now.

There was work to do, after all. I couldn't afford to go back to that vulnerable girl I used to be. I had built walls around my heart for a reason, and I wasn't about to let one kiss pull them down.

We had a kingdom to save, and I had more important things to worry about than love.

I started toward the door, determined to find Aerden and tell him that kiss meant nothing to me, but my knees buckled, and I had to sit down. Why the hell was I so nervous?

I wish we'd had more time to talk through it last night, but after our kiss, the arena had filled with guards under the command of my father, all coming to fight the Stone Guardian. They had been shocked to see us sitting there, Kael's broken body stretched across the arena floor.

The King's Guard had bowed to us then, laying their swords at our feet in awe and gratitude.

And my father? He had fallen to his knees at the sight of Kael's transformed, lifeless body of stone.

He wept an ocean of tears with my mother at his side before he had thrown the diamond-tipped scepter to the ground and ripped the diamond necklace from my mother's neck.

When he finally stepped over to the guardian's body and placed his hand on the broken stone at the being's heart, his power had returned to him, knocking him off his feet for a moment before he stood, once again the tall, commanding king I had known as a child.

His hair was still streaked with white, but his eyes had lost their milky film and had been returned to the clear, strong blue of his youth. The curse had been broken for good, and the king was once again worthy of his name.

In truth, I would have gone through another century of heartache just to see the light in his eyes again. But my joy at seeing it returned was also tangled up with my guilt for leaving him in the first place.

If I had never left the King's City to chase after Jackson and Aerden...

Or if Aerden had just told me the truth back then, he never would have left at all...

I sighed and turned away from the mirror. I could get lost in a web of thoughts like this, but what good would that do anyone now?

The High Priestess's lackey had been killed, and the curse that held this once-great city prisoner was broken. This was a time for power.

And revenge.

It was not a time to think about romance and regrets. It was too late for that now, anyway.

Right?

Then why was I so scared to see Aerden again and tell him that?

The door to my room swung open, and my heart nearly stopped.

My mother's smiling face came into view, and I realized for a moment that I had wanted it to be him. I had wanted it to be Aerden.

I leaned back against the chair, my heart racing.

"Are you okay?" she asked, no doubt scared by the terrified expression on my face.

"I'm fine," I said, bringing a hand to my heart. "You just scared me the way you burst in here like that."

"I should have knocked, but I was dying to talk to you," she said. "Presha told me you were finally awake, and I couldn't wait to see you. You nearly slept the whole day away."

She threw her arms around me the way she used to when I was a shadowling. Tears stung my eyes again, but I pushed them back and pulled her closer.

"I've missed you so much," she said. "You have no idea how hard it was to see you thrown into the dungeons and not be able to do anything about it or tell you what was going on. And the idea of you marrying Kael had me so worried, I spent most of my days dreaming up ways to kill him if he so much as tried to lay a hand on you."

"I missed you, too," I said. "I never wanted to believe you both could have changed so much. Seeing what you'd become broke my heart. I thought I'd lost you forever. Or misjudged you somehow."

Tears glistened in my mother's eyes, and she stroked my braided hair.

"I tried to think of any way to give you some sign, but with that diamond at my throat and Kael always watching, I had no way to let you know what was going on with him," she said. "Not without putting everyone in danger. But you are my clever, strong warrior. Your father told me about the potion you had made so the two of you could talk. I wish I had been so smart."

"You never could have made it work with the way Kael watched you," I said. "But we don't have to worry about him, anymore."

"Thanks to you and Aerden," she said, throwing her arms around me again.

Aerden.

Even just hearing his name sent butterflies through my stomach. I groaned. It was going to be hard to stay mad at someone who made me feel like this.

I swallowed and tried to think of something else. Anything that would get my mind off the way I was feeling.

"What do you think is going to happen now?" I asked her. "How is father feeling?"

"He's back to his old self, Lazalea," she said, taking my hands. "I didn't think it was possible, but it's true. Most of his power has been returned, and he's dying to see you just as much as I was. Once I told him you were awake, though, he said he was going to call a meeting of the Council. There's still so much to figure out."

The Council.

The thought of it put a bitter taste on my tongue.

My father's most trusted advisors, and yet they had let this go on for how long? None of them were wearing diamond pendants around their necks or carrying scepters, were they?

I couldn't wait to hear their excuses as to why they sat back and allowed their great king to be cursed in such a way.

Tatiana especially.

Aerden and Jackson's mother had a lot to answer for, and I couldn't wait to question her.

I briefly touched my hand to my breasts, feeling for the diamond key that still hung there from a chain around my neck.

Tatiana had lied to me about where she'd gotten that key, and I intended to get the truth from her, even if I had to throw her in the dungeons to get it. I smiled at that thought. She wasn't the kind of person who would last long in the dungeons, and if I had anything to say about it, she would be spending a lot of her time there for the things she had done.

"Are they gathering now?" I asked. "This late?"

"We've been waiting for you and Aerden to feel up to it," she said. "He's only just woken up himself. Whatever happened last night must have drained both of you quite a bit."

I swallowed, not wanting to feel this way every single time his name was mentioned, but not entirely sure I could help myself.

"Is he feeling okay?" I asked, needing to know.

"Just tired," she said. "But Lisette was able to heal most of his wounds. He'll be back to himself in no time. I'm just so thankful neither of you were seriously hurt. Word of what you two have done has already spread through the city, and everyone is calling for you to be named Queen. Your father's afraid of an uprising. I still don't understand how you managed to defeat a Stone Guardian all by yourselves when the guards couldn't touch him."

I thought of the strange golem made of light and brought my hand to my lips again.

"I hardly understand it myself," I said as we walked down the hallway toward the throne room, the butterflies in my stomach determined to start an uprising of their own.

SOMETHING YOU COULD LOSE

AERDEN

I woke in my old room, disoriented. For a second, I thought I was dreaming.

To be back here after all this time.

Back where it all began.

It was surreal.

But I wasn't dreaming, and with that, came the memory of what happened last night.

Lea knows the truth.

I threw the covers off my body and dressed quickly, remembering the events of last night with an ache so deep it physically hurt. She'd looked bewildered at first, caught between heartbreak and hope, as our lips had met for the first time after all my years of dreaming.

But we'd been pulled away from each other so quickly after the guards arrived, we hadn't really had a chance to talk about what happened.

And if I knew her, she would be steaming mad today as the realization of what I'd done to her really sank in. She'd be angry and confused and working hard to throw those walls back up around her heart.

I wanted to catch up with her and try to explain myself before she got too worked up to even allow me in her presence.

Not that I could blame her. I'd made so many mistakes, I wasn't sure I deserved a second chance. I had to at least try though. I needed to find her. I needed more time to explain.

I shifted into demon smoke, soaring down the steps and hallways, following a path I hadn't traveled in over a century. The castle was huge, but I remembered the way to her room as if I'd just been here yesterday.

But when I knocked on Lea's door, my breath coming fast and my heart nearly jumping out of my chest, no one answered.

"There you are," a voice said as a pair of arms wrapped around my waist.

I spun, hardly recognizing the face of my younger sister Orian.

A lump formed in my throat. She'd been barely more than a shadowling when I'd left the castle. She looked so grown up now. A total stranger.

"I missed you, brother," she said. "I can't tell you how much."

"I missed you, too, Orian," I said, but the words didn't feel sincere. How could I miss a sister I had barely known?

"The princess isn't here, if that's who you're looking for," she said.

I glanced regretfully at the closed door. "Where is she?"

"They've called a Council meeting, I think," she said. "I'm never allowed to sit in on those, even though Mother says that someday I'll be given a seat on the Council myself if I'm loyal to the king."

I cleared my throat. They'd called a Council meeting and no one had come to tell me? Didn't I at least deserve to be there after everything else?

Old feelings of being tossed aside and powerless reared inside me, but I quickly pushed them back down. I was free now, and I was not going to let them push me aside anymore. If Lea was given a seat at that table, I deserved to be there, too.

I dared them to turn me away.

Besides, I had some questions for the members of the Council. And the king, too.

"You must be hungry after sleeping most of the day. Mother said you used up all your energy last night fighting Kael. I still can't believe he was some kind of Stone Guardian," she said, shuddering. "Come on, I'll walk you to the dining room. Dinner already passed, but I'm sure they'll make something for you if you ask."

"What's this Council meeting about?" I asked.

"I don't know. No one ever tells me anything directly," Orian said. "But I've learned to sneak around this castle and hide in the shadows when the grownups are talking. They never notice a small shadowling hanging around when they're deep in conversation."

I laughed at that. Orian was well over a hundred years old. Hardly a shadowling anymore, and yet in the lifetime of an immortal, she was still considered quite young here in the King's City.

"What have you heard about Jackson, then?" I asked, anxious for news about what was going on in the Southern Kingdom. Had Harper been found?

I wasn't sure how, but I still felt a strange connection to Harper's energy after a century of being linked to her bloodline through the Order of Shadows. For a long time, her energy had felt distant, but now, when I reached out for it, she felt closer. As if she were just around the corner.

Orian stuck her tongue out and twisted her nose. "I hate that name," she said. "Jackson. His name is Denaer. I don't know why anyone insists on calling him that human name."

"Because he likes it," I said. "And after everything he's done for me, I owe him that respect."

My heart tightened as I thought of the last time I'd talked to Jackson. I'd been so terrible to him, and I wanted the chance to tell him I was sorry.

My sister's face grew solemn for a moment before she nodded.

"I will call him that, too, then. If you want me to," she said. "Jackson."

She shrugged, as if the sound of it wasn't really that bad, after all.

"What are people saying about him?" I asked. "Any news about what's happened to him or Harper?"

"I'm sorry, I don't know," she said. "Last I heard, there were whispers about Harper being missing and Den—Jackson —searching for her."

I gritted my teeth and tensed beside her.

That was the last I'd heard, too.

If I could get Lea to talk to me, maybe I could convince her to make a trip with me down to the Southern Kingdom to see them. Although, I had a feeling she would be just as angry at Jackson right now as she likely was at me.

Or worse.

I shuddered to think of just how angry she might get when the dust settled. Last night, I had held her in my arms for a brief moment before the guards had come, and now I wondered if it would be the first and the last time I ever felt her lips on mine.

But I wouldn't lose hope now. I'd waited this long for my chance.

I could wait another century for her to get over her anger if that's what it took.

I turned to head toward the Council's chamber near the throne room, and Orian frowned.

"The dining hall is this way," she said, pulling me in the opposite direction.

"I'm not going to the dining hall," I said, pulling her arm from mine. "If the Council is meeting, I intend to be there."

I expected to see sadness in her eyes, but instead, there was a flash of worry. Fear.

"What?" I asked.

She quickly changed her expression, but I was pretty sure I knew what her fear had meant.

Someone had sent her after me to keep me from that meeting. Mother?

Anger flared inside me like a hot flame. Even after all of this, she was still trying to control me. Well, I was going to have to show her just how wrong she was.

"Why don't you go ahead and try to get them to make something up for me," I said. "I'll join you there later if I can. If not, I'll look for you tomorrow, and we'll catch up, okay?"

I didn't even give her a chance to argue with me. I shifted to black smoke and flew down the corridor to the throne room, reforming just outside the door where the Council was known to meet.

I didn't even bother knocking. I walked past the guards and threw the door open as several surprised faces turned to stare at me.

My eyes locked on those of my mother, though, and refused to let go. Her shock and disappointment at seeing me told me everything I needed to know.

Orian could pretend she was just a shadowling interested in seeing her long-lost brother all she wanted, but I was not as dumb or foolish as I had once been. I had been made to obey others for as long as I could stand, and now that I was truly free, I was never going to cower to anyone else's orders or manipulations again.

Besides, none of them would be sitting here now if it hadn't been for Lea and me having the courage to fight Kael last night. In his Stone Guardian form, he could have ripped his way through this whole city if he'd wanted to.

No, I deserved to be here just as much as anyone else, and I refused to let them discuss what came next without me here.

"See?" Lea said, standing. "I told you he would want to be here."

My mouth fell open in surprise as I shifted my gaze to hers. She met my eyes and then quickly looked away, but not before I saw the mix of anger and loyalty tucked away inside.

I closed my mouth around a smile as I pulled a chair from the corner of the room and sat down beside a member of the Council named Jailan. He nodded to me, respect shining in his eyes.

"I apologize for starting without you, Aerden," the king said with a glance toward my mother. "Your parents insisted you needed a few days to recover after what you had been through."

"I'm actually feeling stronger than I have in a long time," I said, my head held high.

My mother, on the other hand, lowered her eyes.

She didn't want to have to face me after everything she'd done, but I wasn't going anywhere just yet. She deserved her shame, and I deserved some answers.

"What are we talking about?" I asked, reaching for a pastry in the center of the table before leaning back casually in my chair, as if I had always belonged here.

Orian was right about one thing. I was starving.

A quick glance at Lea showed a small smile on her lips that she tried in vain to suppress. She might be angry with me, but we were still a team, and that gave me courage and hope. A dangerous mixture for anyone who dared cross me right now.

"The future of the kingdom," Lea's father said. "I have just explained to the Council the curse Kael placed on me, though it seems no surprise to anyone here. The fact that he was a diamond Stone Guardian in disguise, however. That seems to have surprised everyone."

"How is that even possible?" my father asked. I hadn't seen him or spoken to him in over a hundred years, and yet he'd barely glanced at me since I'd walked in, as if I was nothing to him.

I pushed my own hurt deep down and listened as the conversation erupted into different theories and concerns.

Lea raised her hand, and everyone grew silent. "We don't have to know how it's possible," she said. "Only that it is. Which means any demon in this city could be a Stone

Guardian in disguise. We need to be more careful than ever of who we trust."

She turned her attention to my mother, but before she could say what was on her mind, the king began to speak.

"I did some research last night into the legends about the Stone Guardians, and I couldn't find a single reference to one of these beings having the ability to shift into demon form," he said. "Either this is an ability we simply did not know about, or the magic he used came from the High Priestess herself. It's possible either form was some kind of elaborate illusion. I've given it quite a bit of thought, and I think this is why he chose to slowly drain my power over time, rather than take it for himself all at once. He needed a constant flow of power in order to retain his demon illusion."

"That makes sense," my mother said, and I bristled at the sound of her calm voice. "And it makes it highly unlikely that there are other guardians masquerading here in the city as demons."

"Of course, this is just speculation," the king said. "Until we know for certain, Lea is right. We need to be very careful of who we trust, even among those of us here in the city walls."

"Kael told you the High Priestess herself sent him?" Jailan asked, stroking his cheek in thought. "Did you ever have any proof of that yourself? Besides the fact that he used diamonds to drain your power and control your movements?"

"Isn't that enough?" Lea asked.

"No, it isn't," Jailan said. "Not to my mind, it isn't."

"And why is that?" she asked.

"Because if the High Priestess truly sent Kael here and threatened our princess's life and the life of everyone in this city if the king did not submit, then she has made a direct attack on us here," he said.

"And how is that different from before?" I asked, getting the gist of his argument. It might have seemed logical to him, but it made me furious. "Are you saying you don't consider turning the entire Northern Kingdom into a barren wasteland, destroying nearly every village from the mountains down to the borderlands to be a direct attack on the king and his people? Or is it only those here in the safety of the city who truly matter?"

Jailan cleared his throat and sat stiffly in his chair as he gathered his thoughts.

"I was simply making a point that while—"

"It's true," the king said as he looked at me. There was shame and regret in his ancient eyes. "When I first built the great wall around this city, I truly had the best intentions in my heart. I meant to save as many as I could and have my patrols protect those who could not come to the city. I was a coward, and I made a grave mistake in deciding not to fight the Order of Shadows. A mistake I will not make again."

"Are you saying we have your support now in fighting against the Order?" Lea asked, nearly bouncing on the edge of her seat.

"That's for the Council to decide, isn't it?" my mother asked.

Lea turned a stare full of daggers toward my mother, but before she could say anything, Lea's own mother, the queen, spoke up for the first time since I'd entered the room.

"That's what we're all here to discuss," the queen said. "But now that my husband has been restored to his full power, this Council will not have the power it once had. You all must know that by now."

"We have been loyal to the king, and we will remain loyal," Jailan said, bowing his head. "Even if that means war against the Order of Shadows."

"Now, wait just a minute," my mother said. "I don't think we should rush head-first into a war we cannot win just because Kael claims to have been working for the High Priestess. No one even knows for sure that she exists at all. She could be nothing more than a rumor, and Kael himself could have been a farm boy who found a deposit full of diamonds under the dirt. We need to examine this more closely and discuss it with clear heads before we make a decision that could put every demon inside the walls of this great city in danger."

"Why are you so hesitant to fight the Order of Shadows?" Lea asked, her voice barely more than a growl. "If I didn't know better, I would say you're trying to help them."

Everyone in the room gasped. Everyone except for me.

Chills spread across my skin as if ice had slid down my spine. Lea had a point. One I hadn't considered until this moment. Up until now, I saw my mother's actions as incredibly self-serving, but I hadn't actually imagined she could be working with the Order of Shadows.

Was that even possible?

Hadn't people also believed Lea's father was possibly working for the High Priestess?

When the king seemed to abandon all the demons outside the city walls, Jackson told me that rumors spread about the king's loyalties. Some believed he was scared. Others believed he was weak and greedy.

But a lot of demons believed the king was loyal to the High Priestess.

And his actions would have supported that.

After all, he had been controlled by the High Priestess through Kael's curse.

What if something similar was going on with my own parents?

I needed to talk to her before she started accusing my mother of things that could put her life in danger.

Lea reached for the chain around her neck. A chain I knew held the diamond key I had given her just before I left.

Before she could pull the key free, I stood.

"Lea, can we talk for a few minutes?" I asked, swallowing nervously as she turned her glare on me. As if she hadn't been angry enough, I just had to go and make it twice as bad.

"Please," I said, not looking away, despite the fury in her eyes.

She straightened, glanced at my mother, and then dropped her grip on the chain. "Does anyone mind if we take a break?" she asked through clenched teeth. "I could use some fresh air, anyway."

"Twenty minutes?" the king asked, and everyone stood. "Meet back here when the break is over. We still have a lot to discuss.

Lea hardly took her eyes off me as she stormed out of the room, and my heart pounded so hard, I was sure everyone around us could hear it.

When we were a safe distance away from the others and standing on the steps of the castle's entrance, she turned on me.

"What the hell, Aerden?" she asked. "Do you know how

long I've been waiting to confront Tatiana about this key? My father needs to know the truth. We all do. She's hiding something, and you know it just as well as I do."

"I know," I said, wanting so badly to reach out and touch her hand. To pull her into my arms. To talk about how I was feeling.

But I forced myself to stay on the topic of my mother.

For now.

"Then why did you stop me just now?" she asked. She paced along the first step, back and forth so fast, she was making me nervous.

"Because you've already decided my mother lied to you because she's part of some evil scheme," I said. "What if it's not like that, at all?"

"What do you mean?" she asked. "What other reason would she have to lie about a diamond key? She's potentially putting this whole city at risk. If Kael was working for the High Priestess, what's to say your mother isn't working for her, too?"

"If your father made a deal with the High Priestess in order to keep you safe, who's to say my mother didn't also make a deal? A deal she's bound to honor now, whether she likes it or not?"

Lea's eyes widened, and her mouth opened slightly. She stopped pacing and sat down on the top step.

"I hadn't thought of that," she said. "Do you think that's how she got the diamond key in the first place?"

"I think we have to at least consider the possibility," I said. "Where else would a woman like my mother have gotten a key like that?"

"What about the book, though? What about Trention?"

she asked. "What's her excuse for taking that book away and sending him to the dungeons to die?"

I shook my head, a lump forming in my throat at the thought of my dear friend.

"I don't have all the answers, Lea. Maybe that was part of the deal she made with the High Priestess," I said. "The pages of that book were decorated with the dust of diamonds. Maybe there's something about other continent the High Priestess doesn't want anyone to know about. Maybe part of my mother's agreement was that she had to keep that information hidden. She could be under the High Priestess's control, the same way your father was."

"So, why don't we just go in there and confront her with what we know?" she asked. "I don't see how keeping it secret is going to help anything."

I sat down beside her, wanting so badly to take her hand but terrified she'd punch me in the face for even trying.

"If we bring it out into the open, we aren't going to get any answers," I said. "If she's under some kind of agreement or curse of her own, she won't be able to tell us what's really going on. No more than your father was able to tell you the truth at first. And if the High Priestess has someone watching her the way Kael was watching your father, she'll know we're onto her. It could put my mother's life in danger."

Lea nodded, as if finally hearing me.

"Let's let her believe we buy this story about the shaman in the borderlands. She'll have no idea we suspect her, which means we'll be able to watch her more closely. See if she leads us to new information about the High Priestess," I said. "It's the only way to really find out what's going on. If we confront her, she's going to lie, either because she has to or because she wants to. And we'll never know which."

Lea sighed and let her head fall into her hands.

"When did things become so complicated?" she asked. "Remember when we used to sit here on these steps and just watch the suns go across the sky?"

I laughed. "We used to complain about how bored we were," I said. "Never a dull moment now."

She smiled and looked up at me. "Be careful what you wish for," she said.

The light of the moons shone on her tanned skin, and I itched to move a strand of hair that had fallen across her eyes.

I loved her so much, it ached to be this close to her and not have her. Having the memory of her lips on mine only made it worse.

But at least she was here. She was talking to me. That was better than I'd expected.

And probably better than I deserved.

"Lea—"

"Don't," she said, her body tensing immediately. "I know you want to talk about what happened last night, but I'm just not ready, Aerden. I don't even know how I feel about all of it. Let's just focus on figuring out how to keep the city safe and how to keep fighting the Order. That's what matters most, right?"

I stared at her, my heart wanting to shout that no, nothing mattered even half as much as the conversation she refused to have. But I didn't want to push her, either.

I wasn't sure I'd like what she would say.

She deserved time to figure out how she felt, and I needed to respect that.

"Okay, so how do we keep everyone safe? How do we keep fighting?" I asked. "The emerald priestess is dead, but what about the others? What about the High Priestess? We don't even know what she'll do now that we've killed Kael. She could send an entire army of hunters over that wall any minute in retaliation. We have no idea what her next move might be, but if we hold back on what we suspect might be true about my mother, maybe she'll lead us to an answer."

Lea nodded. "Maybe you're right," she said. "But sooner or later, we're going to have to confront her directly."

"Let's just give it some time. Find out what we can about this key on our own now that we're free to explore the castle," I said. I glanced at her, watching her reaction carefully. "Maybe we could make a trip down to the domed city. A lot has happened since we saw them, and Harper's been missing. We should find out if they need our help. And they need to know what's happened here, too."

She tensed again, which wasn't really a surprise.

"I'm not sure I want to see either one of them right now," she said. "But I do want to know if Harper's home. Maybe we can send a messenger. Besides, if we go anywhere, we should be going to the Underground. If my father is serious about joining us in the war against the Order of Shadows, Andros should be here to speak for the Resistance. We need to join forces against them and fight together."

"I still can't believe Ezrah just sent Andros back to the Underground, instead of telling him to come into the city last night," I said. "What was he thinking?"

Lea shrugged. "I don't know," she said. "I guess he was still worried Andros would have to fight his way inside."

Lea and I had been fleeing the city last night to meet up

with Andros when Kael had intercepted us and tried to kill us. Ezrah—a spy of the Resistance who had risen through the ranks of the King's Guard here in the city—had been on his way to bring Andros and his men to help when Kael had captured him and put him in chains.

When the fight started, Ezrah had managed to get free with the help of a fellow guard. Instead of coming to fight against an enemy like Kael on his own, he'd fled the city, hoping to find Andros waiting.

By the time they'd made it to the city gates, though, word that we'd defeated Kael was already spreading through the city. Once they were sure we were safe, Ezrah had told Andros to head back to the Underground and wait for word from us to decide our next moves.

"I'm just glad he's safe," I said. "Things could have ended up much worse last night."

She gave me a sideways glance.

"Eventually, we're going to have to talk about that thing you created out of light," she said. "I don't even know what to call it? A guardian? A golem? Did you have any idea you could do that?"

I shook my head, still hardly able to believe what I had done.

"I have no idea how I did it or if I will ever be able to do it again," I said. "All I know is that Kael was going to kill you, and I couldn't let that happen. I wasn't going to lose you again, Lea."

Silence stretched between us, full of words we couldn't say. Feelings we didn't know how to express.

I wasn't going to push her, but I also wasn't going to let her live another day thinking she wasn't loved.

"It's time to go back in," Lea's mother said from behind us, making us both jump.

How long had she been standing there?

"We'll be there in a second," Lea said, standing quickly, her cheeks red as if we were teenagers who'd been caught making out.

The thought of it nearly made my own cheeks turn red.

When the queen had disappeared back inside the castle, I turned to Lea.

"If you want to confront my mother about the key tonight, you know that I'll follow your lead and trust you one hundred percent," I said. "But I think we might have a better shot at investigating this on our own. You have your father back, Lea. I'd like a chance at getting my mother back, too. If the High Priestess has someone watching her, it would explain everything that's happened."

Lea paused near the door for a moment before speaking.

"We'll see what we can find out, but we need answers, Aerden. One way or another, I'm going to get them," she said.

I nodded. "Thank you."

She opened the door, but she still didn't move to step inside.

"Aerden?" she said, only slightly turning toward me. I could have sworn her hands trembled slightly for just a second.

"Yes?" I asked.

Slowly, her eyes lifted to mine.

"I'm going to need some time to work through these feelings," she said. "But no matter what happens from here, we're still a team, right? Even if..."

Her voice trailed off, and I saw in that moment just how much my lie had hurt her.

Because of me, she believed, deep down, that love was conditional.

And why wouldn't she believe that?

She'd thought Jackson loved her with the light of a thousand suns one moment and not the next. She'd spent the next few decades blaming herself. Believing she was somehow flawed or unworthy.

I vowed then and there to dedicate the rest of my life to showing her that true love was not something you could lose.

"No matter what," I said. "Even if you never feel the same way about me, I'm here for you, Lea. Forever."

Her eyes glistened with tears for just a brief second before she turned away and disappeared into the castle.

THE LEADER OUR PEOPLE DESERVE

LEA

The rest of the meeting dragged on now that I had agreed to keep my mouth shut about Tatiana's involvement in all this.

The Council talked about ways to protect the city like increasing the patrols of the King's Guard and even seeing about creating some kind of dome the way Harper had in the Southern Kingdom. I didn't want to break it to them, but none of this mattered if another Stone Guardian was hiding here in the city, disguised as a demon.

Or if any of the hundreds of them locked away in that room beneath the castle woke up.

We still didn't know anything about how those rows and rows of Stone Guardians had come to be there or what Kael had intended to do with them, and until we had answers, their existence put everyone in danger.

Maybe Aerden had been right in suggesting we contact Harper and Jackson. This was too complicated and dangerous for me to put a thing like my own pride in the way of winning this war. It didn't matter how angry or foolish I felt. We needed to get in touch with them and see if we could all work together now that my father was free of Kael's curse.

I just hoped Harper was home safely. If not, Aerden was right that we needed to go help them bring her home. She deserved that and much more.

Aerden wouldn't even be sitting here if it wasn't for her.

"Lea?"

My mother touched my arm, and I jumped, realizing I'd been lost in my own thoughts for the last half hour at least.

"I'm sorry, I wasn't listening," I said. "There's just so much going on. It's a lot to process."

"Your father was just wondering what you thought of asking the leader of the Resistance to join us here in a few days to talk about our next moves," she said. "What was his name again?"

"Andros," I said, smiling at the thought of him sitting here in the Council room, eating pastries with all these people he'd hated for so long. "We should definitely be working with him, but just know that he might be reluctant to come here. It might be better for us to meet on neutral ground at first."

"I can't blame him for what he must think of me," my father said. "But if we're going to defeat the Order, we're going to need his help. He knows more about how to fight them than we do."

"We should get Harper and Jackson up here, too," Aerden said. "Maybe call together an official summit or something. All the leaders in one place. Working together, we might really be able to put an end to the Order of Shadows, once and for all."

"Have them bring Illana, too. It would mean so much to

me to have all my children home again," Aerden's mother said, tears shining in her eyes.

I watched her closely, trying to decide whether she was being sincere or not.

I had really been looking forward to exposing her lie about the key tonight, but maybe Aerden was right. Maybe I had misjudged her.

I wondered if she knew about the Stone Guardians beneath the dungeons.

I was surprised my father hadn't brought it up in the meeting, but since he didn't, I didn't either. And when he called for the meeting to end sometime well after midnight, I caught his eye and he motioned for me to join him in his office.

Aerden lingered near the door after everyone else had left, but I shook my head and he reluctantly walked away. He still wanted to talk about what happened last night, but I needed more time to work through my feelings.

I pushed it out of my mind as best I could and followed my father into his large private office.

I stood in the doorway, suddenly overwhelmed with memories of the past.

The room was exactly how I remembered it, even though I hadn't been here in years. Decades. Books lined the walls on shelves carved from elder trees and brushed with gold. A pale silver rug with red threads woven through it like fire lay across an obsidian floor that sparkled when the light from the lamps hit it just right.

A large, leather-bound journal lay open on his desk, a quill made from the light blue and black feather of a winterbird lying across the top of it.

He sat down in the large chair behind his desk and smiled at me.

"What are you grinning at, my princess?" he asked.

I let my eyes travel the length of the room, taking it all in.

"I remember coming in here as a shadowling. You would point me toward the bookcases and tell me to read something while you worked," I said. "I used to sit right there on that bench in the window and read for hours. But mostly, I would watch you and wish I could be just like you."

His eyes met mine, and the clear, honest blue of them nearly brought tears to my eyes.

"You are going to be a good queen," he said. "I always knew you would be."

The smile fell from my face.

"What are we going to do about the Stone Guardians beneath the city?" I asked. "I thought for sure you'd bring them up with the Council."

He sighed and shook his head. "We have to be careful how we deal with this," he said. "And who we tell. If the residents of the city find out there are a hundred or more of those sleeping giants just beneath our feet, there will be mass chaos. Demons will leave the city in droves, making them easy targets for the hunters out there searching."

"We can't sit here and do nothing, though," I said. "If even one of those things wakes up, it's going to be mass chaos, anyway. The demons of the city might have a better chance against the hunters than a group of Stone Guardians."

"What do you think we should do?" he asked.

I sucked in a nervous breath. It was a strange position to be in after the past few months of being treated more like a prisoner than a princess. My father, the king, was asking my advice, as if I were the most important person in the world to him.

As if he truly respected what I had to say.

It was amazing just how much could change in a few days.

"I think we should try to destroy them, if we can," I said. "When I was down there, it looked like someone had been carving the sapphires mined by the prisoners into the shape of hearts for those Stone Guardians. I have a feeling all it would take to wake one up would be to put one of those stones in the right place."

"So, we move the sapphires as far away from there as possible," Father said, nodding. "I can have that done by morning. Then we do some experimental research. See what we have that can harm them in any way."

"Exactly," I said, walking around the room and studying the various books on the shelves. "And if we can, we find out who was working down there, and we put them in the dungeons until we know for sure whether they worked for Kael because he forced them to or because they wanted to."

"It's a solid plan," he said. "As is the plan to bring the leaders of the Resistance and the Southern Kingdom here for a meeting. You know them both, Lea. I think it would be a good idea for you to be the one in charge when they get here."

I glanced up from the book I'd taken in my hand, my mouth open in surprise.

"What do you mean?" I asked.

Father stood and came over to me. "I've been giving this a lot of thought since last night," he said. "I failed this kingdom, Lea, even if my heart was in the right place. I can't turn around now and ask them to trust me after all the mistakes I've made. The demons of the Northern Kingdom deserve a leader who's been fighting for them all this time. Someone who already knows a lot about the war against the Order and has been right there on the front lines, fighting every battle along the way."

"Father, you—"

"You're the leader our people deserve," he said. "If you'll accept it, I'm going to step down and give the crown to you, Lazalea."

I hardly knew what to say. Was I really ready for that kind of responsibility?

Andros had been begging me for years to take the crown by force, saying the demons of the Northern Kingdom would follow me if I was on the throne. And here my father was, handing it to me.

"We need you," I said to him. "You have experience commanding the King's Guard. They're loyal to you."

"They're loyal to you, too," he said. "And as Queen, they'll follow you. They all will."

I turned and paced the floor, trying to wrap my head around this. As if the past twenty-four hours hadn't been crazy and life-changing enough, now I was being asked to take over as Queen?

"Do you really know what you're getting yourself into?" I asked, finally. "As Queen, all the decisions about what to do, who to fight, where to go and who to let into this city would all be mine. I could choose who was on the Council or who was named as Captain of the Queen's Guard."

My father smiled and raised an eyebrow. "I'm fully aware of the types of decisions you'd be able to make on your own," he said. "I trust you to make the right ones, Lea."

"Even if I say I'm going to tear down the wall you've spent the past several decades building?" I asked.

He made a face at that, but he nodded. "Even if you tear down my wall," he said. "Of course, I'd like to still be allowed to advise you as to why that's a terrible idea."

I laughed. "I'm sure you would," I said. "But if you hand that throne and crown over to me, it's my decision in the end."

"The throne is yours if you'll have it," he said. "It's a huge responsibility, but I know you're ready. I wish I had given it to you a long time ago. Things might have been very different. The Order might have already been defeated if I'd fought instead of hiding away like a coward."

I took his hand and squeezed.

"We could spend a lifetime talking about our regrets," I said. "Let's not waste any more time with that. It's a new day. A new chance to make things right."

My father wrapped his arms around me.

"Promise me you'll think about it," he said.

I lay my head against his chest, so grateful to have him back to his old self.

And not quite ready to take his place.

"I will," I said. "But first, let's figure out what to do with these Stone Guardians. Once the city is safe from that threat, we'll discuss it again."

"Deal," he said.

He held me for a few minutes longer, and I wished I could travel back in time to when I was still a shadowling and things were simpler. Before we knew just how destructive the Order of Shadows could be.

Before so many of our mistakes had been made.

TRUTH AND LIES

HARPER

The ruby priestess straightened, her eyes clear as she began to speak.

"One of the main reasons you met no resistance at the emerald gates is that my sisters are busy working on another plan," Magda said. "A plan I have a role in, myself."

I could hardly draw a breath. I was nervous, excited, terrified.

Oh, God, please don't let this be a huge mistake.

"Which of my friends is in danger?" I asked.

"Many of them, I imagine," she said, taking her sweet time spilling the details. "After some discussion, it was decided we should attack on several levels at once. Split your forces and your attention to make you weaker."

I wanted to shout at her that we were not here having tea and that she should just spit it out, but I forced myself to hold onto my composure.

"Some of our instructions came from the High Priestess

herself," she said. "And some of it we decided on our own as a group."

My mouth went dry. This was not going to be good.

"Tell me the plan," I said. "Where will they attack and when?"

I needed to get it out of her as quickly as possible, so I could take the information upstairs and we could decide as a group how to handle it. Jackson would be furious with me for talking to the priestess on my own and making promises, but I could make it up to him later.

If people we loved were in danger, I wanted to know about it.

"First, understand that each of us has a role to play, and like I said, that includes me," she said. "If I don't follow through with my contribution, they will all know I've betrayed them, and it will be over for me, anyway. I told you when we first met that I was replaceable, just like any Prima."

This was getting more complicated by the minute. How would I even know whether to trust her if she was preparing to have her witches attack me or people I cared about?

"Start with that, then," I said. "What's your role in all this?"

"I have placed some bombs in your castle," she said simply, and I nearly fell out of my chair.

There were a few hundred demons and witches upstairs right now celebrating. Jackson was up there. Mary Anne.

"Bombs? Where?" I asked. "When will they go off?"

Then I realized another part of the horror of it all.

"And how the hell did you plant a bomb from inside that cell?"

We had Gregory search her before he threw her in there. We took all her jewelry.

"Don't worry," she said, her voice calm. "It won't go off until just before dawn. By then, most of these demons will be long gone, safely tucked into their beds asleep. It's you and your demon the Order wants most, so one of the bombs is in your bedroom."

I stood. "How many are there?"

"Two," she said. "The other is in the tower room with the Winter girl. That was my sister Alexandra's idea. She always looked up to Eloisa, and she was heartbroken when you killed her. The fact that one of her daughters betrayed her was too much for Alexandra to bear. I tried to tell her the girl might never wake up from whatever is going on inside that cocoon, but she wouldn't listen to me."

Zara.

"I have to move the bombs," I said, starting for the door.

Zara had sacrificed herself to save my life. I couldn't let anything happen to her.

"You can't do that," she said.

"Then walk out of that cell and stop me."

But before I could make it to the first step, she called out to me, her words stopping my feet dead.

"The moment you touch the bomb, it will detonate and kill you. There's no way to disarm it. The bombs will both go off, and there's nothing you can do about it now."

Tears formed in my eyes.

"Then I have to move Zara out of that room," I said.

"If you want to have any hope of her ever coming out of that cocoon, I highly suggest you do," she said. "But I assure you, it can wait a few hours. Or at least until our conversation is over and you hear the rest of the plan. Now, please, sit down."

I almost left the room, desperate to have Zara moved as far away from that part of the castle as possible, but then I thought of the possibility that something just as terrible could happen tonight before I came back. Something I could have stopped if I'd stayed to listen.

"If she dies—"

"Yes, yes. You'll rip my heart out," she said, waving her hand in front of her. "Do you think I'd really let her die when you could just come down here and kill me in an instant? Now, sit down."

I took a deep breath. She had a point there, except that somehow, she'd gotten out of this cell to place those bombs.

I stared at the guard's stool and bit my lower lip.

Gregory.

That's why he was so nervous and jumpy. But why would he betray me? He'd been loyal to my father for a very long time.

"You would be a terrible poker player, my dear," Magda said.

"What?" I asked, pulling myself from my thoughts.

"You wear your thoughts in your expression," she said. "You might as well have been speaking aloud just now. But don't be too hard on poor Gregory. He owed me his life, and he had no choice but to help."

I sat down and closed my eyes, letting my head fall into my hands.

"That's how he survived, then? You found him there in Winterhaven and set him free."

"When it comes to life on someone else's terms or death,

most people will choose life. No matter what they have to do to keep it," she said. Her eyes took on a faraway look and she pressed her hand to her chest.

From the look on her face, I wondered if she was still talking about Gregory.

"What else do you have to tell me?" I asked. "What's the amethyst priestess's role in the attack?"

"Gladys." A sour look crossed her features.

Clearly not her favorite sister.

"She has the best warriors in her coven, having trained many of them from a very young age to be her personal army," Magda said.

"Yes, I've had the unpleasant experience of meeting some of her collared warriors," I said, remembering my fight with them when I was stuck in the past. If Jackson hadn't come through when he did, I wouldn't have survived it.

"Gladys takes her affinity to panthers very seriously," Magda said, nearly rolling her eyes. "Her part of the plan has already been set in motion, I'm afraid. Stopping her is not an option, but you might be able to save the ones she took. She's been instructed not to kill them. Not yet."

My stomach tightened, and I drew my hands into my lap, clutching at my skirt.

"Who?" I asked.

"A small army of demons on their way to the King's City," she said. "I can't remember the name of their leader, only that something about a dragon comes to mind."

I brought a hand to my mouth.

"Andros," I whispered.

She smiled, as if we weren't talking about a dear friend of mine being captured by the Order.

"Yes, that's the one," she said. "She was hoping to get the chance to use his power for herself, but the orders to take him came straight from the High Priestess. Her hunters are to capture and hold him until the full moon. On the human side, of course. The High Priestess has plans for him."

"Where is the High Priestess?" I asked. "Who is she?"

Magda tilted her head and stared at me. "That's a more complicated question than I could answer in one evening," she said. "What I know about the High Priestess will have to wait until another day if you hope to save your friends."

I bit my lip again, nearly drawing blood.

There were no easy answers here, it seemed.

"So, Gladys has Andros and part of the Resistance Army being held by her hunters. What are they going to do with him?" I asked.

"Make him and all of his friends slaves to some of the recently freed demons," she said. "They are planning a mass initiation that can only be done the night of the full moon. I don't know her plans for these new witches they're adding to the coven, but it's something big. They need the power of a great demon for it, which is why they targeted Andros."

I couldn't let them do that to Andros.

"Where are they keeping him?" I asked.

"I don't know, but I know where he'll be," she said. "I can tell you where my sister's home is when the time comes."

I bit my lip. She could also tell us a location that would wind up being a trap.

This whole conversation could be a trap.

I pushed the thought from my mind. We'd figure out how to help Andros without getting caught ourselves once I had all the information.

"And the citrine priestess?" I asked. "Alexandra?"

Out of all the five main priestesses, she was the one I knew the least about.

"Her task is to cripple the rest of the Resistance before they have a chance to go after their leader," she said. "The High Priestess said she would send a demon to Alexandra who knows how to get into their hiding place somewhere in the Shadow World. The Underground, I believe it's called. She's to capture or kill as many demons down there as she can. She won't go herself, of course, but she's to send almost all of her hunters down there."

My entire body tensed in anger and fear.

"There are children down there," I said.

Essex's family was down there.

"Then you should do what you can to save them," she said.

"When is that happening?" I asked, my mind spinning. Where did we even start?

"Tomorrow night," she said. "Of course, you're supposed to die before that in the bombing."

The way she talked about my death so casually and the plan to kill hundreds of others turned my stomach.

But was she even telling me the truth?

I wasn't about to wait around for these things to happen just to prove her honesty, that was for sure.

"Do you know the name of the demon who is going to let her into the Underground?" I asked.

"I'm sorry. I don't know that," she said. "Only that he would be known to the others down there as one of their own."

I let my mind scroll through the list of demons here in the domed city who had once lived in the Underground or who still had family there.

Essex and only a handful of others, none of which could possibly be working for the High Priestess.

It could be any one of thousands who lived down there now. And she'd said '*he*', which meant it was a male demon. That was something, at least.

A needle in a haystack.

"What else?" I asked.

"Isn't that enough?"

She raised an eyebrow and tugged on the sleeve of her shirt.

"As far as our discussion went, the idea was that you and Jackson would be home in your beds after a long day of freeing emerald gates, where you would both be killed, along with the Winter girl. This would cripple the Southern Kingdom's power. Andros and his small army were heading to the King's City to rescue the princess and your demon's twin brother. With Andros gone, however, the twin brother would die in some contest there and the princess would be wed to a demon working for the High Priestess, which I guess was another part of the plan, albeit a much longer-term part.

"The king, apparently, is already under the control of the High Priestess, as well, so getting rid of the princess and the other demon would cripple the Northern Kingdom. All that's left at that point would be to put an end to the fighting spirit of the demons hiding out with the Resistance. Once that was done, the war would be ours."

I cleared my throat, struggling to force breath into my lungs. The king was being controlled by the High Priestess?

Magda was right. This game went deeper than I expected.

"It's a strong plan," I said. "And you still wanted to place your bets with me?"

"We've had strong plans before," she said, lifting her lips into a small smile. "Somehow, plans to kill you haven't worked out so well for us in the past. Even without my help, I imagine you would have taken some losses, but you would not have stopped fighting. And besides, when we talk again about the High Priestess, after you've saved your friends, I'll give you a stronger reason for why I want to help you."

"You won't tell me now?" I asked.

"It's a conversation for another time," she said. "Save your friends, and when you see that I am telling the truth, we can trust each other enough for me to tell you the rest. Just remember. If you do intend to keep your promise to save my life, you have to be careful who you confide in about this conversation and where you got the information you have. If my sisters or the High Priestess find out I told you willingly, I'm already as good as dead. Make up some excuse as to why you weren't in your bedroom, but let them all believe the Winter girl is dead and the explosions came as a terrible shock."

I stood, anxious to get upstairs and tell the others. To have Zara moved from the tower. To form my own army and head to the Underground.

There would be no sleep tonight.

But as I headed for the stairs, I thought of something the ruby priestess had told me when she first got here.

"When I asked you if your sisters knew you were here, you said they didn't." I turned and met her eyes. "If your role in this plan was to plant bombs in my castle, was that a lie? And if it was and they know you're here, how much of the rest of this is lies, too? Are you just telling me this to get me into a position where your sisters can hurt me and the people I love?"

"Clever girl," she said, admiration shining in her eyes. "But

I guess being betrayed enough in your short lifetime makes it easy for you to suspect everyone. That instinct will serve you well."

She shook her head, and I wondered for a moment if she was even planning to give me an answer at all. Finally, though, she looked up at me.

"My sisters don't know I'm here," she said. "They think I passed the bombs on to my spy on the inside. Right now, one of my own daughters is glamoured to look and act like me so that no one knows I'm gone. That is a trick that will only work for a short time longer, but it should hold for a bit, I hope. Harper, I swear on my life that every word I've told you has been the truth."

I gave her a half-smile and shook my head.

Andros caught by hunters. An attack on the Underground. Bombs in my castle.

"I kind of wish you were lying."

I shifted to white smoke and flew up the stairs, the fate of everyone I loved hanging on a razor's edge between truth and lies.

BATTLES YET TO COME

JACKSON

Eloise was dancing with her demon. Torkoth was free.
I hadn't known the demon before he was taken,
but it made me smile to watch him now.

It was so impossible to think of a demon dancing with the Prima whose family had enslaved him for all these years. The two were laughing as if it was the happiest day of their lives.

And for Torkoth, it most likely was.

It had taken my brother Aerden weeks to smile like that, and when he did smile, it didn't stay on his face for long.

But Torkoth had had months to dream of being set free, knowing that the hope of it was real. With Aerden, his freedom had come as such a shock that it nearly sent him into a depression so deep, I was afraid we'd never pull him out of it.

And just when I'd thought things were starting to get better, he'd been taken away and thrown into the king's dungeons in the north.

I missed my brother. If anyone deserved freedom, it was

Aerden, and without him here at my side, I couldn't truly feel free, either.

I turned away from the party and walked onto the front steps of the castle, staring out over the lights of the domed city. Music flooded the streets and demons danced and drank, enjoying one of the rare nights around here that we actually had several reasons to celebrate.

Harper was home. Four emerald gates were free. And for the rest, it was only a matter of time. We could release four to six gates a day. Thanks to the time zone difference, we could set everyone free in a matter of weeks if we kept at it.

Just like we had with the sapphire gates, we would take turns, use the doors in the Hall of Doorways when possible to travel quickly, and free as many witches and demons as fast as we possibly could.

Keeping the master stone safe was routine by now, too. Things were finally going our way again, but for how long?

And without Aerden and Lea here, it still didn't feel complete. Were they safe? Had Andros arrived in time?

I looked down toward the entrance to the dome and wished with all my heart that Andros would walk through that opening with my brother and Lea at his side. Safe.

That was all I wanted. To keep them all safe.

But it seemed that no matter how hard I tried to make sure everyone I loved was here with me, we kept being torn apart.

Someday, though.

Someday, there would be peace.

"Jackson, have you seen Harper?" Mary Anne asked. "Eloise wants to make a toast, but I can't find her anywhere."

I turned and scanned the crowd. She was just here.

Memories of the night she'd disappeared rolled through

me like waves of horror. One minute she'd been right there, and the next she was gone.

Almost on instinct, I glanced up to make sure the magical dome that protected the city was still in place. Immediately, though, I felt silly for being so scared. Harper was probably just talking to someone in the hallway or up in her room.

But as I started for the stairs that led up to the bedrooms, Harper came flying out of another stairway.

The dungeons.

Anger flared inside me. What the hell? Had she gone down there to talk to the ruby priestess without me?

She took human form and looked around the crowded room, her eyes searching for mine. I practically ran over to her.

"What did you do?" I asked. "We talked about this. We were going to wait—"

"You can be mad at me later," she said, out of breath. "We need to talk. Gather the ones we trust the most. Only the inner circle."

She straightened her shoulders and planted a smile on her lips.

"And try not to act like anything's wrong," she said. "We have to talk now, though. Gather everyone you can in the next five minutes and meet me in the war room. Make sure Gregory comes."

She kept the smile on her face, but I could see the fear and impatience in her eyes.

What had that witch told her?

And didn't Harper realize we couldn't trust anything that woman said? We should have waited until morning. After spending a night in the cold dungeons alone, the woman might have been more willing to tell the truth.

Dammit.

She could have at least warned me she was going down there. The last time she went to face a priestess on her own without telling me, I'd nearly lost her forever.

I could do without repeating that experience ever again.

Harper had already walked over to her sister Angela. She also stopped to talk to Brooke, a girl from Peachville who had also been trapped at the Evers Institute in the past with Harper.

I nodded to Mary Anne and disappeared into the crowd to find my sister and Eloise.

Mary Anne would grab Essex, of course.

Mordecai, Joost, Erick, and Cristo stood near the buffet, and when I told them to head up to the war room, they loaded up plates of food and disappeared up the steps.

Unfortunately, Rend and Franki weren't here with us tonight. Rumors swirled that the Brotherhood had finally called Rend and the other vampires in for killing one of their own.

Our very small group would have to do.

I just needed to find Gregory.

Wasn't he down in the dungeons, watching the ruby priestess?

I started toward the stairs and ran into Easton, one of the other guards, on his way down.

"Where are you going?" I asked him.

"Gregory sent me down to watch the prisoner," Easton said. "He told me Harper ordered him to take a break."

She'd been down there alone?

My anger flared again, but I worked to keep my face composed. "Where is Gregory, then? I need to speak to him."

Easton pointed across the room toward the entrance to the guard's main quarters. "He said he was heading to his room. He doesn't look so good, Jackson. I don't know what's up with him lately. I guess the stress must be getting to him."

"Thanks," I said. "Get downstairs and watch that woman like your life depends on it."

"Yes, sir," Easton said and hurried down the steps.

I hurried after Gregory, finally catching him just before he went into his own suite of rooms.

"Jackson," he said with a slight bow. "Is something wrong? Don't tell me something has happened to Harper."

"How could you leave her down there alone with that woman?" I asked. "You should know better."

His eyes widened. "She ordered me to leave."

I gritted my teeth. Was she just trying to cause trouble now?

"Well, now she's ordering us all to meet with her in secret up in the war room," I said. "Come on."

Gregory's body started to tremble, and I stared at him.

"What's wrong with you?" I asked, my nerves pushed to the limit. "Are you feeling okay?"

He attempted to straighten, but his eyes still held a fear I had never seen in him before.

"Let's get up there," I said.

Something didn't feel right about all of this.

The two of us hurried across the throne room, trying not to draw attention to ourselves as we disappeared up the stairs and toward the war room.

Everyone else was already there, worried expressions on each face as they looked to Harper.

Harper stood at the head of the table, her hands just

touching the top of the heavy wooden surface. My anger dissipated as I looked at her.

Despite the scars on her arms she refused to glamour and the strip of torn cloth she wore around her wrist, she stood with her shoulders straight and her eyes clear. Determined. She was still so young to be commanding an entire kingdom and an army, and yet, she belonged exactly where she was.

Queen.

The true ruler of this kingdom, even though she still had yet to officially claim the title in any ceremony.

As much as I wanted to protect her, I needed to remember that ruling was her job, now. It was dangerous, and she wasn't a child, anymore.

Our eyes met across the table, and she nodded to me as I stepped to the side and shut the door behind us.

To my surprise, a guard named Logan stepped out of the corner, steel handcuffs attached to long chains clutched in his hands.

"What's going on?" I asked.

Beside me, Gregory fell to his knees, tears in his eyes.

"I had no choice, my queen. You have to understand. She forced me to do it," he said. "I would have never betrayed you if I'd had the choice. I swear it."

Harper nodded to Logan, and the guard reluctantly placed the chains on Gregory's outstretched hands.

What the hell was going on? What had Gregory done?

"There is always a choice, Gregory," Harper said, a mix of sadness and disgust in her voice. "The fact that you came back here like a snake in the grass, waiting for orders from one of our enemies, is more disappointing than I can say. My father believed in you. Trusted you. And today, you have betrayed his memory, as well as this kingdom."

Gregory seemed to fold in on himself, collapsing onto the hard stone floor at my feet.

"Take him to the dungeons," Harper said. "You can put him in the cell next to Magda Thorn, where he can be constantly reminded of what he has done. Use your cloaking spell to walk through the throne room so that no one sees you."

Logan had an interesting ability to blend in and cloak himself and anyone he touched for a period of time. He bowed and forced Gregory to his feet. The demon steel around his wrists would prevent him from casting or shifting, and once he was inside the cell, his magic would be cut off from him completely.

I shook my head as I watched the captain of the guard be taken from the room in chains.

And as I looked to Harper, I had a feeling this was only the beginning.

When the door was closed again, she motioned for us all to have a seat. She stayed standing, however, as she took in our small group.

"What I'm about to say cannot leave this room," she said. "Whatever preparations we have to make to deal with the things I'll talk about tonight, no one is to utter a word about where we got this information. Is that clear?"

Everyone nodded, the tension in the room now so thick, it was difficult to breathe.

Harper began, telling us about her conversation with the ruby priestess just minutes earlier.

Andros captured. Bombs in the castle, placed because our

own guard captain let that witch out of her cell when we were gone. My brother's death a foregone conclusion without the help of the Resistance. And the Underground, with its thousands of innocent women and children, attacked by an army of hunters.

The Order had never hit so hard before, but after the things we had done to them, I had always known it was just a matter of time before they stepped up their game and came at us with their full force.

"My mother is in the Underground," Essex said. "I must be going to her."

Mary Anne clutched his hand. "What do we do first?" she asked. "Where do we start?"

"We start by moving Zara and blocking off everything close to those two bombs so that no one gets hurt when they go off," she said. "Then, we—"

"Wait," I said, leaning forward. "You're assuming all of this is real. That she's telling us the truth."

"I think she is."

"Why would she plant bombs and then tell us they were there?" Angela asked. "It doesn't make sense."

"Because her sisters and the High Priestess are expecting her to do it," Harper said. "If she doesn't follow through with her part of the plan, that places suspicion on her. We have to let it happen, and we can't let news get out that we knew about it ahead of time."

"We have to consider the fact that she might be lying to try to get us either out of the castle or into a place where there will be an unexpected ambush or attack coming that we don't expect," I said. "She's supposed to give us the location of the amethyst priestess's house, but what if, instead, she gives us the location of a prison or trap? Or what if we all show up and the amethyst priestess already knows we're there? What if they don't know the location of the Underground, and we lead them straight to it when we go?"

Essex ran a hand through his hair. "Jackson has a point," he said. "This could be a trap for us all. I do not want to be putting my mother in more danger, but I also am not wanting to ignore this threat."

I gave him a smile, despite the tension in the room. His English was getting better.

"You're both right," Harper said. "If we act based solely on the things Magda Thorn told me, we could be walking straight into a trap. And if we do nothing, we could live with terrible regrets for the rest of our lives as those we love die to the Order of Shadows. It's up to us as a group to decide what we do next, knowing that either decision could be the wrong one."

I sat back in my chair, realizing the seriousness of this conversation.

Trust the ruby priestess, though? It was unthinkable.

"Okay, there are some things we can confirm the truth of before we go rushing into anything," I said. "The bombs, for one."

"The bombs are real," Harper said. "Before I came here, I went to check on Zara. There is a small ruby the size of a dime attached to the stone that holds the cocoon. There's a matching one in our bedroom, as well."

"And there's no way to diffuse it or stop it from going off?" Mary Anne asked.

"Magda said that if anyone touches it, it will detonate immediately," Harper said. "And she also warned that if we don't let the bombs detonate, it will raise suspicions about her loyalty, putting her in danger, too."

"And now we're worried about Magda's safety?" I asked, shaking my head.

"I promised her, Jackson. In exchange for her help, I will do what I can to keep her alive."

"And she wouldn't explain to you how that's possible? How can we end this war without killing the ruby priestess? We aren't going to just let her entire coven get away with what they've done to demons."

"No, we aren't," Harper said calmly. "But Magda says she believes there is a way."

"Then she should have explained that to you," I said. "I don't like it that she's holding back key information about the High Priestess and the secrets of the Order. Is she in charge, or are you?"

Harper's eyes narrowed, and her body tensed.

I hadn't meant to shout at her like that, but I couldn't believe that just a few days after getting her home, we were already being thrown back into the war.

"I think we should focus on the things she did tell us," Eloise said softly. "We can deal with her secrets later."

"I agree," Angela said. "The bombs are real. What else?"

I sighed. "Andros is missing," I said. "Or at least we haven't had word from him. He was supposed to be heading to the King's City to save Aerden from the King's Games. He should have at least sent word by now."

"Lea told you about the games, didn't she? When you talked to her on the com stone?" Mary Anne asked, looking to me.

"Yes. She said that Aerden was in trouble, but that Andros was coming for them. That was days ago. The games should have already taken place if Andros didn't get to them in time. I think the final round was set for today."

"Aerden is still alive," Harper said. "The connection we shared was severed when he was set free, but there are pieces of it still there. I would know if he was dead."

"I would too," I said. I had to trust that feeling inside me that told me he was okay. "That doesn't mean he's not still in danger. We need to get him and Lea out of there. Magda said the king is under the control of the High Priestess? How is that possible?"

"It makes sense," Harper said. "He's built the wall of the city up so high and abandoned the rest of his people. That never rang true for Lea about the father she knew."

I closed my eyes. Harper was right about that. On top of all the other sorrow Lea faced, the fact that her father had simply turned his back on everyone outside that wall had broken her heart a million times over.

"We have to get them out of there," I said.

"With the wall and the King's Guard standing between us and them, we'll need a strong plan," Harper said. "We won't be able to just waltz up to the gates and demand their freedom."

"Illana, you left the city without permission," I said, turning to my sister. "Can you show us where you went? Maybe we can get in the way you got out."

Illana nodded. "There are usually only one or two guards placed on that exit, and I know them both."

"So, first, we move Zara to another part of the castle, block off any area we feel might be in danger and make sure no one goes near it," Harper said. "Then, we put together a small task force to infiltrate the King's City and save Aerden. Lea, too, if we can, though getting access to the princess might be more difficult."

"Aerden won't leave without her," I said.

"We'll find a way," Mary Anne said.

"Can't Rend help?" Angela asked.

Harper shook her head. "I don't want Rend and Franki bothered with any of this right now. Rend has been called to answer for his actions against the Brotherhood of Darkness. He and Franki have done more than enough to help us over the past year, and I don't want to put them under any extra stress."

She turned to look directly at Mary Anne.

"Please, don't even mention all of this to Franki," Harper said. "We owe them that much peace, at the very least. And I understand if Franki needs your help over the coming days. Be there for her when you can but keep this a secret. Rend saved my life and Jackson's. If I can repay them at all by keeping them out of this added danger, I will do it."

Mary Anne nodded. "They might be pissed when they find out, though," she said with a shrug. "Just saying."

I smiled. She had a point there, but Harper was right. If Rend was being called to answer for his crimes, he and Franki might only have a few days left together. They didn't need to spend it stressed out and fighting the Order.

"We'll deal with his anger later, when he's done with this other mess," Harper said, smiling for the first time since she'd come up from the dungeons.

"And the Underground?" Essex asked.

"That's trickier," Harper said. "We don't want to lead anyone to them, but we can't send just one or two people, either. From what Magda said, it's going to be a dangerous fight. The citrine priestess has been ordered to send nearly all of her hunters."

Eloise moaned and put a hand on her forehead. "Just when I was starting to feel happy," she said, half-laughing. "At least I got a few hours of true freedom."

Harper leaned over and placed a hand on Eloise's shoulder. "You are free," Harper said. "Your decisions and your power are your own now, and that matters."

Eloise nodded. "You're right," she said. "I will see this fight through to the end on my own power. And I know many of the women in my coven will fight with us, if we need them."

"Thank you," Harper said.

"When is the attack on the Underground?" I asked, an idea forming in my mind.

"Tomorrow night," Harper said.

"Then we have to try," I said, nerves tightening my stomach. "We could send Mary Anne and Essex alone tonight. If they're stealthy and careful to be sure they aren't followed, they could warn the demons in the Underground and help them move to safety deeper in the tunnels. There's a whole network of unused tunnels and rooms down there. If they can move everyone deeper in and block off any access to it, the hunters won't be able to get through. The hunters will be counting on a single demon to let them in, which means they'll only be using one entrance. It will be a bottleneck, and they'll have to enter the place very slowly. They'll find the entire Underground empty and have no idea where everyone went. They might even assume the Underground's people moved to a new, secret location."

Harper took a deep breath, as if she hadn't dared breathe at all before that moment.

"That's brilliant," she said. "But they'd have to get started right away. There are thousands of demons down there. Essex, do you think you can convince them to move?"

"I am knowing I can," he said with a nod. "I have many friends in the Resistance who will help."

Harper frowned slightly.

"What is it?" I asked.

"Magda said that it would be a demon from the Resistance who let the hunters inside," she said. "This plan doesn't work if someone on the inside is helping. They'll just tell the hunters where to go."

My excitement waned. She was right. There was no way to know which demon would betray them all, and there wasn't enough time to try to figure it out.

"It's a risk we'll have to take," I said finally. "At the very least, we can move the children and merchants and those who aren't trained to fight to another location. There are hundreds of trained soldiers in the Resistance, and Andros most likely would have only taken twenty or thirty with him to the King's City. The soldiers can stay and fight."

"Maybe when you get down there, you can find a way for the soldiers to hide when the hunters arrive," Harper said to Essex. "If the hunters don't find the rest of the Underground's residents, no one has to fight at all. But if they try to attack and know where the others are hiding, the soldiers can ambush them."

I nodded. "It's our best chance, I think."

"We'll do what we can," Mary Anne said. "Should we go now?"

Harper shook her head. "Let's figure out the rest of the

plan and where to meet up first," she said. "We still need to figure out what we're going to do about Andros."

For the next half hour, we discussed the different possibilities for saving Andros and his army from the amethyst priestess. If the ruby priestess was right, Andros was already captured. He would be alive for a few more days, but Andros as a demon slave? I couldn't stomach it.

We could go to the amethyst priestess's home to stop the ritual, but that only worked if Magda was telling the truth.

And we wouldn't know until we got there.

Finally, Harper held a hand up to stop the conversation.

"We don't have time to go around in circles on this all night," she said. "There is work to be done and preparations to make. When Aerden and Lea are safely out of the King's City and the Underground is safe, we'll meet back here to discuss our next steps."

Angela let out a deep sigh. "We have to consider the fact that disrupting the Order's plans to kill Harper and destroy the Underground could make the amethyst priestess change hers altogether," she said. "It could send her into a rage, and she could kill Andros, anyway. Or she could move him or change the night of the ceremony, knowing that we're coming for her. Is there no way to do everything at once? Rescue Andros now, while we're also saving everyone else?"

Harper sat down and put her head in her hands.

I wanted to pull her into my arms and tell her everything was going to be okay, but I couldn't make that promise to her right now.

Finally, she lifted her head.

"It's a risk we're going to have to take," she said. "If we try to save everyone in one day, we'll be spreading our forces too thin and making ourselves vulnerable. Sending anyone out to try to find where the hunters are keeping Andros would just split our forces. That's exactly what the Order wants us to do. Andros is my friend, too, but he is a warrior. He started the Resistance knowing full well that someday, he might have to give his life for the cause. The demons of the Underground need us more, so we'll focus the majority of our forces and efforts there."

She stood again.

"We'll deal with the castle tonight. Mary Anne and Essex, the two of you will head to the Underground as soon as possible. Be absolutely certain you're not followed, and act as quickly as you can once you're inside. Take several communication stones so we can keep each other updated about what's happening over the next couple of days."

She paused, as if thinking through the plan one more time.

"Jackson and I will put together a small group to infiltrate the castle and save Aerden and Lea. If we can, we'll deal with the king while we're there," she said. "Angela, you'll be in charge of putting together as large an army of witches and demons as you can. Share communication stones with Mary Anne, set yourself up somewhere near one of the entrances to the Underground, but not close enough that you'd be leading anyone straight to it. If Mary Anne needs you and the army, she'll call for you on the stone."

Harper's composure made me love her even more deeply than I had before. When had she grown into such a strong leader?

She was still the person I loved, but I saw now for the first time how our months apart had changed her.

The old Harper would have sent forces to find and save

Andros, no matter what. And it would have been a mistake. Now, she seemed willing to take the losses we might have to take in order to stay strong and survive.

She was still my Harper, but she was different, too.

A part of me mourned for the innocence lost to her over the years since we'd first met, but a larger part of me swelled with pride at just how far she'd come and how much she had survived.

She was a true queen. A true survivor.

And together, we would face the battles yet to come.

Starting with the King's City and bringing Lea and Aerden back home where they belonged.

OUR FUTURE

HARPER

As discreetly as possible, the guards cleared out the entire wing of the castle near my bedroom. After we said goodbye to Mary Anne and Essex, Jackson and I very carefully moved Zara's cocoon to one of the training rooms beneath the castle, far away from the bombs.

It was hard to leave her down there, though. It gave me comfort to know she'd at least had some sunlight and breeze up in the tower with its open archways.

I placed a hand on the cocoon. "I'm not going to let anything happen to you, my friend," I whispered.

I still could hardly believe she was alive.

When my memories had come rushing back to me, all I could remember of Zara was that she had saved my life by sacrificing her own. She'd taken a direct hit of one of the emerald priestess's spells and fallen to the floor.

I wasn't sure how she'd managed to survive it, especially since she'd already been so weak.

Before that night, Zara had discovered a curse her mother,

Priestess Winter, had placed on their entire bloodline, dooming them to turn into hunters if something happened to her. Her curse said that if she was dead, that meant her heirs had failed to protect her. In their failure she would punish them in the most horrifying way possible.

By triggering a curse that would turn each of them into hunters after her death.

The rest of Zara's family, including her two sisters and her aunt, had all already turned by the time Zara's white-blonde hair had begun turning black. Her skin was nearly transparent toward the end, black veins running through her skin, as if the curse were already rotting her insides.

Jackson told me he believed Zara's sacrifice to save my life had broken the curse and that's why she had been wrapped inside the cocoon. Her body was healing so that she could re-emerge brand new.

I hoped he was right.

But until whatever was happening to her inside there was done, we had to take care of her as best we could. And for now, that meant a dark training room in the basement.

"I promise, we'll move you back into the sunlight when this is over," I said softly. "I miss you so much."

"Come on, Harper," Jackson said, taking my hand. "Let's go get everything we might need from our bedroom."

Reluctantly, I left Zara's side and followed him up to the bedroom my father had so lovingly designed for me.

I couldn't hold back tears as I packed my things and prepared to say goodbye to the room with its glass-tiled doors and decorative stones. Its crystal lamps and touches of white roses everywhere. The black fur rug my father had made just for me, because he knew I loved black.

"I know it's a silly thing to be upset about losing," I said as we took one last look at the place, our bags slung over our shoulders. "This space was just one of the only gifts I ever got from him. It's hard to lose it."

"It's not silly at all," Jackson said. "This is your space. Your father created this for you, hoping that someday you'd be a part of his life. The Order has no right to take that from you, on top of everything else."

He took my hand.

"I promise you, as soon as we can, we'll build it back exactly the way it was," he said. "The important thing is that we're going to be safe. If the ruby priestess is telling the truth, we both could have died here tonight. I think you did the right thing talking to her, even though I wish you'd told me what you were doing."

I smiled up at him, shaking my head.

"I knew you'd be mad," I said. "I had to talk to her, though. You understand that, right?"

I thought he was going to lecture me about going off on my own again.

Instead, he set his bag down on the floor and gripped my hand.

"Let's get married," he said, touching a finger to the engagement locket I wore on a new chain around my neck.

I smiled and studied him. "We are getting married."

"I'm not talking about someday," he said, his voice filled with hope and excitement as the idea of it seemed to catch fire within him. "I mean right now. As soon as possible."

The smile faded from my face, and I stared at him.

"Jackson, that's crazy," I said. "We have so much to do. We're basically at war right now, trying to save the people we love who are being attacked. Now isn't the time to think about putting together a wedding."

"We don't need anything fancy, right?" he said. "We could call together a small group in the throne room tonight and say our vows."

I shook my head and backed away. What in the world had gotten into him all of sudden?

"We talked about this," I said. "I don't want to get married when there are still demons out there suffering. They need our help. It wouldn't feel right. We decided to wait until everyone was free so that we could celebrate with joy."

"I know we talked about it, and at the time, I agreed with you," he said. "But things are different now. We've already lost so much. Courtney. Zara. We've been separated from Lea and Aerden, and we don't even know for sure they're okay. Andros is potentially missing or dead. How much more do we have to sacrifice in the name of this war? Our own happiness? For how long? Decades? I don't want to wait that long."

I turned away, hardly believing he was bringing this up right now, when so much was on the line.

"You're talking like you don't think we're going to make it through this war at all."

"We have to face the fact that we might not," he said.

"Jackson." I twirled on him, angry that he could ever say something like that to me. "Don't you dare talk like that. I know we can't assume anything and that every time we push forward in this fight, we risk losing our lives, but we have to at least keep hope alive. We have to believe we can survive this. Sometimes hope is the only thing getting us through the hard times. We can't give up now."

"I'm not talking about giving up," he said. "I'm talking

about taking a small step back and having a moment of joy before we jump right back into the fight. We've earned it, haven't we? After everything? What are we waiting for?"

"Why are you so eager to do it now?" I asked, throwing my hands up. "What's changed?"

"Why are you so against it? You still want to marry me, don't you?" he asked.

I sighed, sorry that I'd yelled at him or made him doubt how I felt, but this was just not the right time to be bringing this up. Why couldn't he see that?

"You know you don't even have to ask that," I said, walking over to take his hand. "Of course, I want to marry you. I just would rather do it when things are easier, and we can celebrate in peace, surrounded by everyone we love. I don't want to get married when we're in the middle of this war, Jackson. Not with all of this hanging over our heads. Besides, don't you want your brother to be here? Maybe even your parents?"

He raised an eyebrow. "My parents? You're joking right?"

I shrugged. "Once the war is over and you get a chance to talk through things with them, maybe you can find peace with them, too," I said. "But at least Aerden should be here. He'd be devastated to miss it."

His sudden excitement was gone, replaced now with a look of fear and regret.

"At least think about it," he said, squeezing my hand.

I curled my fingers around his and gave him a small smile.

"I will," I said softly. "And I do want to marry you. I just want it to be full of joy, Jackson. Not sandwiched between battles and laced with worry."

He looked deeply into my eyes, then, something hidden there I couldn't quite define.

"We could wait a lifetime for a single moment without worry and never find it," he said sadly. "There will always be someone out there who needs help or is being oppressed or enslaved. Being happy doesn't mean we've forgotten them. But we can't deny ourselves joy forever, Harper. We're allowed to be happy even while there is suffering in the world. The joy is what makes the fight worth it."

I nodded. I understood what he was trying to say, but what he didn't understand was that I didn't want our wedding to be something we did out of fear. I wanted it to be a choice we made when it seemed we had an infinite number of choices ahead of us.

"Come with me a second," I said, taking his hand and pulling him toward the balcony.

I pointed down to the white roses and the expansive gardens below.

"Someday, we'll be sitting right down there," I said, almost able to see it. "Our son will be playing at our feet and we will be a happy family. That's our future, Jackson, and we are going to get there someday."

"Harper—" he began, but I placed a fingertip over his lips

"I love you," I said. "But right now, there is work to do. Let's get past this next step and we'll talk about it, okay? Let's rescue Lea and Aerden, save the Underground, find Andres, and finish freeing the emerald gates. Then, we'll see about a wedding. I promise."

He looked like there was something more he needed to tell me, but after a few minutes, he just pulled me into his arms and held me tight against his chest.

"Okay," he whispered, kissing the top of my head. "But let's not put it off forever, Harper."

The fear in his voice sent a chill down my spine as we held each other, and I wondered what had happened that had shaken him up so much.

"We should go," I said. "I don't want to be here when that bomb goes off."

He laughed. "Yeah, you and me both," he said, taking my hand.

I turned to look at the room my father had designed for me one last time before I turned away, leaving it, and the bomb, behind.

CAPTIVE

JACKSON

How could I explain to Harper why marrying her was so important to me?

I needed to tell her about what had happened with Sabine in the Swamp of Nightmares. What I'd given up in order to bring Harper home.

But for some reason, every time I started to tell her, the words just wouldn't come out.

Part of me worried she would lose hope. She relied on that vision I'd had of our future. We both did. We both called on it in times when things seemed difficult, offering it up as proof that someday, we would make it through this.

And now, that promise was gone.

All my visions were gone now, and even though I'd spent a lot of my time cursing them and my lack of understanding, I felt powerless without them. Blind.

As we left instructions for the guards to tell no one where we had gone, we met up with Mordecai, Joost, Erick, and

Cristo near the entrance to the domed city and stepped out into the dark of the night.

Illana had come, too, but she seemed nervous to be heading back to the King's City so soon after she had left.

Most of the residents of the domed city were fast asleep, no doubt exhausted after a night of celebration and excitement. I was mostly just glad to know the castle was clear.

Zara was safely tucked away in the training rooms beneath the castle, Gregory and Priestess Thorn were no doubt having their own little pity party in the dungeons, and all the castle's servants had been instructed to find another place to stay for a few days.

We were careful not to give them direct answers that would explain why we'd cleared out the castle. All we had said was that we had some dangerous people in the dungeons and wanted to make sure everyone was safe.

Tuli, Harper's handmaiden, had been the only one to push back and demand a reason as to why she was being kicked out of the castle. I had pulled her aside and told her that we would explain more later, but that we needed her to go along with this story about the dungeons. I made her promise me no less than twelve times that she wouldn't try to go up to our bedroom for any reason.

Tuli had taken care of me when Harper was gone, making sure I was eating even when I didn't feel like eating, and checking in on me when I could hardly drag myself out of bed some days. If anything happened to her, I would never forgive myself.

Harper and I were already talking about asking Tuli if she'd take a place on the Council, but we just hadn't had time to talk to her about it, yet. She'd been brought to the castle to serve as a handmaiden to Harper by her father, even before he had known if or when Harper might someday come to stay with him.

But over time, Tuli had become a dear friend. And Harper wasn't comfortable having a handmaiden anyway. That was a tradition of the Shadow World Harper kind of hated. She didn't want someone to be called her servant. Especially when she considered them friends.

As soon as we got back, we'd talk to her about it.

When we left the domed city, Tuli was the only one still standing there with the two guards at the entrance.

"Don't be gone long," she said. She lifted a ruby stone into the air. "Keep me updated on when you're coming home."

"We will," I shouted. "Just promise you'll keep everyone out of the castle, okay?"

"I will," she said, shaking her head and mumbling something under her breath.

Harper smiled at me. "Do you think you made her promise enough times?" she asked.

"I just hope she took me seriously," I said. "I don't know what I'd do if anything happened to her."

"She'll be fine," Harper said. "How long do you think it will take us to get to the King's City from here?"

"If we shift and fly, we can be there just before dawn," Mordecai said. "I've made this journey more than a few times, but we'll have to go full speed to make it before the suns come up."

"If we don't, we'll lose the entire day," Harper said. "We can't risk that if Aerden's in danger. We need to go as fast as we can."

"It's going to put us in danger of attracting hunters," Joost said, glancing around. "Are you sure we don't want to be more careful?"

"We don't have time for careful," I said. "We have to get there before dawn, so we can sneak into the city without drawing too much attention to ourselves. I don't know if the final round of the King's Games were supposed to take place yesterday or today. All I know is that we have to get there as soon as possible."

I wished Lea had been more specific about when the King's Games tournaments were being held. All she'd told me when we spoke was that Aerden was participating and that Andros was on his way to rescue them.

I shook my head, worry gripping my chest.

If the ruby priestess was telling the truth, Andros never made it there at all.

"Is everyone ready?" I asked, studying our small but powerful group.

Mordecai, Joost, Erick, and Cristo were some of Lea's best friends. They would do whatever they needed to do to get her out of the city unharmed. Illana, my sister, had recently been smuggled out of the King's city through one of the entrances near the mines. Mines I didn't even realize existed until she mentioned them.

She claimed there had been only one guard patrolling that entrance on the night she left the city, and I hoped the same was true tonight when we got there.

Other than those five, it was just Harper and me. A very small group to be raiding such a huge city, but I figured our chances of getting in and out without attracting too much attention were better if we stayed small and stealthy, rather than bringing an army out to fight.

"Let's get going," Mordecai said. "Everyone follow me. When we get closer to the castle, Illana can show us which way to go."

Illana nodded, but she looked terrified. I had no doubt our parents were furious she'd left in the first place, but having her with me in the Southern Kingdom had helped me to keep my sanity when Harper disappeared.

I touched her shoulder and gave her a reassuring squeeze. "It's going to be okay," I said.

I wasn't particularly excited about the prospect of facing our parents, either, but I was hoping it wouldn't come to that. If we were talking to them, I had a feeling we'd be doing it from behind bars.

And I was going to do everything in my power to avoid that scenario.

Everyone in our small group shifted and soared high into the sky, where we could move even faster. We flew over the swamps in the borderlands and the abandoned villages on both sides of the border. We flew across the plains and the mountains, watching carefully for hunters who liked to hide in the caves along this area.

And finally, after several hours of pushing ourselves as far and as fast as possible, we finally came to the black cliffs, their obsidian rocks reflecting the light of the three moons.

Even at this distance, something lying on the rocks caught my eye. I swooped down and took solid form as my feet hit the ground near the fallen object.

I closed my eyes as my hand wrapped around the cloth.

"What is it?" Illana asked, shifting as she joined me on the rocks.

I shook my head as I stared down at the insignia of a red dragon embroidered on the black band.

There had been a part of me that was hoping the ruby priestess was lying about Andros, but this armband proved something had happened. If not to him, to someone in the Resistance.

And from the blood dried on the nearby black rocks, I was guessing it had been a real battle.

I could only pray Andros was still alive out there somewhere.

"It's an armband worn by members of the Resistance Army," I said.

Harper gasped as she stared at the strip of bloodied cloth.

"I didn't want it to be true," she said.

"Come on, let's get to the castle," Mordecai said. "The faster we get Lea and Aerden out of the there, the faster we can go after Andros and the others. Illana, you lead the way from here."

My sister nodded and looked toward the King's City, it's tall, pointed towers rising into the night.

She shifted, and we followed her, our hearts beating with hope and fear as we approached the city that held my brother and its own princess captive.

A THOUSAND TANGLED MEMORIES

JACKSON

We kept to the shadows just south of the wall, flying low to the ground.

Almost all of us in the group had shifted to black smoke, but Harper's demon shadow was white. She stood out against the darkness of the Black Cliffs, and I kept her close to me, hiding her within my own shadow so the light of the moons didn't catch her.

As we crept toward a secret entrance near a mine Illana said existed near the back of the city's wall, my eagerness to see Aerden increased. We'd been apart too long, and I prayed he was okay.

What kind of foolishness had caused him to enter the King's Games in the first place? Or had he been forced into it?

And how, exactly, was the king being controlled by the High Priestess?

I hoped that when we found my brother and Lea, we would also find some answers.

Please, let them be okay.

Illana's shadow paused near a section of the wall just before a sharp curve, and the rest of us stayed back, careful not to make any sudden movements or attract unwanted attention. If we could, we would neutralize any guards stationed back here without having to kill them.

When she took solid form and walked up to the edge of the wall, my entire shadow hummed with anticipation. What was she doing? She was going to ruin our one advantage by showing herself.

I prepared to shift at any moment in case a guard appeared and attacked her.

She disappeared from sight around the corner, and I slowly followed her, careful to stick to the darkest of the shadows. I could feel the others just behind me, ready to strike as soon as any guards appeared.

"Warin," Illana whispered. "Are you here?"

I tensed. What if a different guard had been stationed here tonight?

"Warin?" she called again, louder this time.

When she stepped forward along the wall, two silhouettes materialized beside her in the darkness, a single spark of magic lighting against the night as they grabbed her.

I didn't hesitate to act, flying toward them as fast as I could and bringing the tip of my spear to one of the guard's throats. I smiled as the blade of Harper's sword gleamed against the throat of the second guard.

The two demons lifted their hands from Illana's arms, releasing their magic quickly.

"If you don't resist us, I promise we won't hurt you," I said. "How many guards are just inside this entrance?"

I pressed my spear's icy tip against the demon's throat hard enough to come just shy of drawing blood.

"No one," the first guard said. "Not until morning."

"And the arena's dungeons?" I asked. "How many guards will we face between here and there?"

The second guard dared to turn his head and peer at me through the darkness. Harper's body tensed, ready to do what had to be done if he moved against me.

"Denaer?" the guard whispered. "Is that you, old friend?"

I nearly lost my grip on the weapon in my hand, hearing the sound of my old name on the tongue of a demon I hadn't seen in decades.

"Cenhelm?" I asked.

We had been friends as shadowlings here in the King's City, training together since we were old enough to hold a sword.

"I don't want to hurt you, but I have to get inside the city walls to my brother," I said. "Do you have news of him? Have the King's Games completed?"

It was dark out here, but with my vision, I could see as clearly as if it were day. Cenhelm carefully lifted his head and smiled at me.

"You obviously haven't heard the news," he said, his shoulders relaxing.

"What news?" Harper asked, not lowering her sword, despite this demon's relaxed stance.

"The final round of the games were cancelled. The king is back to his old self, and your brother is a hero of the city," Cenhelm said.

I tensed. What kind of trick was he playing on us here? Something to get us to relax so that he could attack. I glanced toward the entrance the pair had been guarding, checking to see that no one else waited there in the shadows to ambush us, but there was no movement anywhere that I could see.

"You don't have to fight your way into the city," Cenhelm said. "You could have walked right up to the front gates, and the king would have welcomed you all with open arms. I can take you up to the castle myself and prove it to you."

Harper's eyes searched mine, looking for some sign of what to do next. Did we trust what this demon said and possibly walk into a trap? Or did we dare hope he was telling the truth?

I shook my head. I didn't have an answer yet, and I didn't want her to let down her guard.

We had too much to do to allow ourselves to be captured.

How could we be sure?

If he was telling the truth, Aerden would no longer be trapped in the dungeons. He would be in his old chambers or somewhere up in the castle.

But there would also be tons of guards near the castle. It was too risky to try to start there.

"Take us to the arena," I said, finally. "We'll check the dungeons for ourselves, and if Aerden is there and we find out you were lying to us, our promise not to hurt you is off."

Cenhelm lifted his hands into the air again. "I swear it, Denaer. Your brother is not in those dungeons."

"Then you have nothing to worry about," I said. "Now, move."

Cenhelm and the other guard led our small group into the King's City. We kept to the shadows as we moved first through a secluded section of sapphire mines well-hidden from the rest of the city by a smaller wall.

Then, coming through a large doorway, we entered the

streets of the King's City, the familiarity of it hitting me across the face with the force of a thousand tangled memories, each laced with sorrow and joy and the feelings of home.

"Let's keep moving," I said, my eyes now locked on the oval shaped stands of the arena just ahead in the distance.

We were almost there.

BRAVE WARRIORS

AERDEN

I planted my feet firmly on the dusty floor of the arena's battlefield.

The guards and servants had done their best to erase all evidence of last night's fight with the Stone Guardian, but I could still feel the energy and tension of the fear that had filled this place. The rage.

I closed my eyes and tried to relive those moments just before Kael had turned his attentions to Lea, meaning to kill her with a single sweep of his stone arm.

I let the same fear and love flood my heart and spill over into my magic, and when I was sure I was close to the same mix of emotions and power, I threw my hands forward, willing the giant golem of light to appear.

A small spark fell from the tips of my fingers to the dirt below, but nothing more.

I widened my stance and closed my eyes again, allowing my own frustration to fuel my power. Somehow, in the moment of my greatest need, I had accessed a power I never even knew existed inside of me.

And if that power was strong enough to bring a Stone Guardian down when a dozen guards had failed to so much as touch him, I needed to know exactly what I'd done.

And I needed to be able to do it again.

I took a deep breath and imagined Lea's face. I filled my heart with every drop of emotion and love I had toward her, letting it surge through me like a rushing river until I felt it from the tips of my toes to the very top of my head.

I imagined a giant stone hand coming toward her, taking aim at her face and meaning to crush her. I let my fear ignite the love inside me, and with a single step forward, I pushed it out of myself with a groan that echoed through the empty seats of the arena.

When I opened my eyes, hoping to see the same light I'd created last night, there was only a dim flash like lightning that illuminated the area for a split second before disappearing again.

But that second had been enough to reveal the figure standing at the arena's entrance.

I nearly fell to my knees, wondering if I'd imagined him in my attempt to conjure something meaningful. But as he shifted and flew toward me, I realized he was actually here. My brother had come for me.

Again.

He reformed just as his shadow collided with my body, and I stumbled back as Jackson threw his arms around me.

"You're alive," he said, nearly crushing me.

I laughed and hugged him back, thinking I'd never been so happy to see him in my life.

"What are you doing here?" I asked. "Did Andros tell you what happened?"

Jackson stepped back, releasing me. "Andros? Have you seen him?"

"No, but Ezrah told us Andros would spread the news about what happened here last night," I said. "Maybe he just hasn't gotten to you yet."

Harper flew into the arena, followed by several others I couldn't make out from this distance. I didn't have the same gift of sight my brother had, but as the group approached, I smiled at them. My old friends were a welcome sight.

Brave warriors to have come here expecting to fight the entire King's Guard alone just to rescue me.

And I had no doubt they would have been successful if it had come to that.

Harper threw her arms around me. "I can't tell you how good it is to see you standing here and not in chains in those dungeons," she said.

"Where have you been?" I asked her. "I could feel you, but you were so distant for a long time."

I took her hand and noticed the horrible crisscrossing of deep scars all along the skin of her arms. God, what had she been through?

"It's a long story," she said. She glanced around the arena and smiled. "But I think you just might have a story of your own to share. Is it true the king has been released from a curse and Lea is safe in the castle?"

"It's true," I said.

The guard standing behind Jackson relaxed. "I told you it was true," he said, bringing a hand to his throat, as if he'd been afraid he might lose his head.

That's when I noticed the woman who stood behind the guard. She smiled as our eyes met.

"It's good to see you again, brother," she said. "We seemed to have switched places. I went south after I heard you were free, and you came north. I'm glad we can finally stand together again."

"Illana," I said, pulling her into a hug. I hadn't seen either of my sisters in over a hundred years, and yet I'd seen them both now in one day.

It was a good day.

"Come on," I said. "Let's go up to the castle and find Lea. Then we can all share our stories."

I didn't warn Jackson that Lea might not be as excited to see him as I was, but I'd let him deal with that when the time came.

Together, we all shifted and flew toward the castle. I had a feeling she might still be in her father's study, and as we approached the throne room, the guards stationed at the door confirmed it.

They stood straighter, tentatively reaching for their weapons as we approached.

I held up my hand. "We need to see the king and the princess," I said. "It's urgent we speak to them. Please let them know the Queen of the Southern Kingdom is here."

The guards glanced at Harper, their eyes wide with surprise. The demon on the left gave a quick bow and disappeared quietly into the king's study, emerging a moment later to usher us inside.

"Only Denaer and the queen," the guard said. "The others can wait out here."

Mordecai nodded, and the four of them settled onto a row

of benches just outside the door with Illana.

The study was almost more like a library with its rows upon rows of books that lined the walls. I wasn't sure I had ever been inside this room more than once a very long time ago, but stepping into it now, I felt the tension radiating from Lea all the way across the room.

"Queen Harper," the king said, lowering his head in a bow as he approached. "I cannot tell you what an honor it is to finally meet you. As you know, things were not always good between your father and myself, but I hope our two kingdoms can work together once again."

Harper straightened, then bowed her head to the king, as well. "King," she said. "The honor is all mine. I haven't officially taken the title of Queen just yet, but I intend to soon. One of the guards informed us that things here at the castle had changed, and I know we are all anxious to hear what's happened."

She stepped toward Lea, smiling.

"I'm so glad you're safe," she said.

Lea held out a hand, as if the two of them had only just met.

Jackson looked at me, questioning, and I shrugged. It was too much to try to explain here.

"Thank you," Lea said. "And you, as well. We heard rumors you had been captured by the Order."

Lea's gaze swept over Harper's arms, and the first sign of true emotion since we'd walked into the room shone in her eyes. Worry. Concern.

I couldn't blame Lea for being angry at all of us, but she still couldn't hide the fact that she cared. Even for Harper.

"It's been a rough few months," Harper said with a small smile. "For all of us, I imagine."

"What are you doing here?" Lea asked, her gaze moving to Jackson. Her jaw tensed, and I could only imagine all the things she wanted to say to him right now and might have if her father hadn't been in the room.

"Well, believe it or not, we came here to rescue you," Jackson said, laughing. "I can't tell you how glad I am to see that you don't need rescuing."

The smile fell from his face just as quickly as it had appeared.

"I only wish the same could be said for all our friends."

I stepped forward to stand at Lea's side and face my brother.

"What do you mean?" I asked. "What's happened?"

"We have reason to believe Andros and his elite squad have been captured by the amethyst priestess," Harper said. "And that an attack against the Underground is imminent."

Lea laughed. "That's not possible," she said. "Ezrah just saw Andros last night. He had come here hoping to rescue us, too, but when they saw we had defeated a Stone Guardian and restored order to the city, Ezrah told him to head back to the Underground. Everything was fine when Ezrah left him. I'm sure he's back in the Underground by now."

I suddenly understood Jackson's surprise when I'd mentioned Andros earlier.

Shaking his head, he reached into his pocket and pulled out a tattered strip of black cloth.

The red dragon embroidered on the fabric was a symbol of the Resistance, and the blood smeared across it was a sign that war had found us once again.

AVENGE ME

LEA

I nearly fell to my knees as I reached for the tattered cloth in Jackson's hands, but Aerden reached out to steady me.

I clutched the black armband in my fist, the red dragon insignia torn to shreds but still recognizable despite the blood smeared across it.

"Where did you find this?" I asked, daring to look into Jackson's eyes for the first time since he'd entered the room.

My petty anger suddenly seemed incredibly childish compared to the threat that faced one of my best friends. We had to find him.

"Just beyond the city's walls on the Black Cliffs," he said. "Lea, there was blood everywhere."

I glanced at my father, and he nodded. He shared my ability to see the memory of an item when it was charged with great emotion or conflict.

Sometimes it was more difficult to get a clear memory of an item when it had been removed from the location where the act had taken place, but I had a feeling this armband would be so emotionally charged, I would have no trouble locating the vision.

The question was, was I ready for what I might see? What if he was dead?

Or worse.

"Lea, are you sure?" Aerden asked, stepping toward me with worry in his eyes. "I know you got some rest this morning, but last night was hard on both of us. You're drained. Going into such a violent vision so soon could leave you unable to fight if it comes to that."

I didn't care. When it came to my friend, the leader of the Resistance, and the others I had trained with for so many years, I would find whatever will I needed to fight. But we wouldn't have the slightest clue what—or who—we were up against without seeing the attack.

"I'm here with you," my father said, placing a hand on my arm. "We can enter the vision together. If we combine our power, it shouldn't take too much energy to make it appear."

I shuddered, thinking of what we might see. Jackson had said there was blood everywhere, but what did that mean?

Andros couldn't be dead. He was one of the strongest warriors I had ever known, and with all this talk about father stepping aside to make me Queen of the Northern Kingdom, I assumed Andros would be by my side as the Captain of the King's Guard, if he would take the job.

I couldn't let anything happen to him.

And why had Ezrah said he was okay? Was Andros taken on his way back to the Underground?

I had to find out.

"Stand back," I told the others. "And don't touch me at any point until you're sure I'm back."

I could take others with me into a vision, but tricky things happened when someone tried to join a vision that was already in progress. Father warned me that sometimes people could get stuck in the spaces between.

Aerden placed a hand on Jackson's chest and they all stepped back several steps, giving us space.

I closed my eyes and tightened my hand around the dragon armband as my father held tightly to my wrist.

I tried to clear my mind and see only the face of my friend. It took a minute to clear myself enough to embrace the power within me, but goosebumps broke out on my arms, and when I opened my eyes, I was there.

My father stood at my side, able to let go of me now that we were here in the vision together.

It was dark out, but I could see the shadows of at least forty demons standing in rows before Andros. They were dressed all in black, the only hint of color the red of the dragons at their bicep.

"This is where we wait until Ezrah comes for us," he said. "Judging by the placement of the moons, he should be here within the next fifteen minutes. If he's not here in half an hour, we go in on our own. We'll be using a side entrance near the sewers, but it will be guarded by at least two members of the King's Guard. If anyone here has a problem killing tonight, you can leave now with no shame. These are fellow demons we'll be fighting tonight, not witches."

No one moved a muscle. The group before him was so silent, I wouldn't have known they were there if the moons had been behind shadow tonight.

"We have two priorities," Andros said. "We are here to rescue Aerden, brother of Denaer, and we are here to free our princess. We all have our feelings about the king and the other members of the Council, but tonight is not a night for heroics and snap decisions based on our emotions. The only thing that matters is that we save Aerden and Lazalea. If you object to this or have other plans, speak now and make your ideas known."

No one spoke, but there were so many in Andros's elite squad who hated my father and what he had failed to do for his people. I prayed for the chance to explain the truth to them. To convince them that my father would fight for us now that he was whole again.

"If Ezrah fails to show, we will split into two groups. You all have your assignments," he said, walking down the rows as he spoke. "Red Group. You're in charge of rescuing Aerden. He's locked away in the dungeons of the arena, two floors down in the last cell. Kill any guards you meet along the way and search them for weapons and keys. Do not give them a chance to sound the alarm."

Andros walked back up a separate row.

"Dragon Group. Your job is to rescue the princess. Ezrah said he would be meeting with her inside the arena, but it's possible she could be locked away in her room. You've each been given the chance to study a map of the castle," he said. "Get to her room using back stairs that are less likely to be guarded. Kill any guards you meet, but if there are citizens and servants along the way, incapacitate them with whatever magic you have available. If you can avoid severely hurting them, do what you can. If not, do what you must."

Andros came back around to the front of the group.

"Do not be afraid when you approach the wall of the King's City, built to keep us, its true citizens, out. Remember what you have trained for. Remember who we fight for," Andros said. "Someday, shadow willing, we will see these lands restored to their former glory. Tonight, we take another step forward in that journey. Fight well, and leave your fear behind you."

The rows of demons standing before him raised their left fists but remained silent.

I looked around, searching for some evidence of their attackers, but the night was still. The Black Cliffs reflected pieces of moonlight back toward us, but there was no movement that I could see anywhere.

I turned to see the King's City with its obsidian towers rising against the backdrop of the dark blue sky. When I was a shadowling, there was no wall around the city. The streets and markets welcomed everyone equally.

Now, the massive wall enclosed the entire city in its dark embrace, a symbol of what the Order of Shadows had done to us all. They had separated us from each other. They had caused us to build walls around our hearts that no magic could break through.

The wall hid the intricate beauty of the castle's entrance with its gleaming steps and veins of gold the way the Order's evil hid the beauty of a shadowling's smile.

They turned us against each other, and while we were trying to save ourselves, they stole us in the night.

Soon, I would tear that wall down, just like I would tear the Order down. Piece by piece until there was nothing left of it.

"There," my father whispered. "Is that Ezrah?"

I followed my father's gaze to see a single shape walking toward us in the moonlight. Only, there was something strange about its movements. This was not a demon swirling in shadow, but it wasn't a man, either.

This creature hovered over the obsidian of the Black Cliffs, as if flying. My heart tightened, and I shouted to Andros, forgetting for a second that he couldn't hear or see me.

"Hunter," I shouted.

Andros seemed to realize it just as I did, and he gathered a dark red power in his hands.

But with everyone's attention on the single hunter coming toward them in the darkness, no one noticed the fifty others coming up behind. I screamed as their rotting faces were illuminated by the red energy of Andros's first spell.

The Resistance was outnumbered against the group of hunters. It was hopeless, and I fell to my knees, preparing to watch the death of one of my dearest friends.

But the hunters had not come to kill.

They had only come to capture and to hurt.

I watched as the Resistance fought with everything they had, downing several of the hunters before they were overcome. Each hunter carried chains that glinted silver in the moonlight. Demon steel to bind their magic.

Andros was the last to fall, and by the time he was brought to his knees, chains wrapped around his body, his face was covered in blood.

"You may try to kill me, but you will never stop the Resistance," he said, his head held proud even then. "Our friends will come for us, and when they do, you'll wish you never saw my face."

The hunter who had chained him lifted her hands and pushed him back with a spell made of air like a tornado.

Bruised and bloodied, Andros tried to pick himself up as the hunter came to stand over him.

She leaned down and gripped his face with one bony, decayed hand.

"You will never see your friends again," she said. "By the time they figure out you're gone, you'll already be trapped inside the body of a witch for all eternity. They won't even know where to look."

Andros looked up at her and smiled, his eyes showing no fear.

The hunter pushed him back to the ground as hard as she could.

"Why are you laughing?" she asked angrily.

But I knew why.

When the hunter had reached for him, the sleeve of her tattered robe had lifted to reveal a bracelet made of pure amethysts.

The hunter turned away, giving orders to the others, and as she did, Andros leaned over and ripped his black armband with his teeth, quickly spitting it to the ground before anyone noticed.

He had left a clue. A trail for me to follow.

"If you can get free, find me, Princess," he whispered, almost as if he could see me standing here. "And if it is too late, my friend, avenge me."

With that, the vision disappeared, and I was once again back in the study of my father's castle.

"Someone find Ezrah," I said, rage trembling in my voice. "And bring him to me in chains."

HE CAN'T BE TRUSTED

HARPER

"What did you see?" I asked when Lea had returned from the vision with her father.

The anger and worry in her eyes scared me. What if the ruby priestess had lied? What if Andros was dead and Lea had just been forced to watch it happen right before her eyes?

"He's been taken," she said. "By hunters of the amethyst priestess."

It wasn't good news, but it did line up with what Priestess Thorn had told me.

"I've never seen a hunter up close like that before," the king said, obviously shaken by what he'd witnessed. "And never so many of them in one place. They had to have known he would be there."

"And how many demons he would have with him," Lea said. "They came with every drop of information they would need to defeat him quickly, before any of the guards near the castle could see what was happening or go out on patrol."

"It's exactly like she said," Jackson whispered to me.

"Like who said?" Lea asked, stepping forward.

I had no idea what was going on with her, but she hadn't exactly welcomed us with open arms. She seemed pissed when we showed up, actually, and I had no clue why.

Now, though, she was downright angry.

So nice of her to be grateful we had come to her aid, despite everything else we were facing right now.

Jackson opened his mouth to tell her everything, but I placed a hand on his chest and shook my head slightly. If she was already in a mood like this, the last thing I wanted to do was tell her we'd gotten the information from one of the Order's priestesses. We could explain it later.

Besides, if her father had been under the control of the High Priestess, I needed more details before I started talking about the ruby priestess's involvement in all of this.

"Someone warned us of a three-part attack," I said. "One attack will involve bombs in my domed city, but we've taken precautions to make sure no one is hurt. The next attack was what you just witnessed with Andros. As far as we've been told, he's to be kept alive until the High Priestess gives her further instructions."

I decided to just leave it at that, without giving too much information just yet.

"And the third?" Aerden asked. "Something about the Underground?"

I nodded. "The citrine priestess is expected to send almost her entire force of hunters down into the Underground where she's supposed to kill or capture as many as she can," I said. "Mary Anne and Essex are already there now, moving everyone to safety before the attack, which we believe is supposed to occur tomorrow night. With any luck, the place will appear empty by the time the hunters get there."

Lea studied me, her eyes reduced to slits. "And just how did you come across this powerful information?" she asked.

"That's not important," I said, ignoring Jackson's sharp look. "What matters is that we do everything we can to save them. Once the Underground is secure, we can head for Andros's location."

Lea scoffed. "And it's just going to be that easy, is it?" she asked. "We've only been searching for the location of the different priestess's houses for decades. I'm sure it will be simple to just locate her home and walk right in like we owned the place."

"I know where to find him," I said, not giving her more than that.

I could feel Jackson's eyes on me, but I didn't care if he was confused. If Lea was determined to keep things professional and distant between us, as if we barely knew each other, then I was simply following her lead.

I certainly didn't need to hear her judgments right now about the decisions I made in my own kingdom.

"How?" she asked. "Are you seriously not going to tell me?"

The door to the study opened, and two guards rushed in, their heads lowered.

"Ezrah's nowhere to be found," the first guard said. "His stuff has been cleared from the barracks. One of the guards at the front gate said she saw him leave earlier this afternoon."

Lea's eyes widened. "He's gone?" she asked.

"Ezrah is the guard Andros placed here in the city?" I asked. "Someone from the Resistance?"

"Yes," Aerden said after Lea hesitated. "He's been helping us communicate with each other and with Andros since we were thrown in the dungeons."

The king shifted his weight uncomfortably, and I wondered what the full story was here. He'd been the one to throw them in the dungeons in the first place, and supposedly, he'd been controlled by the High Priestess with some kind of curse until last night.

Apparently, we all had a lot to talk about when things slowed down a bit.

"He lied to me," Lea said. "He told me he saw Andros and told him to head home, but that's not what I saw in that vision. Andros was still waiting for Ezrah to arrive. He hadn't spoken to him or seen him yet when those hunters arrived."

"And those hunters knew exactly where to find him," the king said. "It was an ambush."

"Ezrah was the only one who could have possibly known where he would be," Lea said.

My heart tightened in my chest, and I fumbled in my pocket for one of the communication stones. I held one in my hand and rubbed a finger across the top of it. As soon as it connected with Mary Anne's stone, it began to glow with a deep red light from within.

"Harper? Are you safe? Did you find Lea and Aerden?" she asked.

"They're here with me now," I said. "We're all safe, but I need to know how you guys are doing. Mary Anne, there's a demon from the Resistance who may have betrayed Andros to the amethyst priestess. His name is Ezrah. Is he there with you?"

"Ezrah?" she asked, whispering now. "Harper, he arrived

here even before we did. He's been taking control here, telling people which rooms to go into, even though we wanted to move them deeper into the tunnels. Ourelia said he was one of Andros's most trusted friends."

I closed my eyes, trying to think through the possibilities.

If Ezrah was the betrayer, he would be moving everyone into danger zones, not away from them.

"He can't be trusted, Mary Anne," I said. "You need to tell Essex. The two of you need to restrain him somehow. The hunters can't get into the Underground unless someone lets them in. If you restrain him now, he won't be able to—"

"He's gone," she said, panic in her voice. "He was just standing here in the room a few minutes ago. I don't see him, Harper."

"Find him," I said. "Grab Ourelia and a few others and search for him. Make sure he doesn't get to any of the entrances. We're on our way to you as soon as we can get there."

Screams rang out through the com stone as horror swept through the crowd near Mary Anne.

"They're already here, Harper," she shouted, spells blasting in the distance. "Hurry."

And with that, the stone went dark.

NO MATTER WHAT

LEA

"N o," I shouted, reaching for the stone in Harper's hand as if I could somehow teleport through it to help my friends.

The stone went dark before I could reach it, not that it would have made any difference. There was nothing I could do from here.

"You said the attack would be tomorrow," I said, shaking my head. "We have to get down there."

"It was supposed to be, but maybe Ezrah moved up the timeline when Mary Anne got there," Harper said. She grabbed Jackson's hand. "Aerden is safe. We have to go to the Underground."

He nodded and looked up at me. "Will you come with us?"

Whatever anger I felt toward him melted away in the face of danger, and I nodded.

The demons of the Resistance and those who lived in the Underground had been our family for a time, once, when we had nowhere else to turn. I would do whatever I needed to do to keep them safe.

"Father, how many of the King's Guard can you spare?" I asked.

"Wait," Jackson said. "You're absolutely certain it's safe to trust him. No offense, King, but you haven't exactly been a friend to the Resistance all these years."

"I am a friend to you all now," my father said. "Lea, tell Mazrock to gather three hundred of his best soldiers and follow you to the Underground. How many hunters are you expecting down there?"

Harper shook her head. "I'm not sure. Potentially all of the citrine priestess's hunters. It could be close to one hundred, if all of them show up."

I cursed. A few hundred against thousands of untrained shadowlings and merchants? It would be a slaughter.

At least Andros had only taken forty or so of his most elite squad with him last night, which meant there were at least a thousand soldiers left behind in the Underground to protect the rest of the demons locked inside.

But would it be enough to stop them?

It sometimes took five or more demons to kill a single hunter.

We needed to get there as soon as possible, and though I was grateful for three hundred soldiers from my father's army, it wouldn't do any good unless we got there in time to stop those hunters.

We moved quickly, shouting orders to Mazrock and gathering our weapons. My bow was up in my bedroom, but I made my way there as quickly as I ever had, my heart pounding as I flew through the castle.

"What's happened?" Presha asked when I reformed and started changing clothes and shoving things into my backpack.

I wasn't going to be much use to anyone in a dress.

"An attack on my friends in the Underground," I said. "I have to go."

I didn't stay to explain more than that.

By the time I made it back to the throne room area, Mazrock's three hundred guards had already assembled in the hall, waiting for my command.

Behind him, four of my best friends stood, their eyes wide as they looked at me with pride.

Tears threatened to fall as I threw my arms around Mordecai and Erick's necks, then reached over to hug Cristo and Joost. The five of us had spent decades together in the human world, seeking out as many of the Order's gates as we could find and turning as many witches as we could into our allies.

I owed them my life a hundred times over, and I had missed them.

"Thank you for being here," I said, hoping we all had a chance to catch up once this fight was over.

"Harper and Jackson have already gone," Mordecai said. "But I know which entrance to take. I can lead you there."

I nodded, noticing that Aerden had stayed behind with me. Our eyes met, and he nodded, the axe from his battles in the King's Games strapped across his back with a leather cord.

I stood in front of the soldiers and explained to them as quickly as I could just what we were about to face. Although many of the King's Guard soldiers had been out on patrols where they faced hunters over the years, for the most part, these soldiers had not seen true combat at this level in decades.

Some, probably never outside of training.

I gave them a quick rundown of the way hunters fight and the layout of the massive tunnels of the Underground. I commanded them to get as many of the Underground's citizens to safety as possible, no matter what it took.

"Protecting me is not your mission, is that understood?"

The soldiers nodded in unison, and I looked to Mazrock.

"I'm going to push us as fast as we can go," I said, checking to be sure my bow was secure across my back. "Keep up."

With that, I shifted and flew through the castle's massive arched doorway and out into the streets of the King's City. The heavy gate that barred anyone from entering this city without an invitation opened with a massive creaking sound, as if it had been decades since it had opened.

And I realized with a start that it probably had been. Guards passed in and out of the city through small doorways, but the main gates of the King's City wall had not been opened to let anyone in or out in a very long time.

But now was a time of change, and as our massive force flew through the open gate, I vowed to return as soon as I could and make sure those gates were now opened to any demon of the Northern Kingdom who wanted to seek refuge within the walls.

We flew as fast as we could, pushing our demon shadows as hard as possible as we flew high into the air and traveled great distances. But before we'd even made it halfway to the nearest hidden entrance to the Underground, a massive explosion lit up the night, throwing fire and rock into the air.

Even at this distance, the force of it was enough to nearly knock me out of the sky as the heat blossomed across my skin.

What the hell had just happened?

The guards behind me paused as I held back, studying the plumes of fire that rose into the air from several locations across the Shadow World. I made a few calculations, and realized, with a sinking feeling deep in the pit of my stomach, that nearly every known entrance to the Underground, guarded and secret and inaccessible unless someone below brought you through the black roses, had just been blown to pieces.

HOLD THE LINE

JACKSON

We had almost made it to the Underground's entrance near the forest when a massive explosion shook the ground and erupted in the night like a volcano.

Harper was thrown backward against a nearby tree, and my face stung with burns as I fell to the ground at her side.

"What the hell happened?" she asked, climbing to her feet as the flames caught on and spread through the forest around us.

I stood and stepped toward the entrance to the Underground, my eyes wide as I realized the ring of black roses that used to be there had been replaced by a massive hole the size of a bus.

I coughed and blinked against the heavy smoke rising around us. I had to do something about these flames, or we'd be killed just from the smoke.

I crouched low and closed my eyes, connecting easily to the enormous power here in the Shadow World. It was so much easier to reach it here than it was for me in the human world, and I drank it in, allowing the energy of this place to fill my body.

I inhaled, breathing in the power.

As I exhaled, a chill passed over my lips, covering the entire area surrounding us with a light frost that extinguished the flames in an instant. The smoke that went along with it quickly disappeared, too, and Harper and I moved to the Underground's entrance.

"I think they just blew up every entrance," I said.

"Which means hunters can get in from anywhere," Harper said. "We have to find them."

She shifted to smoke and flew through the damaged entrance. It was pitch-black down here, but without missing a beat, she conjured a bright orb of light that zipped through the tunnels ahead of her.

The small tunnel opened up into a massive marble staircase that led down to a huge hall.

At first, the entire marketplace seemed deserted, which is how it was supposed to look when the hunters arrived, but as we traveled deeper into the Underground, the sounds of fighting and screams soon reached us through one of the main tunnels leading back to the apartments.

"This way," Harper shouted, tearing off down the hallway.

It didn't take us long to find the fight, but down here in the smaller tunnels, it was difficult to push our way through to help.

Mothers grabbed their shadowlings and shifted, flying toward the main hall or ducking into apartments where they could hide, but for every group that flew past us, another lay injured and bleeding on the floor.

Smoke filled the hallways and screams filled my ears.

I stopped to help as many as I could with my healing light, but there were too many injured, and I had to save some energy for the hunters.

Finally, after fighting our way through the fleeing crowds and bringing down three hunters along the way, we finally pushed into the heart of the fight.

Mary Anne had brought the majority of the demons of the Underground through a small tunnel past these apartments and into a secret cavern that was rarely used except by the army for special training. The ceiling in this area of the Underground was nearly as high as that of the main market, and the room itself was about half as big, running the length of several football fields.

For a place to hide, this was a great location as long as no one knew where to find you.

But for a battleground, it was horrible. There were only two ways in or out, which meant that as the hunters poured in through one side, there was only one possible escape, and that was through the halls and apartments we'd just run through.

Only a few demons could push through at a time, which meant the rest of them were all sitting ducks for the wrath of the hunters.

The inside of that room was pure chaos as the Resistance Army fought to hold the hunters back. The bodies of those who had fallen littered the stone floor of the room, and the smell of blood and smoke tinged the air.

I searched for any sign of Mary Anne or Essex, but it was impossible to make them out amongst the fighting. I just had to pray they were okay.

It was also possible they were settled in a different part of the Underground. She'd told Harper that Ezrah had tried to separate them. I would find her as soon as I could, but for now, I joined Harper as we flew to the front lines of the battle, our weapons raised as we met the hunters who threatened to destroy everything this place stood for.

Swords clashed against decaying bone, and spells exploded around us. Something burned as it collided with my shoulder, but I didn't have time to even care what had happened. There were so many hunters, all I could do was keep fighting with everything I had.

I would not let this place fall.

"Hold the line," Harper shouted. "Don't let any of the hunters through."

Her rallying cry seemed to spark hope in the demons fighting, and we reached deep inside, giving everything we had to the fight even as our allies fell at our feet.

I don't know how long we fought. Hours, maybe, before the screams of the hunters had faded and their green and black blood dripped like thick tears from the obsidian walls. By the time the last hunter on the line had fallen, my body was covered in blood.

A mix of my own, the demons fighting at my side, and the hunters who had fallen to my spear or my spells.

I fell to my knees as I turned to see so many injured and dying. Hundreds calling for help and raising their hands to the sky, screaming in horror and pain.

How could the Order of Shadows be so cruel?

I wanted to cry out in sorrow. I wanted to heal as many as I could, even though I wasn't sure how I could find the energy to heal even one.

But even as I tried to stand, I heard a cry from deeper

within the Underground. A cry followed by a chorus of screams that could only have come from a fresh group of hunters.

I looked over to meet Harper's gaze, praying it was just some echo in my head. That it wasn't real. But from the horrified look in her eyes, I knew my prayers had not been answered.

Somewhere deeper inside the Underground, even more hunters had arrived to fight.

Harper stood, her knees trembling for a moment before she steadied herself and lifted her sword.

"We fight until the last hunter is down," she called, and with a strength I admired more than ever, she disappeared through the doorway in search of the fight.

I DON'T KNOW HOW

AERDEN

In all the stories I'd heard of the Underground, this place had been portrayed as one of great strength and solidarity. A city built from the ashes of the Northern Kingdom as those the king abandoned came together as one.

The Resistance Army was over a thousand soldiers strong, trained to fight the toughest hunters and to protect those who could not protect themselves.

I'd wanted to visit this place so many times since I'd been set free, but my own fear of traveling back to the Shadow World had kept me from it.

Now, as I stared out at the destruction, I wished I had come in more peaceful times, when I could have known the safety and community of this place. As we ran to join the fight, I knew that it would never be the same again, even if they could manage to rebuild.

No one would ever forget the blood that stained the walls or the screams of the hunters mixed with shouts of terror and the screams of children.

I stayed close to Lea's side as we led the King's Guard through the halls and tunnels, searching for the main fight. This place was massive, built by the trolls thousands of years ago, and though Lea seemed to know exactly where she was going, the halls were difficult to navigate in places, and I could feel her frustration mounting.

"There," she shouted, pointing toward a massive hole in the wall at the end of one tunnel that opened up into a large room with high ceilings. "They're in the training rooms."

We flew to the end of the hallway and stepped into a fiery hell as hunters unleashed the worst of their magic on rows of soldiers. On the front line, I caught sight of Jackson briefly as he thrust the tip of his spear into the neck of a hunter.

Lea commanded the guards to join the fight, then turned to Mordecai and Joost.

"We have to help everyone get to safety," she said. She pointed to a spot on the wall. "Through here is another set of tunnels that leads back to the market. Do whatever you have to do to open this up and give them another way out of this room. We have to keep this other side clear to get my army inside as fast as we can."

The two demons nodded and went to work, blasting the stone with magic until cracks began to form.

"You're with me," Lea said, reaching for my hand and shifting as she flew toward the front lines.

When we reformed just shy of the first row of guards who had joined the fight, she turned to me, her eyes locked on mine. I could hardly hear her over the destruction of battle, but she seemed to speak directly to my soul.

"Whatever you did last night, I need you to do it again," she said. "Whatever that thing was—that golem—could bring down this entire line of hunters in a matter of minutes. Aerden, I need you to bring him back."

I shook my head. "I can't," I said. "I tried to do it again tonight, but I don't know how. I don't know what I did, Lea."

"You have to try," she said, grabbing my hand.

I closed my eyes and imagined one of those hunters heading straight for Lea. I tried to imagine its bony hand wrapping around her neck, and I poured all my power into that feeling of fear and my desire to keep her safe.

But when I opened my eyes, there was no great light. Only a dim spark of energy crackling on my fingertips.

"I can't control it," I said. "I'm sorry."

She cursed and took her bow from her back, nocking an arrow made of green light. Poison.

"Then fight, dammit," she shouted, running forward toward the fight as she let the first arrow go.

For a minute, I lost her in the throng, catching sight of her arrows flying as my axe found its way into my hands.

I ran into the chaos, half-searching for her in the crowd as I severed the head of one hunter and turned to the next.

Harper had said she expected a hundred hunters, but there had to be twice as many in this room alone.

I hadn't even realized the Order commanded so many. Where had they all come from?

A hunter's hand grabbed my shoulder and an icy chill ran down my spine as her magic flowed into my body, almost freezing me to the spot where I stood, but just as suddenly as she'd grabbed me, she let go in a scream of horror as the tip of a spear sliced through her temple.

Bones and dust fell to the ground as thick blood oozed from the hunter's eyes.

I turned to see Jackson at my side, giving me a quick nod of his head before he pulled the spear from the hunter's body and moved on to the next. He was covered in blood, and I wondered just how many of these things he'd already faced.

I turned to follow him, but just as I did, Lea caught my eye and stopped. She lowered her bow as a hunter stepped forward, a spell of pure flame gathered in its hands.

I screamed for her to move, but she just stood there, determination in her fiery gaze.

What the hell was she doing? If she didn't move, she was going to get herself killed.

She raised an eyebrow, as if urging me to get with the program, here.

She was taunting me. Forcing my hand. Putting herself in death's way just to push me to the edge.

If she survived this, I was going to kill her.

The hunter released its spell, and time seemed to slow down. Lea didn't move at all. She just stared at me. Waiting.

I reached deep within my own soul to access some hidden part of my power I had never even known existed until last night.

I closed my eyes and screamed, my fists balled tightly at my side as my fear and love sparked hotter, more intensely than ever.

The force of my scream echoed even over the noise of the battle, and all around me, gasps of surprise filled the air. When I opened my eyes, he was there.

My golem, conjured from pure love and desperation, held the hunter's ball of fire in one massive, radiant hand. At my command, he flung the spell back toward the hunter, and it exploded in a huge eruption of light that traveled down the row of hunters who remained.

I lifted my axe and ran toward the hunters as the King's Guards backed away, unsure whether to trust the golem or fight against it.

Wherever I aimed my axe and my power, the golem moved to strike, too, taking out hunter after hunter in quick succession.

In minutes, Lea's arrows joined the fists of my golem to my left while Harper's sword gleamed with light as she fought on my other side. Jackson stood next to her, his spear and conjured blades of ice slicing through the hunters with greater force than I'd ever seen him use before.

We moved as a team, our strength as a group unstoppable.

And when the last of the hunters had fallen and the battle was truly over, the golem I'd conjured disappeared in an instant. Exhausted, I fell to the ground, the world around me blinking into darkness.

CRYSTAL CLEAR

JACKSON

I ran to my brother's side as he fell, screaming for help.

"Get Angela," I shouted to Harper. "See if you can find her."

There were so many who needed our help with healing, but I could only focus on Aerden. He'd been through too much to die now. What the hell had he done, anyway? Where had that being of light come from?

There was no way he'd created that.

Was there?

Lea placed a hand on my shoulder. "Angela won't be able to help him," she said softly. "I'll help you move him into one of the empty apartments just down the hall. All he needs is rest. Let Angela help the demons who are injured. And if you have any energy left, you can help her. I'll keep an eye on Aerden."

I looked up at her, shaking my head.

"What did he do?" I asked. "I don't understand."

"Let's move him," she said, glancing around at all the destruction in the room.

Together, we lifted him and brought him into the first empty apartment we found that actually had a bed in it. The room was dusty, as if it hadn't been lived in for a very long time, but it would do.

"I'll stay with him," Lea said, pulling up a chair and barely glancing at me.

Not exactly the way I'd expected to be treated by her after all this time.

"What's up with you?" I asked. "You've been giving me the cold shoulder since we first walked into your father's office. If you're upset we didn't come for you sooner, you have to understand—"

"What do I have to understand?" she asked, looking up with ice in her eyes. "That you had someone you cared about more than both of us combined to search for, instead? You don't have to go making apologies to me. Everything is crystal clear now, Jackson."

I took a step back.

"I knew where you were," I said. "I knew you guys were safe, even if you weren't exactly comfortable. Of course, I had no idea your father was somehow working for the High Priestess until recently, but that's something you'll have to explain to me, because it doesn't make a whole lot of sense. Harper, on the other hand, was kidnapped by the emerald priestess and in danger of being killed."

"Like I said, you had your priorities," she said. "Who am I to question that?"

"What the hell is your problem?" I asked. "Last time I spoke to you, just a couple of days ago, really, you said you were looking forward to coming home and catching up on everything that had happened since you guys were captured. What's happened since then to piss you off so badly?"

She stood, finally looking at me, instead of avoiding my eyes.

"I found out the truth," she said, her body trembling with anger as a tear slid down her cheek. She wiped it away so fast, I was afraid she'd scratched herself. "I found out that you've been lying to me for a hundred years, letting me follow you around like a lost puppy, begging for scraps. Letting me believe that I'd done something to upset you or displease you. Letting me believe that I had gone from the most important thing in your life to practically nothing. How do you think that made me feel all these years?"

Her words nearly knocked the breath from my lungs. I fell back against the wall, shaking my head. I didn't even know what to say to her. There were no words strong enough for that kind of apology.

"I'm so sorry. It wasn't my truth to tell," I said, all the anger fading away. Everything she said was the truth, and she had every right to be mad. "I had no idea if we would ever see Aerden again, and he made me promise to take care of you. I did everything I could to live up to that promise, but I failed you both, Lea. I'm so sorry. I never meant to hurt you. I swear I didn't want that."

"But you did hurt me," she said, her tears flowing freely now.

It broke my heart to see her like this. She was always so strong and untouchable, but now, after the battle and everything else that had happened, both of us were raw and vulnerable.

"I know," I said, my heart breaking for all the pain I had caused her. "I'm sorry."

"You should have told me the truth," she said. "You should have told me that day when I opened the locket and saw that light."

"I know."

"You had every opportunity to tell me the truth at any point over the past one hundred years. To set me free from this ridiculous belief that I was somehow undeserving of the love you used to have for me," she yelled. "Do you know that I used to lie awake at night, trying to pinpoint the exact moment when I'd lost you? And I couldn't fathom it. I couldn't understand how something so strong and pure could be lost. All I could come up with was that I had somehow come up short. That I just wasn't the person you needed me to be, despite walking away from everything for you. For both of you."

"I should have told you," I said. "But with him trapped as a Prima demon, I thought it would only torture you more. And I felt that I'd be betraying his memory. His truth. Lea, I know it's no excuse, but I was trying to honor my duty to you and my promise to him. I failed you in that, and I can't tell you how sorry I am."

She turned away, her shoulders shaking with sobs. I had never seen her so openly upset, and I had no idea what to do. I wanted to wrap my arms around her and help her see that I had never meant to hurt her, but I knew she didn't want my comfort right now.

"It would have been easier for me if you had both been honest from the start," she said softly. "It would have been easier for all of us. If I had opened that locket to see an ordinary light inside that heartstone you gave me, I would have been okay with that. I would have accepted that and honored our commitment. Instead, that light gave me hope. It made me see everything differently."

"I know," I said again, feeling helpless.

"It would have been a lot easier to understand how we drifted apart if I had not thought you loved me with such a strong passion," she said. "It wouldn't have hurt so damn much when I lost you."

How did I explain to her that I was hurting, too? I had lost my twin brother, and I didn't truly know if I would ever get him back. I was lost without him, determined to do nothing more with my life than fight the Order who had stolen him from us.

But the difference was that she hadn't caused my pain the same way I had caused hers.

I owed her a lot after all of this, and I didn't even know where to start.

"I'm glad you know," I said softly. "Even if it means you'll hate me forever for what I did."

She turned, her eyes still glistening with tears.

"I don't hate you," she said. "I'm just hurt. Confused. I'm..."

She searched for the right words, her eyes landing on Aerden's face before she turned away again.

"I'm furious," she said. "But I don't hate you."

There was so much I wanted to say to her, but I wasn't sure she'd really be able to hear me right now. I wanted her to know that even though the light had not come from me, the light itself was not a lie.

It was real, but it was Aerden's truth, not mine.

The light.

I gasped and brought a hand to my forehead as I looked down at my sleeping brother.

"That golem," I said in a whisper.

Lea sniffed and turned around, almost laughing as she walked over to Aerden's beside. "Can you believe that's how I found out?" she asked. "Some giant golem made of light that suddenly appeared to save my life last night? I would have recognized that light anywhere."

I studied her face and the way she looked down at him, hope swelling in my heart.

She loves him.

She might not be ready to admit it, even to herself, but I could see it written in her expression.

I wanted to pick him up off the table and dance around the room with him. There was hope for them, yet, and after the battle we'd just been through, we needed all the hope we could get.

A golem made of pure light. Pure love.

Holy crap.

"I didn't even know it was possible to conjure something so strong," I said. "I've never heard of another shadow demon able to do anything like it. I certainly can't, and I'm his twin brother."

"I didn't, either," she said, pulling her gaze away from his face. "But it could be very useful for us as we face the Order. We'll have to figure out how to train him to use it."

When she faced me again, she had wiped every trace of vulnerability and sorrow from her face and replaced it with the logic and reason of a leader. A skill that would serve her well when she was queen.

I had a feeling that moment for her was coming sooner

than any of us expected, and I hoped she didn't push Aerden away out of her own sense of duty to the kingdom.

She would be a great leader, but she deserved to be happy, just like all the rest of us.

Lea had grown used to sacrifice, though. And pain.

Because of me, she had gotten totally out of practice when it came to believing in love or prioritizing her own happiness.

I glanced down at Aerden. Convincing her to believe in it again was his job, now, though. Not mine. I didn't envy him the task, but it was going to be one hell of a ride to watch it happen.

"I'm going to check on the others," I said. "See where I can be helpful now that I've had a few moments of rest. I'll see you later?"

She nodded, her eyes clear and her head held high, as if she had never even shed a tear.

Damn, she was strong and stubborn. A dangerous mix when it came to a demon like Lea. I was glad to know, at least, that though she was angry, she didn't hate me.

It was a relief to have that secret out in the open. I had carried it for so long, it had become a weight on my shoulders.

I hoped that over time, she would learn to forgive me for the lies I'd told.

That she would learn to forgive us both.

I squeezed my brother's hand. "Let me know when he wakes up."

"I will," she said.

She sat down by his side, leaning back in her chair but not daring to meet my eyes.

Whatever moment we had shared was over, and for now, there was nothing more to say.

DIAMONDS

HARPER

"**G**et at least two guards on every single entrance," I said. "And a runner, if we have enough demons able to do the job. We need someone to run back here and alert us if any hunters appear at that entrance."

Mazrock nodded, apparently willing to take orders from the Queen of the Southern Kingdom in the absence of his own princess. Where the hell had Lea gone, anyway?

The last time I saw her, she'd been standing over Jackson and Aerden as I ran to get help. When I got back, the three of them were gone.

I bit my lower lip, looking around for them one more time. I didn't have time to go searching the whole Underground. Even though I wasn't the leader down here by any means, in Andros's absence, many of the demons were looking to me for help and instructions.

Ourelia, Andros's wife, had already begun setting up a makeshift hospital in one of the larger training rooms deeper inside the Underground, leaving me here to sort through the rest of our defenses.

Essex and Mary Anne had been helping to move the wounded and separate those who needed immediate attention from those who could wait or be cared for by a loved one.

I was relieved to see Essex's mother following him around, tearing strips of cloth from a large roll of fabric to help bind wounds and stop minor bleeds.

But not everyone here had been so lucky.

I brought a trembling hand to my forehead, wincing at the pain that blossomed in my side as I lifted my arm. I had been struck by several spells and a few blows along the way. Nothing serious, but it was enough to leave some bruises for sure.

It was nothing compared to the injuries some of the others down here had suffered.

Such a senseless loss of life. And why had there been so many of those hunters?

"Has anyone seen Ezrah?" I asked. "Does anyone know if he was captured or hurt?"

I was hoping he was alive so that I could hand him off to Lea, but no one seemed to know where he was. Which meant he had probably gotten away in the chaos.

Coward.

I didn't even know the guy, but I wanted the chance to tell him exactly what I thought of him.

How could a fellow demon allow this to happen? What could possibly motivate him to offer up so many of his own people for slaughter?

I couldn't even imagine it.

But I knew from experience that the Order was good at threats and manipulation, sometimes kidnapping or threatening a demon's family in order to force them to betray their friends. I'd seen it too many times to count now, so was that what happened with Ezrah? Had the Order taken someone he loved and threatened to kill them if he didn't betray the Resistance?

Or had they promised to free someone he cared about if he did this one thing?

It wouldn't make it forgivable, but at least it would make sense. Sometimes, people did horrible things when they were desperate to save the ones they loved.

I shuddered as I thought about the things Jackson told me he had done to some of those hunters in an effort to get them to say where I'd been taken. Even though they were hunters he was torturing, I couldn't help but think about how even hunters had once been little girls with hopes and dreams. They were usually turned into hunters because they'd disobeyed the Order, and although many of them eventually came to thrive on the death and enslavement of demons, most of them had originally been good people with good hearts.

The Order had a tendency to twist everything, though. Even hearts.

The ruby priestess had said it herself.

It's amazing the distasteful things you can get used to doing when you have no other choice.

I wanted to believe I was above making those kinds of choices, but who knew what I would be willing to do if someone had Jackson by the throat. Would I let him die if there was something I could do to stop it?

I turned away from the blood-soaked floor of the first battle room now that it was mostly empty except for the putrid bodies of the dead hunters.

If there was one good thing that had happened tonight, it was that the Order of Shadows had lost at least two hundred of their hunters.

I paused in the doorway before leaving and suddenly turned back, just wanting to see for myself if each of these hunters carried tokens from their citrine priestess. I held my breath and bent down toward the nearest hunter, using the tip of my sword to push what was left of her around as I searched for some sign of a stone.

Not all hunters carried trinkets that gave away which priestess they worked for, but many of them did. A lot of the times, the stones they wore allowed them to communicate with their priestess or the Prima who ruled over them. And sometimes, the stones gave them special abilities like speed or stamina in battle.

I saw no sign of a stone on the first few hunters I checked, but the sixth one was the lucky one. I heard the stone drop from the pile of rags she had worn, and I got down on my hands and knees to search for it among the debris and blood on the floor.

I gasped as the diamond sparkled in the light of the conjured orb floating above my head.

The ruby priestess told me nothing about there being diamond hunters here today. Was that why there had been so many?

I looked at the dozens of hunters decaying on the floor in rows backing up to the hole they'd crawled through to get in, and I motioned to several of the guards near the door.

"Gather a team of five and go through the bodies of these

hunters, here and throughout the entire Underground," I said. "Look for any sign of diamonds or other gemstones like this."

I pulled the strip of cloth from my wrist and used it to pick the diamond stone off the floor. I showed it to the guards.

"It can sometimes be a necklace or a ring. Sometimes just a loose stone," I said. "Be careful not to touch any of the stones directly with your skin. Sometimes these stones are cursed or charged with powerful magic that can kill you instantly, so be as careful as if your life depended on it."

"What do we do with them once we've collected them all?" the guard next to me asked.

He stared at the decaying bodies at our feet with a disgusted look on his face, and I couldn't blame him. This was not going to be a fun job, but it was important.

"Bring everything you find to me as soon as you've finished," I said. "I'll send another team behind you to clean everything up."

The guard gave a slight bow of his head and called out to two more guards near the door.

Diamonds. Dammit. What else was the ruby priestess wrong about?

Or had she lied just to lure us into a trap they never thought we'd survive?

I shook my head. Why was I so eager to believe she'd been trying to help me? Even now that I'd just watched one of the most horrific attacks on demonkind there had ever been?

I needed to find Jackson, Lea, and Aerden, if he was awake. Together, we needed to figure out how to secure the Underground or get these demons to safety, and then we needed to make a plan for how to rescue Andros before it was too late.

I just prayed that chance had not already passed us by.

IT WORKED, DIDN'T IT?

LEA

A good princess would have been out there with the King's Guard, giving orders and helping everyone clean up, but I couldn't seem to force myself away from Aerden's side.

He was going to be furious when he finally woke up, because even if no one else realized what had happened tonight with that golem, he knew what I had done.

Of course, I was already mad at him, too, so this would make us even. For a few minutes, anyway.

I paced the room, trying to remember what all I had said to Jackson in my anger. I hadn't meant to even talk to him about the heartstone tonight. Not after all the death and destruction we'd just witnessed. But it had all just come pouring out of me.

I guess I'd held my pain in for so long that it had a will of its own at this point.

And it had felt good to cry. To just yell at him for a change, instead of bottling everything up and pretending I was okay.

My anger and hurt at seeing him again was different, too.

For so many years, all I saw when I looked at him was my own failure to hold onto his love. Now, though, the truth made me see him in a whole new way. Instead of holding him up as this ideal I had somehow let slip through my fingers, I saw his failure now, too. His flaws.

His pain.

I shook my head and groaned. God, I didn't want to admit that I could see how this must have been hard on him, too. And on Aerden.

In our culture, when a princess was promised to someone, there was no backing out of it or choosing another. It was decided when we were born, and we were taught from a very early age that it was our duty to honor those decisions.

If Aerden had told me the truth back then and asked me to betray my duty to be with him, instead, what would I have done? What could I have said to him?

I sighed. I didn't want to see this from his point-of-view. I wanted to be able to hold onto this anger for a very long time. My anger had served me so well over the years, keeping me from having to face the truth of how I'd come up short.

And now that I realized I had never failed or lost anything, I didn't even know how to react.

I kicked the chair, and Aerden sat up with a startled gasp.

"Oh my God," I said, running over to him. "I'm sorry. I didn't mean to wake you up. You need to rest."

He narrowed his eyes at me and leaned back against his elbows. "You," he said.

"What?" I asked, backing up a couple steps.

I pressed my lips together, trying so hard not to smile. It was ridiculous, because I knew he was furious, but at the same time, I honestly couldn't help myself.

"What?" he asked, pushing himself up to a full sitting position. "You know exactly what. Were you trying to get yourself killed? What the hell were you thinking?"

I raised an eyebrow and leaned back against the wall with a shrug. "It worked, didn't it?"

For a second, I thought his eyes were going to pop out of his head. "Do you think this is some kind of a joke?" he shouted. "A game? If it hadn't happened, or if I had just been a few seconds late, do you realize what might have happened?"

"I suppose I'd have been turned into barbeque," I said. "Good thing your friend decided to join us when he did."

Aerden brought a fist to his forehead, his eyes closed as his body trembled with anger. "You are going to put me in an early grave if you ever do that again," he said. "And this golem is not my friend. I don't even know for sure where he comes from or how I manage to bring him out. I certainly can't control him, and it's not worth putting your life on the line just to try to force it out of me. All it will take is one time when I can't make it happen, and I'll lose the one thing—"

He cut himself off and looked away, his chest rising and falling with each labored breath.

"The one thing, what?" I asked, my heart racing.

I knew I shouldn't push him, because I might not be ready to respond or react to whatever he might tell me. But I needed to know what he was going to say. I wanted to hear it, so I could feel my own reaction, because right now, I had no idea if I could really trust these thoughts racing through my brain.

Or the urges running through every inch of my body.

"Nothing," he said. "Just don't do it again. I'm begging you."

"If you don't want me to do it again, then you're going to

have to learn how to control that ability," I said, holding my chin up. "I have never seen anything so incredibly powerful, and an advantage like that could turn the whole war around."

His head snapped toward me, a hurt expression on his face.

"Is that all this is to you?" he asked. "A tactical advantage?"

"No, that's not what I meant. It's just that whatever this power is, it's incredibly important," I said. "Think of what's possible if you truly learn to control it. If this is what's been hidden inside you all your life, just think of the potential. What if there's more you don't even know about yet? What if this is just the beginning?"

He looked at me like I'd slapped him across the face.

"Well, then what are we waiting for?" he said, wincing as he put his feet on the ground and attempted to stand. "Why don't we head out there and find someone else who wants to kill you. Maybe that will force my hand. If we find something dangerous enough, who knows what we might discover?"

"Aerden, don't be an asshole," I said, pushing him back onto the bed. "You need your rest, and you know that's not what I was trying to say. Of course, this means more to me than just some power or ability we can use in battle. Is that what you need me to say?"

"Not if it isn't true." He stared into my eyes, and I had to look away.

We were standing too close, and I wasn't thinking straight.

"I'm glad you're awake," I said, heading to the door. "I need to go see what I can do to help. There are so many injured, Aerden. It's a mess. We have to do whatever we can to put an end to this. And what about Andros? What if he's really gone forever? It's just too much. I don't know what else to do if we aren't pushing ourselves as hard as we can."

He tried to stand again but decided against it after a few seconds.

It took everything I had to stay there by the door instead of going to him, but I wasn't sure I could trust myself to be that close to him right now. I didn't want to move things forward when I wasn't sure I could follow through.

And things were way too complicated for me to even trust what I was feeling.

"I have to go," I whispered.

"Lea," he called out, but I shut the door quickly and kept moving, knowing that I wouldn't be able to put off that conversation forever.

But now was also not the time.

There was work to be done and friends to save.

There would be time for figuring out our feelings later. For now, though, it was time to figure out how to make the Order pay for what they'd done here today.

TRUE LOYALTY

HARPER

"Are you guys okay?" I asked, putting an arm around Mary Anne's shoulder.

Essex and his mother were working to clean up the materials from her shop that had gotten destroyed or messed up during the attack. Most of the merchants here in the market had simply stored their things here in hopes that the hunters would think everyone had left. No one expected the fight to get this far.

"We're fine," Mary Anne said. "But so many lives were lost. If you guys hadn't gotten here when you did, I hate to think what might have happened."

"Why was the attacking early?" Essex asked. "I was thinking we have until tomorrow."

"I thought so, too," I said. "I don't know. Maybe Ezrah told them to come early."

I didn't want to mention anything about the ruby priestess since we were trying to keep that part of our information secret, but I had a feeling she had been truthful about what she knew.

But something had gone wrong.

What I wanted to know was why?

"We need to get these demons to safety," Mary Anne said, pulling me to the side where Essex and his mom couldn't hear us. "I don't know that we have room for everyone in the domed city, though, Harper. Or food and supplies. What are we going to do?"

"I don't know," I said, biting my lip and looking around. "But they can't stay here. Not with all the entrances blown open and the black roses system completely destroyed. How did that even happen?"

I looked up at the ceiling where there were once black roses lining every piece of rock.

"Something Ezrah did, I think," Mary Anne said. "Some kind of bomb or device that linked all the entrances together or targeted only the black roses. I'm not sure, but whatever it was, it was freaking powerful. Ourelia says there's no easy way to rebuild that system to keep everyone safe. And she thinks the whole place could be compromised. It's not safe here."

I shook my head. Dangit. The Underground's brilliant use of black roses to teleport people in and out through an exchange of energy had kept thousands of demons safe for nearly a century.

And now, all that was gone in a single evening.

"I think we could afford to move about a thousand demons into the domed city right now," I said. "I can have Willow work to extend the reach of the dome itself, but that's going to take weeks. As for food and supplies, I have some in reserve for times like this, but I think a thousand extra mouths to feed is about all we can handle."

"That's not enough," Mary Anne said, her eyes growing wide. She gestured to the large groups of people huddled in corners. "There are several thousand down here. We can't just leave them here without protection."

"They can come to my castle."

Lea walked up beside me and gave me a nod.

"We have room," she said. "There's an entire wing of my father's castle that was used for servants a very long time ago. The area was damaged in a fire, and though it will need work to be repaired, I think we can move some beds into those rooms and house at least a thousand demons there for now. Maybe more. And the citizens in the city will offer rooms, too."

Mary Anne threw her arms around Lea. "Thank you," she said. "God, it's good to see you."

Lea smiled and hugged Mary Anne back. "I missed you, too."

"This isn't exactly the happy reunion I'd been dreaming of, but it is good to have us all back together," I said, choking up a little when I thought of Courtney and Zara. Not everyone who had lived with us at Brighton Manor for all those months after the fall of the sapphire gates had made it this far, and it broke my heart that we would never all be together again.

"We have a lot to talk about, and we need to start figuring out a plan to rescue Andros," Lea said. "Are you ready to tell me where you got this information about the attacks? Or am I going to have to beat it out of you."

Mary Anne whistled, and I tried to glare at Lea but I couldn't help smiling.

I kind of missed having someone to threaten and joke with

like this and while there was still some tension there between us that was real, I could tell that deep down, she was just as relieved to see me safe as I was her.

Still, I had a feeling things would never quite be the same for us as those days at Brighton Manor when we all felt like one big family. My heart ached for those days, even though things weren't easy. We were all working toward a common goal back then, though, and I hoped that much, at least, still remained.

"I'll tell you where the information came from and where things stand with the Order of Shadows from my point-of-view, but I'm not sure you're going to like everything I'm about to tell you," I said. "And we do need to call a small meeting to figure out our next moves, but we need to be very careful who we invite to attend. True loyalty is in short supply these days."

"Tell me about it," Lea mumbled. "Ezrah was the one person who was there for me through this whole ordeal since Aerden and I were taken. It's hard for me to believe he could betray the Resistance. Yet, here we are."

I touched her arm.

"A guard loyal to my father for decades betrayed us all," I said. "Sometimes, people do horrible, unthinkable things when they feel they have no other choice. And death—even an honorable one—doesn't feel like a choice for some."

"Gregory?" she asked.

I nodded. "So, we only call on those we know we can trust with our lives, and that's a very small list," I said. "Mary Anne, tell Essex when you can get him alone. Lea, if you can find Mordecai and the others. I'll make sure to tell Jackson and Illana. Is Aerden awake?"

Lea nodded slowly. "Awake but still very weak. He's going to need more time to recover."

"Awake is good enough. We need a meeting room," I said. "It should be relatively quiet and out of the way, but big enough that we can fit our whole group around a table comfortably."

"The library," Lea said, the excitement of a new idea spreading across her features. "Let's meet in the library. Fifteen minutes?"

I nodded. "I'll see you there."

I said goodbye to Mary Anne and went to look for Jackson, but as I walked down the hallway, the guard I'd tasked with searching the hunters walked up to me and bowed.

"Our search is complete," he said.

I grabbed his arm and pulled him over to a deserted corner in the shadows. "What did you find?"

He glanced around and pulled a strip of bloodied cloth from his pocket.

"Twenty of the hunters seemed to have no trinket or gemstone on them at all," he said.

He opened the strip of cloth to reveal a small pile of yellow stones. Some were rings made of gold or silver, while others were bracelets or loose stones.

"Sixty-two citrine stones were found," he said.

Those numbers seemed to match up pretty well with what we had expected.

"And the other?" I asked, taking the citrine stones and covering them back up in the cloth. I placed the bundle in my own pocket.

The guard's hand trembled as he pulled a second bundle of cloth from his pocket. This one was bulkier, and the sight of it made my mouth go dry. I could feel the power radiating from that bundle even before he opened it.

"A hundred and thirty diamond stones, Your Highness," he said, moving the cloth to the side to reveal a pile of loose stones, earrings, bracelets, pendants, and other settings.

Over one hundred diamond hunters? Where the hell did they all come from?

"Thank you for doing this," I said. "And I trust you'll keep this to yourself?"

I almost laughed as the word trust came out of my mouth. Right now, I couldn't trust a quarter of the people here. Even those whose loyalty went back hundreds of years couldn't be trusted if the Order managed to find their weak spot and turn them against us.

"I won't tell a soul," he said.

"You did good," I told him. "Thank you."

"What orders do you have for me now?" he asked. "I told our small group to stick together in case you had another task for us."

I gave it a brief moment of thought before turning back to the guard.

"Choose a thousand demons to come to the Southern Kingdom," I said. "Keep families together. Tell them to pack as sparingly as possible. Only the essentials. They'll be leaving with me to head to the Southern Kingdom in about two hours."

"In the middle of the night?" he asked. "Forgive me. I don't mean any disrespect to an ally queen, but these demons have been through a lot. There could be more hunters out there, waiting for them. Shouldn't we give them time to rest before such a long journey through the borderlands?"

"The borderlands aren't as bad as people think they are," I

said, remembering how afraid Jackson and I had been the first time we traveled to the Southern Kingdom. "And as dangerous as it may be, time is a luxury we don't have right now. We leave in two hours."

The guard bowed and hurried away, leaving me standing there in the hallway staring at a mound of cursed diamonds and wondering how many diamond hunters were still out there.

WHAT WE DIDN'T EXPECT

HARPER

The library had been a good choice. The black, round table Andros often used for his own Council meetings sat among rows of shelves that extended from floor-to-ceiling, hundreds of books pressed neatly together on each shelf.

Our group was small, but as trustworthy as I could imagine ever finding.

"Thank you all for coming," I began. "I know many of you have questions about where I got the information regarding this attack and the capture of Andros, and I'm only going to explain it here to you now under two conditions. One is that you respect my decisions about my prisoner and how I choose to handle her. And two is that you promise to tell no one outside of this room who that prisoner is. Do you all agree?"

Of course, many of the people in the room already knew about the ruby priestess, but several of them didn't. I knew I would receive some criticism for working with and believing a high-level member of the Order of Shadows, but I had to do what I felt was right.

When everyone in the room agreed to my conditions, I laid it all out on the table, explaining how the ruby priestess and I had met, when she had come to me, and everything she told me when we talked last.

"She lied about the attack, then," Ourelia said. "There were twice as many hunters as that, and they attacked earlier than expected. Why would she tell you about it at all if she was going to lie about it?"

"I cannot believe you have the ruby priestess in your dungeons and you haven't ripped her heart out," Lea said, standing. "What are you thinking? You could end another priestess in an instant."

I sighed. I knew there would be some harsh criticism from her, but now that it was here, I completely understood where she was coming from. It was risky and crazy. Maybe even stupid.

"I don't want to take up all our time trying to justify my decisions, but from the way I see it, we can kill her at any moment we choose," I said. "But as long as she's willing to talk, she's an asset to our cause. She can give us key information that will help us to bring down the Order much faster than we could without her."

"I just don't see what she's getting out of it," Ourelia said. "Why risk her life to help us? It seems much more likely that she's trying to trick you and lure you into a trap."

"My thoughts, exactly," Lea said.

"That's why one of my conditions was that you respect my decisions," I said. "I went through all of these thoughts and arguments in my head and with Jackson and my Council before we made a decision, and we decided to let the ruby priestess live so she could prove useful to us with information."

"But she lied," Ourelia said.

"I don't think she did." I pulled the two bundles of cloth from my pockets. "I had a group of guards search the dead hunters for trinkets and gemstones. Sixty-two of the hunters carried citrine gemstones. Along with the twenty or so who carried nothing, that number proves to be about what the ruby priestess told us to expect."

The group around me nodded.

"But what we didn't expect was this."

I pulled the cloth away to show the items from the second bundle.

"Over a hundred of the hunters who died were carrying diamonds," I said. "It's possible the ruby priestess had no idea those diamond hunters were going to show up."

"It's also possible she lied so that we would only prepare for half the hunters who were supposed to be here," Lea said. "We walked right into a trap, and if we hadn't shown up, it might have ended very differently."

"She has a point," Jackson said. "Lea and Aerden were supposed to be taken care of, according to the Order's plan. Aerden should have fallen in the King's Games and Lea was to be married to a demon named Kael."

"A demon who turned out to be a Stone Guardian in disguise," Aerden said.

My mouth literally fell open. Had I heard him right?

Aerden explained about Kael's transformation and Lea explained to us how Kael had held the entire King's City under the High Priestess's control in exchange for her safety.

"Are we sure we can trust the king to fight with us?" Ourelia asked.

Lea nodded. "I'm sure of it. It never felt right to see my father completely abandon us that way," she said. "At first, I think he hesitated to get involved due to fear and underestimating what the Order was capable of. Then, when it was clear just how much destruction they could cause, it was too late for him to act. It's going to be different now, though. I promise."

"So, the Order's plan to take us all out in a matter of days has already been upset," I said. "Obviously, Jackson and I won't die in the bombs the ruby priestess set in our castle. Lea and Aerden survived the King's Games and Kael is dead, meaning the king is also back to his full power. And now, despite sending extra hunters here to destroy the Underground, we fought back and killed them. As far as I know, no one else was captured and taken."

Ourelia shook her head. "Too many have lost their lives, but everyone is accounted for. Except Ezrah."

"The only part left that we know about is Andros," Lea said. "You think they're going to alter their plans for him, because of everything else?"

"I think it's possible," I said. I glanced at Ourelia. I hated to say this in front of her, but it needed to be discussed. "Priestess Thorn told me her sister Gladys was told to keep Andros alive, but now that we've messed up so many of their other plans, it's possible they will either move up their timeline or change their plans for Andros altogether. Priestess Thorn says the ritual they plan to perform with him has to be on the night of the full moon, though."

"When I saw him in my vision," Lea said, "the hunter told

him that their plans were to put him and the rest of the elite squad into the bodies of witches."

Aerden shuddered, and I couldn't blame him. He knew more than any of us just how horrible it was to be locked inside the body of a witch.

"She said that even if we searched for him, there would never be any way for us to know whose body he'd been placed into," Lea said. "We have to find him before that happens."

"So, what do we do?" Ourelia asked. "How can we get to him?"

"We have to take a chance on what the ruby priestess has told us," I said. "I know you guys think it could be a trap, but if it wasn't for her, we wouldn't have known any of this would happen. A lot more demons would have died tonight in this attack."

Lea couldn't argue with that. I hated to think what might have happened if they'd had to fight on their own.

"Jackson and I will move as many demons to the domed city as we can tonight, and while we're there, we'll talk to the ruby priestess. Get information about the amethyst's house and any traps she might have set for us there."

"And if it's a trap?" Mary Anne asked.

I took a deep breath. We were playing with fire here, and we all knew it.

"Once we scout out the amethyst priestess's house, I'm planning to use my ability to astral project to search inside," I said. "We won't go inside until we know for sure that it's the right place and the ritual is happening that night."

"I'll move the rest of the Underground to the King's City," Lea said. "But when you go to rescue Andros, I want to be there with you."

I nodded. "Of course," I said. "Mary Anne will pass out fresh communication stones, so we can all keep in touch. Let us know of any new developments along the way."

Jackson stood. "We've made it through so much, and it's important to remember that the reason the Order is hitting us so hard is because we've hurt them. We've hit them harder than they ever dreamed possible. They had no idea their priestesses could be killed, and now we've killed two of them. We have a third in custody, and if she's telling us the truth, we may have a shot at killing amethyst in a few days, too. We have to keep our heads up and keep pushing forward. We will put an end to the Order of Shadows."

I touched his hand as I stood.

"Jackson's right," I said. "They're getting desperate, but that means they're going to throw everything at us. So far, we've only directly faced one priestess at a time, but if they start working together or the High Priestess gets more involved, we don't know what they might be capable of. It's important not to underestimate them, but it's also important not to lose hope, no matter what we might face along the way."

Everyone stood, determination and fear on their faces. There was no telling what we might face in the coming weeks, and even though we had the victory of freeing the emerald gates, there were no guarantees we would be able to free the remaining three.

All we could do was keep putting our whole selves into this battle. Keep risking it all to see freedom restored.

"Keep in touch, and be safe," I said. "Hopefully, we'll be meeting up again soon with Andros by our side."

Ourelia came over to hug me, tears in her eyes. "Thank you for being here for us all," she said.

"I'm just sorry we didn't get here sooner," I said.

"It's good to have you home, Harper," she said. "Andros will be excited to hear you're safe, too. I know we will bring him back. We have to."

"We will," I said. "Where will you go? To the King's City?"

She nodded. "Sasha will be excited to see the inside of the city," she said with a smile. "She's been daydreaming of it for a long time, and I honestly wasn't sure we'd ever see the day when we would be welcomed there. But I believe she will be safe in the King's City."

"I'll see you soon," I said to her with another hug.

Almost everyone filed out of the library to make preparations for the journey ahead, but Aerden, Lea and Jackson all stayed back.

The four of us waited until we were alone, and for a moment, there were no words between us. There was just a knowledge that we had all fought with everything we had to find our way back to each other. And now, we were parting again.

Jackson told me that Lea knew the truth about Aerden's heartstone, and I understood now why she'd been less than thrilled to see us when we'd first arrived, but a lot of that tension had disappeared over the past few hours, as we all remembered what it was like to fight at each other's side.

"I've missed being together as a group," I said, finally daring to disturb the silence. "Do you think we'll ever recapture the way it felt when we lived together in Brighton Manor? I don't think I fully appreciated those days until I realized they were truly gone."

"I heard it was burned down by the emerald priestess," Aerden said, sadness deep in his blue eyes. "Is that true?"

I placed my hand on his and nodded. It had been his home far longer than it was ever mine, but it had meant a great deal to all of us for different reasons.

"And Courtney?" Lea asked, shaking her head. "Zara?"

"It's still hard to believe Courtney is gone," Jackson said. "I did everything I could to save her, but it just wasn't enough."

"Zara is alive," I said. "We just don't know when she'll wake up or what's happening to her inside that cocoon. All we can do is wait and hope, but I feel in my heart that someday, she'll come back to us."

"It's crazy how fast everything has changed," Aerden said. "I feel like I spent an eternity trapped as a Prima demon, but once things changed for me, they just kept changing. I think I'd like to go back to simpler days for a while. Maybe take a vacation."

I laughed. "Here's hoping," I said. "Let's make a pact that as soon as the last priestess is dead and all the gates are free, we'll work together to rebuild Brighton Manor, bigger and better than before."

"And we'll spend a month's vacation there every summer. All the old crew," Jackson said.

Lea stuck her tongue out. "Not summer," she said. "Not in Georgia. Change that to October, and you've got a deal."

"We can have a Halloween Ball there every year to celebrate the end of the Order and the peace of two worlds restored," Aerden said.

"I'm so there," I said.

And I held that promise in my heart, tucking it away so that I would never forget.

Someday, we would return to simpler times and celebrations. Someday soon.

A DARK STORM

AERDEN

"Before you guys go, there's something else we need to talk to you about," I said, glancing toward the door of the library. "We didn't want to bring it up in front of everyone, because we don't want people to panic or start to draw their own conclusions about things when we really don't know for sure what's going on."

"What is it?" Harper asked, sitting back down.

She'd just been getting up to head out and lead a group of demons back to the Southern Kingdom, but she needed to hear this first.

I explained everything we knew about the diamond key my mother had given me before I left the King's City all those years ago. The key I had given to Lea that she recently discovered also opened a room far beneath the castle.

"A room full of Stone Guardians?" Jackson said, shaking his head and pacing the room. "That's terrifying. We can't send several thousand demons with you to the King's City when there's a threat like that sleeping just beneath their feet."

"They're inactive," Lea said. "Sleeping. I think they can't be activated without gemstones in their hearts. My father is already working to have the sapphires moved out of the city so that the guardians can't be awakened."

"And what if you're wrong about that?" Harper asked. "What if they don't need the stones to wake up? Even a handful of those things could destroy the entire city from what I've heard about Stone Guardians."

"There's still so much mystery surrounding the ones in the basement," I said. "I don't think they're exactly the same as Kael. I have a suspicion he created them somehow, and I'm hoping that now he's gone, the ones in the basement are nothing more than statues without his magic to wake them up."

"That's a pretty big risk to take with the lives of everyone in the city," Jackson said.

"You're right," Lea said. "But we can't evacuate the city, either. We're talking about millions of demons. We'd have nowhere to go, and right now, it's safer than anywhere outside the wall. When I get home, we're going to start some experiments to see if we can destroy the ones in the basement without compromising the stability of the area beneath the castle."

"Please, keep us updated on what's going on," Harper said. "In the meantime, I'm going to get all my best shielders working on the dome. If we can extend it far enough out, we can work to build a city big enough for all the demons in the Shadow World."

Lea laughed and shook her head. "My father wants us to all work together, but I'm not sure he's willing to move under your roof and share the ruling of our people with you."

Harper shrugged. "The dome isn't impenetrable, anyway but it's what we've got," she said. "And if I can, I want to build a refuge strong enough and big enough to house everyone who needs us."

I could see the respect in Lea's eyes when she looked at Harper now. Something had definitely changed about Harper since we'd seen her last. She was more sure of herself. Stronger, even if it came with a harder edge.

We'd all been through a lot.

"There's more," Lea said.

We explained about the book my friend Trention had found.

"There's another continent across the Sea of Glass?" Jackson said. "How is that possible? Everyone knows there's just a wall of darkness that no ship can pass through. Sailors and fisherman call it The Storm."

"Maybe it's a magical barrier," I said. "I've been thinking about it ever since he first mentioned it. What if there really is a huge continent over there and someone blocked us off from it?"

"And then destroyed every mention of it in the history books," Lea added, as if she could read my mind.

"But why would they do that?" Harper asked.

I shook my head. "That's what we need to figure out," I said. I glanced at Jackson. "And we need to figure out what role our mother has in all of this. Why would she be trying to keep that information secret? And where did she really get that key?"

Jackson ran a shaky hand through his hair. "I don't like where this is going," he said. "What if she's being controlled by the High Priestess the same way the king was?"

"That's what I'm worried about, too," I said. "Maybe she didn't come after me, because she couldn't. Maybe she was bound to some kind of promise, the same way the king was."

"Do you think she could have made a deal to get that key in the first place?" he asked.

There was hope shining in his eyes, and I completely understood how he was feeling.

For so many years, we'd felt that our mother—one of the only people in the world who was supposed to truly love and protect us unconditionally—had just thrown us to the side for no reason other than her own fear or desire for power.

It had never made sense to me how she could do that to both of us, but seeing the change in Lea's father had given me hope, too. If we could find a way to free our mother from whatever curse or promise was binding her and keeping her from joining us in our fight against the Order, it could change everything.

"We have to figure this out," I said. "Maybe we can help her."

"We were going to do some research about the key and the book before you guys showed up, but we didn't have time," Lea said. She pulled the key out of her shirt and held it out for us to see. "I've tried to use my ability to see the past on this key, but all I ever see is the moment Aerden gave it to me. I haven't been able to see anything beyond that, but this key must have a history. If I can get my father's help, he might be able to help me unlock whatever's hiding there. He's always been better at finding visions locked deeper inside items that were moved from their original locations."

"And I'm going to spend some time here in the Resistance library," I said. "My friend Trention that I told you about was a scholar in the city for centuries. One of his unique abilities was that he could read any language, even if it was brand new to him."

A look of recognition flashed on Jackson's face. "I remember that demon," he said. "He used to come to some of my tutoring sessions back when everyone was trying to prepare me to be the husband of the queen."

He said it with a laugh, but I quickly looked to Lea to make sure she was okay. I hated when anything brought up those tough memories of what she lost when we all left the city, but to my surprise, she laughed, too.

"Turns out you were studying the wrong kingdom's history all this time," she said. "If only we had known."

Everyone kind of stared at her, unable to believe she'd actually just made a joke about Jackson's intention to marry Harper that hadn't included some kind of dig about her own pain.

"What?" she asked. "It's true."

Jackson and I looked at each other for a long moment, and he finally shrugged, but there was a growing smile on the corner of his lips.

"I remember Trention," he said. "He was a good man."

"He died in my arms," I said, a lump forming in my throat as I said the words. "And in his final moments, he passed a spark of his own power and spirit to me. I think I may be able to decipher some of these old texts in here that the Resistance scholars have been working on for years. I'm at least going to try. If I can find any reference to the continent across the sea, I'll let you know."

"If it exists, we need to find out why someone's trying to hide it from us," Lea said.

"And how to get through a dark storm that seems to swallow up any ship that tries to pass through," Jackson said.

"The fact that the book Trention found was dusted with diamonds makes me feel that it's somehow related to the Order," I said. "We just have to figure out how. It could be the piece of the puzzle that's been missing all along."

"Never a dull moment," Harper said with a laugh. "We have so much to do and figure out, but I can't tell you how happy I am that you are both okay."

"Where were you, by the way?" I asked her. "I can still feel my connection to your family, even if it's not as strong as it used to be. It's like we're still linked in some small way, and while you were gone, I could feel that you were still alive, but you were so distant. I tried to explain it to Lea, but I couldn't. Where was the emerald priestess keeping you?"

Harper laughed and self-consciously touched the scars on her arms. "1951."

My eyes widened. "What? Are you serious?"

She shrugged. "It's hard to believe, but I think that's a story for another day," she said. "The important thing is that another priestess is dead, and we're all safe and back where we belong. I'm sure I don't have to say this, but both of you are welcome in the domed city any time."

Wow. I was still hung up on the fact that a priestess had somehow trapped Harper in the past. She was right when she'd said we couldn't afford to underestimate them, because I never would have imagined a priestess could be capable of such a thing.

"Hopefully, we'll be seeing you both soon when we go to rescue Andros," Lea said.

Harper nodded, and I pulled her into a hug.

"I've missed you," I said. "Please, stay safe."

"I feel the same connection to you, too," she said. "Be careful. And take care of Lea."

"She can take of herself," I said with a laugh. But then I thought of the determined look on her face as she stepped in front of that hunter earlier and lowered her bow, forcing me to find the strength to summon the golem of light. "I'll keep an eye on her, though. You never know what kind of trouble she's going to get herself into next."

I gave Lea a pointed look, and she just shrugged, but there was a hint of a mischievous smile on her face at the same time.

We all said our goodbyes, and when Harper and Jackson had gone to take a thousand of the Underground's demons back to the domed city, Lea and I started our search through the library, looking for books whose pages were decorated with the dust of diamonds.

ANOTHER LIE

JACKSON

The journey back to the domed city was not easy with over a thousand demons to protect along the way, but we managed to make it to the borderlands just a few hours after sunrise.

We stopped to take a break near a stream. Many in our party were injured and couldn't travel at full speed. Several couldn't shift at all and had to be carried by others.

I could tell from the looks on many of the faces that despite our assurances that the borderlands were not haunted, some of them were still scared to pass into the Southern Kingdom. I laughed and shook my head, causing my sister, Illana, to come over and ask me what I found so funny.

"Remember the stories of the hauntings in the borderlands?" I asked. "Dumb stories people made up to scare us. So much of life is about perception and the stories we've been taught to believe, but when you really look closely, a lot of that stuff is a lie meant to control you."

Illana's eyes widened, and she shook her head.

"Well, that was a deeper answer than I expected," she said. "But you're right about that. People can be made to believe just about anything if the story surrounding it is good enough. Most people aren't really willing to look past their fear."

"Not until they're forced to," I said, looking toward the swamps of the borderlands. "Harper and I never would have willingly come this way. Not unless we felt we had no other choice. And when we were pushed to the point of facing that fear, we saw it for what it was. An illusion. A lie."

Illana nodded. "Deep thoughts by Denaer," she said with a laugh. "I mean, Jackson. What's got you in this kind of mood, thinking about lies and perceptions?"

I shrugged.

There were things I wanted to ask her about our mother, but I didn't want to drag her any deeper into all this than she already was. Illana had spent a lot more time with our mom over the past century, though, than I had.

"Why do you think Mom didn't come after Aerden and me when we left?" I asked. "Why just leave us to our fate?"

Illana sighed. "Are you still hung up on those questions after all this time?" she asked. "I would have thought you'd eventually come to terms with it."

"It's hard to come to terms with something you can't understand," I said. "Did you know she gave Aerden a diamond key before he left the city?"

She gave me a strange look and shook her head. "Where would Mom have gotten a diamond key?"

"That's a very good question," I said, studying her face to see if she looked genuinely surprised.

She didn't act like she even believed I was telling the truth.

"It was supposed to protect him from the Order," I said.

"Did you also know the king made a deal with the High Priestess in order to keep Lea safe?"

Illana's mouth dropped open slightly, and her eyes cleared as if she'd just understood something that had puzzled her for a very long time.

"That's why he changed so rapidly," she said in a whisper. "Everyone in the city seemed to believe it was his own sorrow and regret for what was happening to his kingdom that had changed him, but she did something to him, didn't she? The High Priestess?"

"In a way," I said. I told her about Kael.

"I never liked him," Illana said. "He's part of the reason I wanted to get out of that city. There was talk for a while of marrying him off to one of us. I guess Lea coming home changed that, but I wasn't about to stay there and marry a demon who made my skin crawl."

My jaw tensed. "They were going to force you to marry him?" I asked.

"Me or Orian," she said. "Orian was kind of swooning over him. He was handsome, and she was too young to really see past that, but when I tried to get her to come with me to the Southern Kingdom, she said she couldn't imagine leaving our parents. It's a relief to know Kael's dead, though. I knew there was something going on with that guy. I never guessed it was that bad, though."

We sat in silence for a minute, eating some berries and muffins for breakfast that one of the bakers from the Underground had brought along with them.

"You could go back now, though," Illana said quietly. "We both could. I know Mom and Dad would be so happy to see you now that they would be free to actually be themselves, instead of feeling like they had to cower before a king who had seemed to lose his mind."

"The king hadn't yet made that deal with Kael when we left the city, Illana," I reminded her. "They can't hide behind that as an excuse for refusing to help me find Aerden all those years ago."

"Things were different then," she said. "I know it won't do any good to try to explain it to you all over again, but back then, no one believed you could get someone back once they were lost to the Order."

"I know," I said. I'd heard that argument a thousand times, but it hadn't stopped me from trying to save my brother. It hadn't stopped Harper. "I was just wondering if there might have been more to it."

"Like what?" she asked.

"Like maybe mom made a deal with someone the same way the king did," I said carefully. "Maybe she made some kind of binding promise in order to get that key in the first place. Something that kept her from coming after us?"

Illana's eyes opened wider, and she sucked in a huge breath. "Oh my gosh, do you really think that could be why?" she asked. "Do you think she's in danger, somehow?"

"I don't know," I said. "Aerden's going to look into it more when he gets back to the city. If the Order has any power over her, though, maybe we can help her. Do you think if we asked her to come stay with us in the Southern Kingdom for a while, she would come?"

Illana smiled. "I don't know, but she might," she said. "I mean, she is a high-ranking member of the king's Council, and I doubt she'll want to give that up, but it might be worth asking her. Oh, Jackson, let's go home. Let's go see her and talk to her about all of this. If we ask her, maybe she'll just tell us whatever it is she's done. Wouldn't that be simpler than trying to figure it out on our own behind her back?"

"Not if whoever she made that deal with is watching her," I said. "We don't want to put her in more danger. But if we could convince her to come stay with us in the domed city, we could keep her safe from whoever that is. At least, it's worth a shot."

Illana grabbed my hand.

"I know that Mom never wanted to lose either one of you," she said. "She acts strong, but that's just because she was raised to act that way in public. In private, behind closed doors, I've seen just how much it tore her apart to lose you both."

Her words touched a place deep in my heart I hadn't allowed myself to feel in a very long time. I had closed myself off from thinking about my mother and father, feeling so much hurt for so long at their callousness when Aerden disappeared and when I left.

But knowing there could be a bigger reason behind it gave me hope.

"When Andros is home and we're through this next attack, we'll talk about going home to talk to her," I said.

Illana smiled. "You promise?"

"I promise," I said.

"We need to get going," Harper said, coming over when she was done making her rounds and checking on the injured. "Now that it's full daylight, we need to make good time to the domed city. The more time we spend out here in the open, the more we put ourselves at risk for another attack."

I nodded and stood, finishing off the last of the berries.

"Then, let's go home," I said.

And I realized as I said it that I was currently standing between two homes. My old one and my new one. I had stopped associating that word with the King's City, because I had felt that everyone there abandoned me.

But now?

Now, I wondered if that had just been another lie the Order had convinced me of for all this time. Another meaningless heartache that could have been avoided if only I'd been able to see the truth.

"You coming?" Illana asked, pulling on her backpack.

I nodded and reached for my own backpack, but before we headed into the swamps of the borderlands toward home, I turned and glanced one last time in the direction of the King's City.

TO THE KING'S CITY

LEA

After Aerden stuffed as many books from the library as his new backpack—courtesy of Essex's mother— would hold, we formed a caravan of more than two thousand demons, the likes of which the Shadow World had never seen, and began our journey to the King's City.

The three-hundred King's Guard soldiers were stationed at even intervals surrounding all sides of the caravan, ready to protect us if hunters attacked along the way, but I had a feeling we would be allowed to make our journey to the city safely.

There was no way the Order expected us to annihilate over two-hundred hunters last night.

No, they had expected us to fall.

The question was how many more hunters did they have at their command?

We used to think there was only one hunter per gate. That would still have been a lot of hunters, but from the display we'd seen last night, there had to be more than we ever feared.

And where had all those diamond hunters come from?

There had been rumors of diamond gates, but we'd never once, in all our travels, seen one.

And yet, now I'd fought many diamond hunters in battle. First when the hunters attacked the domed city just before Aerden and I were captured, and now in the Underground.

So, who was commanding them? And if there were diamond gates out there, where were they?

These were all questions that needed answers sooner rather than later if we hoped to have a chance at winning this war.

Yes, we'd come this far, but Harper and Jackson were right. The Order's attacks were only going to get worse, and since they'd always underestimated us in the past, it made me wonder just how little they had tried.

What if we'd only scratched the surface of what the Order was capable of?

I shuddered and looked back at the caravan of demons following us to the city.

These and the demons who had been allowed to live in the King's City were practically all there was left now of the once-thriving Northern Kingdom of the Shadow World. We had lost thousands of demons over the years, and now our numbers had dwindled to just these few.

We couldn't afford to lose more. No matter what else, we had to keep them safe.

And the way to do that was not to build a stronger wall or a bigger dome.

The only way to do that was to put an end to the Order of Shadows forever.

But for now, the wall around our great city would have to be enough.

I sent a pair of guards ahead in the night to warn my father to begin preparing in the abandoned wing of the castle, but I had a feeling he would still be shocked when we appeared on the horizon, one massive train of demons fleeing the Underground to take refuge in a city that had once turned them away.

Times were changing, that was certain, and I had a feeling I was about to find out just how certain my father was about handing that crown down to me.

If he thought I was truly ready to lead, then he would welcome these demons with open arms and not question my decision to bring them here.

It took the full day to get to the gates of the King's City, and when the first of our group arrived, I was relieved to see the massive gates swing open.

My father stood on the steps of the castle as I approached, a look of awe and bewilderment on his face as he drew me into a hug.

"The guards told me what you faced when you got to the Underground," he said. "We heard the explosion from here, and I thought I might have lost you. I don't know what I would have done, Princess. I don't know how I could have survived getting you back after all this time, just to lose you again."

"The explosion happened when we were still on our way there," I said. "But every entrance to the Underground was blown wide open, leaving everyone inside vulnerable. We can try to rebuild the entrances, but it's going to take time. I didn't want to leave everyone down there vulnerable to attacks in the meantime, and there would have been no good way to protect them with the Underground in that state."

"I understand," Father said. "I've done as you asked and

had the abandoned wing set up with beds and supplies. It will
be a bit crowded in there for a while, but it should at least be
safe."

"Thank you," I said, so relieved to hear that he actually
agreed with me and had taken the steps I'd asked him to take.

It was almost too good to believe.

The other citizens of the King's City filled the streets,
watching as the refugees poured in from the Underground.
Every once in a while, members of families or old friends
recognized each other and ran to meet.

Several of the demons coming in from the Underground
were offered rooms in the homes of those who had lived here
for decades.

I couldn't help getting a little choked up at the sight of this.

The demons here in the city had felt like prisoners here,
too, but today was a day of coming together and of unifying our
once-broken kingdom.

To someone else, it may have looked like helpless, injured
demons having to flee from terror, but to me, it looked like the
beginning of our freedom and our strength. If we learned to
fight as one kingdom and put all our forces toward ending the
Order and protecting everyone who still remained, we could
truly make a difference.

"Have you had any rest?" my father asked. "You look
exhausted. Why don't you go back to your chambers? I'll have
Presha bring some food to your room."

I shook my head. "I won't rest until everyone has a safe
place to lay their head." I said. "You had an infirmary set up,
too?"

He nodded. "In the arena," he said. "It isn't elegant, but it
will work until everyone is healed."

"Thank you," I said, putting a hand on his wrist. "I can't thank you enough for this."

"I should have done this a long time ago," he said. "Opened these gates to everyone. Maybe we could have saved so many more."

"There's still time," I said. "Three priestesses still remain, and if we can end their lives, we can free the thousands of demons still trapped in the human world inside the bodies of witches. There's a long road ahead of us, Father, but with you by my side and all of us finally working together, I know we can do this."

He kissed my forehead.

"Go," he said. "Do what you need to do to help everyone get settled. I'll be here until the last of the demons are inside the gates. After that, you and I need to have a talk about what's hidden in the basement."

I nodded, glancing around to make sure no one had overheard.

"I'll find you when I have a free moment," I said.

Aerden waited for me at the top of the steps, and we flew together to the once-abandoned wing, now teeming with life and laughter as the demons of the Underground settled into their new homes.

"May I speak with you for a moment," Mazrock, the head guard, asked.

I had been helping a large family find a set of rooms next to each other, so they didn't need to split up. I excused myself and followed him to a set of rooms near the end of the hallway.

"What is it?" I asked.

Mazrock nodded to an older demon who stood at the end

of the hallway, his hat in his hands. He shook his head and mumbled something to himself.

"Dorlar. Tell her what you told me," he said, keeping his voice low.

I recognized the older demon by his name. He was what some people called a spellweaver. Others called them builders. This particular builder had been working for my father since before I was born.

Dorlar shuffled into the last room on the left and glanced around, ducking his head as if he expected the ceiling to come crashing in on him.

And honestly, from the looks of it, it very well could have.

I knew parts of the abandoned wing were in disrepair, but that was only because no one had ever taken the time to fix things up and reopen this part of the castle. In advance of our arrival, my father had called on every builder in the city to fix the rooms up here. In just a few hours, the entire wing was expected to be completely finished.

"What's wrong?" I asked, following his gaze up to a spot on the ceiling that was discolored and cracked.

"I've tried to cast my building magic in this particular room more than a dozen times," Dorlar said. "But this room has been...resistant to my powers."

"Resistant?" I asked. "How so?"

"I can feel the weaving of the spell, and I know it's working," he said. "At first, the room seems to shift and change, but after a few moments, it..."

His voice trailed off, and he frowned, as if he couldn't quite explain what had happened here.

"It what?" I asked. "Just do your best to explain it in your own words."

He looked up at me then, and his eyes were filled with terror.

"It pushes back on me," he said, shaking his head. "I've never experienced anything like it, and it's put a bad taste in my mouth. Like...well, like something that happened here was touched by evil, Princess. I know how strange that sounds, but every time I try to touch the old wounds here with my own magic, I can feel something even stronger and darker seeping into me. I can't do it again."

I studied the discolored wall and the cracked ceiling. There was a faint smell of sulfur in the air. It wasn't in any kind of shape for a family, but there had to be something he could do.

"We can't afford to lose even an inch of space right now," I said.

It wasn't that I didn't believe this demon. I knew he was a good demon who had done many great things in service to the king. But an evil that pushed back against his magic? That didn't seem likely.

"What if you brought several builders in here with you?" I asked. "Do you think you just need more power to heal this room?"

His eyes widened with fear, but he quickly bowed his head. "If you would like for us to try it, I will obey you, Princess, but..."

His lip trembled as his words failed him again.

"I will try," he said, bowing again and hurrying from the room.

Mazrock shrugged and followed the old demon, but I stayed back, wanting to get a closer look at that wall.

At first, it looked as if the stone itself had been singed with fire. Green fire, perhaps.

But that should have been easy enough to repair.

However, when you looked at it from certain angles, the wall almost seemed to disappear, as if they were invisible in places. Or maybe...

I stepped closer and nearly tripped over a small stone on the floor. I reached out to steady myself, touching the dark scar on the wall.

I cried out as the diamond key pressed against my skin seemed to erupt in flames, but before I could reach for it, the room went completely black, and I was pulled down into a darkness so deep, it consumed me.

And then the vision began.

THE DIAMOND KEY

LEA

The memory was old. Much older than me. Possibly older, even, than my own father.

I'm not sure how I knew, but I could sense it, somehow. The age of it. The weight of it.

And similar to the room I had just been standing in, with its wound on the wall that couldn't be repaired, this memory seemed to be damaged, too.

Rather than being one, continuous memory, this one came in bits and pieces, followed by stretches of darkness.

In all my years since I'd discovered I had this ability and my father had taught me to use it, I had never encountered a memory quite like this. It almost felt as if it was torn somehow, although I wasn't sure if that was the right word for it.

Maybe it was the age of it that unsettled me so much. Slipping this far into the past had consequences. My father had warned me not to stay too long in a deep memory of the past. It drained power faster than a recent memory could, and if I allowed too much of my energy to be drained, it could be a long time before my body recovered.

If ever.

I shuddered and took a deep breath. If it hadn't been for the fact that the diamond key around my neck that I'd been trying to research had obviously reacted to this location, I would have forced myself to wake up right away.

But this could be my chance to see something important.

To find the true origin of the diamond key.

Determined to focus, see what there was to be seen, and then get the hell out of here, I turned around, careful to move very slowly.

But as I turned, the memory jumped locations. Startled, I stepped backward as the ground beneath my feet started to sway and tilt. Rain pelted my skin, and a roaring wind blew my hair back from my face.

My stomach flipped, and I reached for something to steady myself, finally latching onto a wooden railing.

At first, I couldn't see anything. It was too dark, as if someone had slipped a black cloth over my eyes.

But then, someone standing in front of me conjured a small orb of light.

I was standing on the deck of a large ship. It appeared to be deserted, except for the woman who had conjured the orb.

She lifted her arms into the air, and the wind increased at her command.

I stepped closer to get a better look at the woman, hoping to see her face and figure out how the key played into all of this, but it was too dark, and the memory too faded to see it all clearly.

Nausea rolled through me, and I knew it was from more

than being on a ship. The memory was pulling too much from me. I needed to wake myself up.

But just as I made up my mind, a bolt of lightning struck the sky, and I saw that there, on a chain around the woman's neck, was a key with a diamond embedded in its center.

I took a step toward her, but the moment my foot hit the ground, the memory shifted again.

I squinted against the bright light of four suns. I was standing in a market this time, and although the rest of the area looked completely foreign to me, the castle where I'd grown up looked exactly the same.

The glint of a diamond catching the sun made me turn my head just as a cloaked woman rushed by me, her face covered in shadows. She gripped the key and stuffed it into the collar of her dress, hiding it from view as she turned and raced through the crowd.

I tried to follow, but the memory jumped again. Pain cramped my stomach, but I held on, wanting to see a little more.

I needed to see her face, just once. I needed to know who she was.

When I steadied myself enough to open my eyes, I was once again standing in the room of the abandoned wing. Except this time, the room was not damaged at all. In fact, it looked brand new. The wooden floors gleamed, and a beautiful new rug made from red and gold thread covered the floor at the foot of the bed.

The cloaked woman shut the door behind her and leaned against it, taking several deep breaths. The vision lurched, and I leaned against the wall.

Dizzy and weak, I held on, watching as the woman—

dressed differently this time—locked the door of her room and quickly fell to her knees by the bed. She pulled up one side of the rug and pulled up one edge of the floorboard to reveal a small, secret cubby underneath.

With another glance toward the door, she lifted a box out of the cubby.

I gasped and fell to my knees, but the memory tore again. I was losing control of it.

I looked up, determined to hold on just a little longer.

If I could only see her face. Just once.

This time, the woman was sitting on her bed when a second woman entered the room. This woman wore a white cloak, the fabric pulled down so far over her face, I could see nothing but shadows inside the hood.

There was no mistaking the large diamond amulet hanging from a chain around her neck.

I've seen that amulet before.

The woman on the bed screamed, but before she could do anything to protect herself, the white-cloaked woman threw her hands up and white flames erupted throughout the room, melting even the stone on the walls.

I fell to my knees, sure that I could feel those flames burning my own skin.

The vision shifted again.

A diamond key retrieved from a box under the floorboards.

White-hot flames spreading throughout the servants' quarters as demons screamed and ran.

The thick fabric of a white cloak gliding across the floor, the flames never touching it.

The flames themselves dying to nothing, and leaving

almost no evidence of their existence behind, save a few key details.

The scar on the wall, as if the stone itself had been wounded.

The smell of sulfur.

And there, in a pile on the floor by the bed where the woman had stood, a grey servant's dress.

These pieces came to me like pictures being placed on a table, one-by-one.

And then, just before my power completely disappeared, there she was. Tatiana, standing in the gardens of the castle, weeping. She looked up, surprised.

The vision blinked out.

A woman in white, walking toward her.

The vision blinked again.

Tatiana, handing a diamond key to her son.

Blink.

Aerden, handing the key to me.

Then, knowing I had done too much and pushed too far, the vision disappeared, and everything went dark.

FAR FROM OVER

HARPER

I expected to come home to a castle in chaos. The bombs were supposed to have already gone off, destroying the tower and half the residences in the castle.

Instead, the only surprise and chaos was from the demons making their way through the surrounding forest to the city's entrance.

Even though we had room in the castle for more demons, I couldn't risk putting anyone in there. Not yet. I needed to find out why those bombs hadn't gone off when they were supposed to and why there were inconsistencies with the ruby priestess's story.

After a full day's journey, though, we were all exhausted and hungry.

Everyone needed rest.

I called a city meeting, asking all the residents of the city who could to come to the steps of the castle. Using magic to amplify my voice, I addressed them as a group for the first time since I'd come home.

"Thank you all for coming," I said. "As you may have already noticed, I brought some demons with me today from the Underground. Last night, they were attacked by the Order's hunters. Some are injured. Others are scared. All are currently without a home. We need to make room for these demons in our city. If you have an extra bedroom, I'm asking for you to offer it up to a family for the night. Any extra space or supplies you are willing to offer would be greatly appreciated."

I knew the humans and demons of our city would come together to help provide for the others. That was simply the nature of this place my father had built. We would work together to make the best of it.

"Tomorrow morning, I need everyone who has ever worked on the creation of the dome and the plans for this city to join me in the throne room," I said. "We will be starting an expansion project in the coming days, hoping to make more room for everyone who might need to seek refuge under this dome. It's no secret here that we've brought down another priestess of the Order of Shadows—"

I had to pause there, because the cheers from the crowd were too great. I loved to hear them celebrate, but anxiety slithered around in my stomach like a poisonous snake, just waiting to strike.

"But the harder we attack them, the worse their attacks will get, as well," I said. "The weaker they get, the more desperate they will get. We need to be vigilant. Report any suspicious behavior to the guards. The Order plays dangerous games, and that often means the people standing right next to us are our greatest enemies. Anything strange you see in the forest, no matter how small, let us know. If anything at all seems off to you, don't hesitate to come forward. Sometimes it's the smallest clue that tells us trouble is coming."

I looked out at the citizens of my kingdom, wishing I didn't have to say things that would make it harder for them to sleep at night, but we couldn't afford to become complacent or to think that just because we'd killed two priestesses, we had won this war.

The war was far from over.

"We have to stick together. As we welcome new demons into our community, there may be some growing pains," I said with a smile. "We may be crowded. We may have to share in ways we aren't used to sharing. But as your future queen, I'm asking you to keep an open mind and an open heart. To remember that this situation is only temporary. We've been through so much already. I know we can make it through whatever is coming next, as long as we do it together."

"Here, here," someone shouted from the back, and the crowd erupted in applause.

I took a deep breath. Everything was going to be okay here.

"If you have a room to spare, I'll ask you to form a line here to speak with one of the guards," I said. "If you are just coming in from the Underground, I'll ask you to form your line on this opposite side. The guards will pair you up according to space, and we will do everything we can to keep all families together. Thank you for your kindness and your patience."

Jackson took my hand, and we waved to the crowd as they moved into lines on opposite sides of the castle steps. I gave instructions to the guards, asking them to let me know if any trouble arose.

When everything seemed to be settled, we both headed inside to get some food and some rest.

"No bombs," Jackson said. "Do you think she's lying to us?"

"I don't know," I said. "But I'm going to find out. Maybe they're scheduled to go off tonight while we're sleeping, and she was just wrong about the timeline? Have Gregory brought up from the dungeons first. I want to talk to him."

I had just sat down to eat when Gregory entered the dining hall, his head lowered and his eyes ringed with red. Had he been crying?

"Your Highness," he said. "I don't have words to say—"

"What I want to know is whether the priestess has been talking to you while the two of you were locked away down there. Did she tell you anything that might be important for me to know?"

It was a long shot to even ask him, and it would be hard to believe anything he had to say, anyway, but I figured it couldn't hurt to ask.

"She just blathered on and on about how someday, she was going to be free of the Order of Shadows and how she couldn't wait to buy an apartment in New York City," he said.

"New York?" I asked.

"Yes, apparently, she's always wanted to live there. She hates California," he said. "I honestly am not sure how much more of her chatter I could put up with. She doesn't seem to ever stop talking."

I suppressed a smile. "Well, that's a good start for your punishment, then," I said.

Horror crossed his face. "I'm begging you," he said. "Put me anywhere else. Just don't put me back in that cell next to her."

Wow. He genuinely acted like he'd just been tortured for two days straight.

The truth was, we really needed Gregory's help right now with the refugees. He knew this city better than anyone.

"I'll give you a little break from the dungeons if you agree to help get the refugees settled into their temporary homes," I said. "And you know where all the extra food and blankets and things are stored, so I'll need you to help ration those out."

"Refugees?" he asked.

"From the Underground," I said. "They were attacked, and now we've got a thousand of their demons living in our city. If you agree to help them, I'll let you do that for the rest of the afternoon. There will be two guards stationed to watch you at all times, though, and if you so much as hint at trying to run away, I'll tell the ruby priestess she can trigger that curse she placed on you."

Gregory closed his eyes.

"I'll do whatever you ask of me, I swear," he said. "I intend to spend the rest of my life trying to make this up to you."

"Well, this is a good place to start," I said. "Go."

Easton and Gregory bowed and headed out to help with the distribution of supplies.

Jackson gave me a sideways look, and I just brushed it off. It wasn't that I trusted Gregory, but I understood why he did what he did. He wasn't going to give us more trouble.

Besides, he was the one who knew the most about the extra supplies here in the castle.

Just as Gregory left, Tuli appeared, carrying a tray full of food.

She smiled when she saw me and placed the food down on the large dining table. "I'm so excited you're home, Harper," she said. "What you've done for those demons is very brave and kind. I want to help, if I can."

I stood up and gave her a hug. "Thank you for taking care of things here while we were gone," I said. "I don't know what I'd do without you."

Jackson and I wanted to talk to her about the possibility of joining the Council as caretaker of the castle, but there were too many people around now that Mary Anne, Essex, and Angela had all joined us to eat.

"If you have time, you could help Gregory with the blankets and other supplies," I said. "And later, when you have a spare minute, I want to talk to you about something important."

A look of concern crossed her normally-tranquil face and she tugged at her long, black braid. "Is everything okay?" she asked.

"Yes," I said. "It's good news. I promise."

She bowed—something I still wasn't used to from others—and left the room to go help with the supplies.

The rest of us started to eat as we chatted about our plan to rescue Andros. In the middle of it, though, the door swung open and Gregory led Rend and Franki inside. I hadn't seen either of them since I'd gotten home, but I could tell from the worried looks on their faces that something terrible had happened.

Rend explained the Franki's best friend, Katy, had been attacked by the Mother Crow—the witch who had killed my mother—and was locked inside some kind of sleeping curse.

Jackson started to mention the things we'd been going through, but I stopped him. Rend had saved our lives and already given so much to keep us safe. What he was going through right now was enough. He didn't need to know how bad things had gotten here for us.

Since things seemed to be under control here for now, I sent Angela, Mary Anne, and Essex back with him to try to help Katy. I reminded Mary Anne to be back here tomorrow to help set another Emerald Gate free, but really, I wanted her back in case we had to go find Andros.

Mary Anne's eyes sent a quick apology, but I waved her off.

Her mother was still out there somewhere, and since Mary Anne herself was a crow witch, she needed to be a part of whatever was going on with Franki and the Mother Crow right now.

I couldn't ask her to stay here in the castle with all of that happening, too.

I promised Essex I would take good care of his mother and saw them all off through the portal of white roses.

With a sigh, I headed back toward the castle, but just before I passed under the stone arches, Tuli called my name. I looked up to see her standing on the balcony of my room.

How many times had I made her promise not to go up there?

"Harper, we can't seem to find the extra pillows and blankets. Do you remember—"

"Tuli, get out of those rooms. I told you—"

A huge explosion rocked the entire castle, sending chunks of stone and debris through the air. I cried out as pain tore through my leg. I struggled to stand, blinking against the ash and smoke as red flames consumed half the castle on this side.

"Tuli," I screamed, crawling over the rocks, desperate to see if the balcony was even still there.

My ears were ringing, but I heard someone shouting my name. It was like being underwater. The sounds were muffled and distant.

"Tuli? Tuli, I'm here," I said. I tried to stand, but my leg had been partially crushed by one of the falling stones.

I tried to shift, instead, but it was no use. I was in too much pain to focus.

Hands grabbed me under my armpits and dragged me from the area as more shouts rang out.

Jackson knelt at my side, cradling my head in his lap. He was saying something I couldn't quite make out and running a soothing hand down my cheek.

I tried to tell him about Tuli, but the pain was so awful, I couldn't focus.

Jackson placed both hands on my crushed leg, and I opened my eyes as freezing cold energy rushed through my body. It was both painful and soothing at the same time, and when it had passed, I found that the ringing in my ears had stopped, too.

Guards all around us worked to clear the area, and Jackson started to lift me into his arms.

"Tuli," I said, finally catching my breath. "She was up on the balcony in our room, Jackson. You have to find her."

"What?" he asked, his eyes wide.

He shifted and flew toward the stone that had fallen from above. We both worked, using magic to lift and remove stones, searching for her and calling her name.

When I moved a large slab of stone and tile, her body came into view, and I dropped the stone to the side, falling on my knees beside her.

Jackson placed his hands on her forehead and closed his

eyes. He shook his head and gripped her face, leaning down, closer.

"No," he said. "This can't be happening. What was she doing up there?"

I began to sob. "I asked her to look for blankets and supplies, but I meant in the storerooms. The bedrooms were supposed to be blocked off. I'm so sorry, Jackson."

He cried out, lifting her into his arms and shaking his head. He held her close as a white mist hovered over her body, shimmered with a great light, and then disappeared, her spirit passing from this world to the next.

"Why did the bombs go off now?" he asked. "It was supposed to happen in the middle of the night. No one was supposed to be up there."

I touched his arm, but he pushed me away.

"It's all her fault," he said. "I'm going to kill her, Harper. We never should have let her inside the dome."

At first, I wasn't even sure who he was talking about, but as soon as he lowered Tuli's body to the ground and shifted, I realized he was heading for the dungeons.

Jackson was going to kill the ruby priestess.

RITUAL ROOM

JACKSON

I had come down here to kill her, but instead of finding the ruby priestess sitting idly in her cell, she hovered three feet in the air, clutching her neck and gasping for breath. She seemed to be alone in her cell, and yet something— or someone—was attacking her.

A red vapor poured from her mouth and snaked down her body, disappearing into the floor near her feet.

Her wide eyes sought mine as I entered the room, and she reached toward me.

"Help me," she managed to whisper.

Harper stopped just behind me and gasped. She shifted again and disappeared up the steps.

As I stepped closer, the air around the ruby priestess shimmered, as if she were surrounded by an open portal.

But that's impossible.

The dungeons were shielded from anyone except members of the royal family to be able to cast magic of any kind. Even demons.

As long as you were on the outside of the cells, a demon could shift into shadow, but even if I'd wanted to, I wouldn't have been able to actually cast a spell or connect to the main source of my power down here.

And no witch should have been able to cast anywhere in the domed city. It was part of the protection placed on the dome when Harper's father had built it.

And yet, something was happening to the ruby priestess. Something I had absolutely no explanation for.

Harper flew past me, a set of keys clanging in her hands.

"What are you doing?" I asked.

"I'm going to help her," she said. "We can't just let her die."

Harper finally got the right key in the lock, threw open the door, and rushed inside, but the moment she stepped inside that shimmering space, she disappeared.

It really was a portal.

Cursing, I ran after her, stepping into a room that felt both familiar and foreign at the same time.

Walls coated with jagged crystals replaced the damp stone walls of the dungeons, and the plain stone floor had been replaced by onyx carved with intricate, swirling patterns. I could see now that the red mist of energy pouring out of the priestess was actually flowing into a ruby stone just under her feet. A stone that matched the size and shape of the master stones Harper had pulled from her sisters' chests.

Only there was one important difference.

This stone was embedded in the floor of the strange crystal and onyx chamber and was one of five in a pentagram carved into the floor. Each point of the star held a similarly-sized gemstone, one in each of the five colors of the Order's covens.

Sapphire. Emerald. Amethyst. Citrine. Ruby.

It was a ritual room. That much was clear.

The design of the space matched those of the Order's ritual rooms, but instead of a large demon gate in the center of the pentagram, this room had an onyx column covered in rough gemstones.

Atop the column at about waist-height sat the most massive diamond I had ever seen in my life. Twice the size of one of the Order's master stones, that diamond pulsed with a light so bright it seemed to burn me when I looked at it.

Harper rushed around, trying to pull the ruby priestess down or set her free, but I couldn't stop looking at that stone.

The power radiating from it nearly knocked me off my feet, but at the same time, it called out to me. Urging me closer.

I reached for my connection to that deep well of power within me, and the moment I tapped into it, my entire body buzzed from head to toe. The power filled me so quickly, I thought I might explode into a million tiny pieces.

I wanted more.

The ruby priestess let out a deep, guttural sound as she clawed at her throat, held there by some invisible force.

"Jackson, help me figure out how to get her down," Harper said.

Reluctantly, I stepped away from the diamond stone in the center of the room and walked toward Priestess Thorn. Seconds ago, I had been determined to end her life myself, but now I was going to have to save her just to find out where the hell this place was and how she had ended up here, despite being in the protection of the dungeons.

"Quickly," she sputtered, her eyes darting toward something behind me.

When I turned, I expected to only see the bars of the cell standing open in the dungeons of the castle, but instead, there was an arched doorway with a multi-colored waterfall cascading over the top of it. From behind the water, a figure made of pure, white light seemed to walk toward us.

"Please," Magda said, gasping for breath. "The dagger. Cut me free."

"Jackson, help me find it," Harper shouted. "Hurry."

I joined her at a large glass table covered in ritual items. Cups, necklaces, rings. Multiple of each, embedded with a common stone.

Diamonds.

"Here."

Harper pushed the chalices to the side and reached for the diamond dagger, but I grabbed it first.

I walked up to the ruby priestess and placed the tip of the dagger just over her heart.

"Why did you lie about the timing of those bombs?" I asked.

Her eyelids fluttered open, and she shook her head. "I didn't lie," she said. "They were supposed to go off last night."

"Bullshit," I said. "You were the one who planted those bombs. You waited until we got home to set them off somehow. You killed my friend."

I spoke through gritted teeth, pressing the dagger into her skin until I drew blood.

"Jackson, don't," Harper said, but when I looked at her, she backed away.

"Tell me the truth," I said. "There were over two-hundred hunters waiting for us at the Underground. Most of them had diamonds on them. It was an ambush. You lied to us."

Magda shook her head violently, her legs thrashing.

"No," she said. "I swear. Cut me free, and I'll explain."

"Why? So you can lie to us again? Send us into another trap? I don't think so."

"Harper," Magda said, her eyelids fluttering and her shoulders drooping.

The red mist pouring from her throat seemed to dim, as if her energy had nearly been drained from her body.

"Cut her down, Jackson," Harper said, touching my arm. "We don't even know what this place is or what's happening to her. If she dies, it needs to be on our terms. Not here. Not like this."

My jaw tensed, and I struggled to hold myself back. I wanted to plunge the dagger into her chest and rip that stone out so badly. I wanted to make her pay for Tuli and Andros. For every demon who had died in the Underground.

"If you kill her, we have no chance of finding the amethyst priestess," Harper said. "She needs to pay for what she's done, but we still need her. Dammit, Jackson, give me the dagger."

I closed my eyes and struggled against my rage.

But Harper was right.

We left before the ruby priestess had told us where to find Andros.

Reluctantly, I pulled the dagger away and handed it to Harper.

I wasn't even sure how Harper was supposed to cut her down. There were no ropes or chains binding her that I could see. Only the red mist.

"What do I do?" Harper asked, slapping Magda's face to wake her up. "I don't see anything holding you up. Tell me what to do."

"The stone," she said, her voice now hardly a whisper. "Sever the connection."

Her eyes rolled back, and her head fell forward.

Harper dropped to the floor and thrust the dagger toward the red mist of energy that poured into the stone at Magda's feet. I expected the dagger to pass through it the way it would through mist or fog.

But instead, it made a sound like flesh as Harper sunk the dagger into it.

Magda drew in a shrieking breath as a bright red light shot out of the hole the dagger had made. A moment later, she fell to the ground, her red skirt pooling on the floor like blood.

"No," a voice behind me cried.

For an instant, I felt a white-hot heat approaching, as if the devil were standing at my back.

Harper dropped the diamond dagger and went flying backward.

I reached for her, and a bright blue light seemed to extend from my hands. I couldn't explain what it was. It was unlike any magic I'd used before, but it seemed to just pour out of me.

I used the light to scoop Harper and the ruby priestess up, pulling them toward me.

The portal that surrounded us seemed to shrink, and with one last glance at the glowing diamond, I jumped through, taking us back to the cell where it had all began.

The portal closed and the glowing blue light around me disappeared, dropping Magda and Harper to the floor.

"Are you okay?" I asked.

Harper sat up, rubbing her shoulder. "I think so."

Priestess Thorn rolled over, her body trembling as she drew in several labored breaths. The area around her neck was red and swollen, as if someone had been choking her with a braided rope for hours.

I stood there for a moment, waiting for my hands to stop shaking.

What the hell just happened?

I closed my eyes, picturing every detail of that room and committing it to memory. There was no doubt in my mind that place was important. Vital in our war against the Order.

And what was that diamond? Why had it seemed to call out to me like that?

I felt almost empty now that it was gone.

"Thank you," Magda said, her voice rough and hoarse.

The ruby priestess struggled to a sitting position and rubbed a tentative hand against the burn around her throat.

"You both saved my life," she said.

When she looked up at me, a tear fell down her cheek.

I slid down the wall until my butt hit the floor and shook my head.

"I was coming down here to kill you myself," I said. "But it seems someone else almost beat me to it."

She laughed, and then winced, her breath hitching in her throat.

"Not my best day," she said.

"Magda, what was that place?" Harper asked, her voice barely more than a whisper.

"That place," Magda said, "is where the true Order of Shadows was born."

THIS IS WHAT WE DO

HARPER

Chills spread across my skin, as if a ghost had just entered the room and walked right through me.

Magda's words stirred me to my core, and I suddenly wondered if all those secrets she'd been promising to share were about to come pouring out of her.

"What do you mean that's where the Order was born?" I asked.

Magda sighed and scooted back until she was able to lean against the bars of the cell. The three of us sat there with the door wide open, each catching our breath.

"That's a long story," she said. "One I'm afraid you don't have time for today. Not if you want to save your friend."

Jackson stood and paced the floor. "How can we believe anything you say?"

"Do you think the High Priestess would have risked exposing herself to you by opening up a portal like that if she didn't want me dead as fast as possible?" Magda said. "Do you think that's how she would choose to reward me if I had done what she asked me to do? What you really should be asking is how she found out I was here. How did she know to send extra hunters to the Underground? Think about it. She knew you were coming."

"She knew because you told her," Jackson said.

But I shook my head. "No," I said. "If Magda had done what the High Priestess asked, she wouldn't have just tried to kill her or transfer her power. That's what she was doing, wasn't it? She was going to drain your power and give the ruby gates to someone else."

Magda brought a hand to her throat.

"Yes," she said. "She's threatened it before, but she's never actually tried to follow through on it. She wanted me dead, because the things I know are dangerous in your hands. Can't you see that?"

"Then tell us what you know about that room," Jackson said. "That diamond."

Magda shook her head, running a hand along her skirt to smooth the fabric.

"You promised me you would do what you could to keep me alive, and then you told someone close to the High Priestess that I was here," Magda said. "To me, that's not living up to your half of the promise."

"I made no promises," Jackson said, narrowing his eyes.

I stood and sighed. "I made that promise, and I intend to keep it," I said. "But the only people I told about you were the most trusted people in my Council."

Magda raised an eyebrow. "And despite everything you've been through, you think there's no one on your Council who would betray you to the High Priestess?" she asked. "Can you trust every single one of them so much you know without a doubt they haven't been coerced or manipulated into giving away your secrets?"

I suddenly felt sick to my stomach.

I knew better than to say that I could trust anyone without a doubt. Jackson. Aerden. That was it, really. I wanted to say I could trust Rend, Mary Anne, Angela. Everyone. But would Mary Anne betray me if she was told that Essex would be tortured if she didn't give away my secrets?

In a world where ritual sacrifice could mean anyone could obtain a permanent glamour that no one could see through? Not even Jackson? How did I even know Angela was still really Angela and not some spy made to look like her?

There were no guarantees of loyalty in this game the Order played.

"I didn't think so," Magda said. "Someone you trust told the High Priestess I was here. They told her I was spilling her secrets, so she improvised. She sent her own personal hunters to the Underground, hoping it would be enough to destroy you all."

She cleared her throat, touching the red spot again.

"The only way those bombs went off at a different time than the one I set is if they were manually changed, using a spell I created myself," she said. "Which means someone in your castle got the spell words from the High Priestess and used them to change the timing. It's the only explanation. You can bet she knows your plans to save your friend Andros, as well."

I was so frustrated, I wanted to bang my head against the wall.

But Magda smiled. "Lucky for you, I held some information back from you about that, just in case."

"What?" I asked. "You lied?"

She raised a finger. "No, I did not lie," she said. "I just didn't tell you the entire truth. I don't know where Andros is being held by those hunters, but I know where he's going to be. I can help you create a plan that will trick whoever is betraying you. I'm good at tricks."

There was literally no way to know if she was telling the truth or not. It was possible Rend could make some kind of potion that would let us know, but he was currently unavailable, dealing with the Brotherhood of Darkness.

And he'd told us once himself that someone with a high-level of magic might be immune to potions like that.

So, what were we supposed to do? We were running out of time.

"I'm sorry, Magda, but we need to talk for a second," I said.

I connected to my power and waved my hand toward her, grateful for the fact that someone with royal blood could still use magic down here in the dungeons.

"What did you do?" Jackson asked.

I looked over at Magda, who now had a swirling black shadow wrapped around her eyes and ears.

"She can't hear or see us now," I said. "It was the fastest way to get some privacy."

"We can't trust her," Jackson said. "I think we should kill her and take the stone. One less priestess alive. Thousands of demons saved."

"Okay, but we kill her now and we have no idea where Andros and his squad are being held," I said. "Not a single clue, other than the fact that the amethyst priestess's hunters took him. We have no idea where the amethyst priestess lives.

There's no way we could find him in time. The ritual is tomorrow, Jackson. We kill her. We kill Andros."

Jackson slammed his hand against the wall.

"If she tells us where the amethyst priestess lives, we'll be walking into a trap," Jackson said. "Even if she's telling us the truth about everything and it really is someone in our castle who is talking to the High Priestess, it's still a trap now. We've lost the element of surprise."

I walked over and took his hands in mine.

"Then we walk into a trap," I said, looking into his eyes. "This is what we do. We see the danger and we go anyway, because it's the only way to save the people we love. When the emerald priestess captured you and demanded I bring Zara to Winterhaven, I knew it was a trap, but what choice did I have? It was either step into the trap and try to win anyway or let you die."

I reached up to touch his face.

"I wasn't going to let you die without a fight," I said. "And we aren't going to let Andros die, either. We're smart and we're strong. We won't go in without a plan. We'll figure it out together, just you and me, because you're the only one I trust with my whole heart and soul. What do you say?"

His eyes searched mine, and I could see the struggle there. It was never easy to step into danger willingly, but we couldn't stop now. We couldn't abandon our friend.

Finally, he nodded.

"I don't trust her, but I trust you," he said. "And if we're gonna go, we need to go as soon as possible. Let's bring Andros home."

I squeezed his hand. "Okay, let's do this."

I waved my hand again, and Magda let out an annoyed sigh.

"Was that completely necessary?" she asked. "That was extremely unpleasant, I'll have you know."

"Good," I said.

I pulled her stool over and set it in the middle of the cell.

"Now, tell us everything we need to know about your sister Gladys and her amethyst fortress," I said. "Looks like we're about to spring a trap."

RICH WITH DIAMONDS

AERDEN

I lit another candle and set it on the table near Lea's bedside.

She'd been asleep for several hours now, hardly moving at all since we'd brought her back to her own bed.

The shaman, Lisette, had been in to check on her every hour, but she said there was not much she could do. Lea had taken herself beyond the point of exhaustion by stepping into some kind of memory or vision in that damaged room of the abandoned wing, and until her body and mind got the rest it needed, she would almost be in a coma.

The king had come to see her right away, but after placing a hand on her head for a moment, he had relaxed and nodded.

"She'll be okay," he'd said. "She didn't go deep enough to get lost there, but she definitely pushed herself too far."

I agreed to let him know as soon as she woke up.

Some of Lea's handmaidens had thought it highly inappropriate for me to want to be in her private chambers when Lea was sleeping, but I finally convinced them to give us some privacy so that I could read quietly.

The truth was, I didn't want anyone to see what I was reading.

I'd managed to smuggle about fifty books out of the Underground's library thanks to a special backpack Essex's mother had made for me, and it was going to take time to get through them all.

Luckily, I had some time to spare.

I set the first book on the table and started to skim the pages, amazed at how easy the text was to read, despite the fact that I'd never seen this language before. There were parts of it that were still hard to make out entirely, and I wished more than ever that Trention were still alive to read these books himself, but for now, I just had to be grateful to have even a small piece of his power.

Several more hours went by, and I slowly made my way through three more books.

Each of these books were written in the same foreign language, and I had chosen them because their pages sparkled with the dust of diamonds, just like the book Trention had described to me before he died.

But so far, I'd found nothing interesting. A fictional story about a hero journeying through time. A boring account of a family's estate and legal dealings. A thin book that seemed to be a cookbook.

I tossed that last one back in the bag and rummaged inside for the next.

This one proved to be more promising. It was a travel journal, describing cities I'd never heard of filled with demons.

These were not cities from either kingdom on this continent, I was sure of it.

I leaned forward, devouring the pages, eager to find something that would tell us more about this land to the west. Were there really cities there five times larger than the King's City?

It would mean millions.

What could we do against the Order with allies like that?

A line near the bottom of the hundredth page caught my eye, and I ran my finger over the text, making sure I'd translated it correctly.

Today, I travelled from Mirogul to Planshar, a large city near the mountains. The diamond fields near Planshar are rumored to hold the most beautiful, clear white diamonds in the Shadow World. These diamonds are said to be a major source of the Shadow World's inherent energy, and many demons travel here from all over the world to be healed and refreshed.

Then, later, on page one-hundred-seventy-six.

When my friend invited me to travel across the Sea of Glass to visit his homeland, I never expected to find a land so rich with diamonds. They are rare stones in my country, but they are more plentiful here than any other stone. I feel certain this is why the air here seems to hum with an energy that lifts my heart.

This book was filled with passages like that, and with the frequent references to things I recognized like the Sea of Glass, I knew with my whole heart that the author of this journal was describing this mysterious land to the west.

A land rich with diamonds, he'd said.

A land now blocked off from us by a wall of storms so dangerous, it consumed any ship that got close to it. There was no reference to the storm in this book, though, which made me believe it didn't exist when it was written.

I kept paging through and was about to reach for the next book in my bag when Lea moaned and lifted a hand to her head.

Slowly, her eyes fluttered open, and I instantly moved to her side.

"Take it easy," I said softly, reaching for a cool cloth on her bedside table. I carefully placed it on her forehead. "Just take your time. Rest."

"What happened?" she asked. "Where am I?"

"You're back in your bed. You passed out in the abandoned wing," I said. "Your father said you used your power to see visions. That you went too deep."

"How long have I been asleep?" she asked, trying to sit up.

I shook my head and placed a firm hand on her shoulder. "You need to rest, Lea. If you ask me to move, I'll move, but you should know you've been knocked out cold for more than eight hours now. Your body is weak. If you push yourself now, you're going to be putting your life in danger."

She groaned and lay back.

"I've lost the whole day," she said. "How are the refugees? Is everyone settled? Do they need me?"

I smiled and moved the cool cloth around her face.

"Everyone is doing great," I said. "And before you ask, no. There's been no word from Jackson and Harper yet."

Her eyes opened. "I have to be able to go save Andros," she said.

"You will," I assured her. "Rest. That's the only way to get better. Not even a shaman can do much to help exhaustion like this. What were you trying to see in that room, anyway? Dorlar said he walked out of the room and five seconds later, heard your body hit the floor. I've never heard of a vision taking you in so deeply."

She shook her head slowly. "I wasn't trying to see anything," she said. "All I did was touch that wall and it pulled me under."

She frowned.

"There was something important," she said. "Something about a ship. And a woman. I need to remember."

"Don't push yourself," I said. "You can remember tomorrow. Are you hungry? Do you want me to call for something to eat?"

I started to stand, but she reached for my hand and pulled me down to her side.

"Stay," she said, her eyes closing. "Just stay with me."

She fell asleep again, her hand curled around mine.

After a few minutes, I stretched out to grab the next book, pulled it into my lap, and started to read, never once letting go of her hand.

NOT EVEN DEATH

HARPER

After more than an hour of taking notes about the amethyst priestess's home, the types of magic she liked to cast, the traps she tended to set, I was becoming more terrified about what we might be walking into.

We would need to be very careful about every single step we took inside that place when we got there.

If Magda was telling us the truth, though, only a few of us would ever have to go inside that fortress the amethyst priestess called Blackwood.

Jackson and I needed some time to work through our plan, but I didn't want to leave the ruby priestess down here where she might be attacked again. If the High Priestess truly wanted her dead, she wasn't going to stop trying until she'd achieved that goal.

"How did the High Priestess open that portal earlier," I asked Magda. "Did someone leave something down here with you that opened it? Or does the High Priestess just have the ability to reach you whenever she wants?"

Magda shook her head. "I'm not sure," she said. "She's only done something like that once before. I'm assuming it's the master stone in my chest that allows her to open the portal to me. This stone is connected to that room you saw."

"The ritual room?" Jackson asked.

Magda nodded. "Yes, the other half of this stone is there," she said. "I think it allows her to reach me when she wants to, as long as she knows where I am."

I sighed. "Well, that's going to present a challenge for us," I said. "You're only good to us dead if we get to keep the master stone. And honestly, even if everyone else disagrees with me, I think you're more useful to us alive."

"Well, thank you for that, at least," Magda said.

"We have to figure out a way to block whatever signal that stone in your chest is sending out," I said. I looked to Jackson. "Any brilliant ideas?"

"Willow," he said. "She's our best shielder."

I shook my head. "If shielding worked, the dome would have prevented the High Priestess from opening that first portal."

"Good point," Jackson said. "We have things that prevent people from casting, but I don't know of anything that goes the other way."

"Why did you say you think she needs to know where you are for it to work?" I asked.

"I don't know for certain, of course, but when the High Priestess found out Hazel had taken you to a secret location where she could run experiments on you, she was furious," Magda said.

"Why would she care about one of her priestesses running

experiments on me? I would think she'd be happy you guys were torturing me."

Magda laughed. "Oh, she wasn't angry you were being tortured," Magda said. "She did say she wanted you kept alive for some reason, but I think she was more upset that she didn't know where Hazel was. She knew that if you ever got a chance, you would kill her emerald priestess the way you'd killed her sapphire. I got the feeling she wanted to put an end to Hazel and transfer the emerald gates to someone else, but she couldn't find her. It's just a theory, but if the High Priestess has no idea where I am, I don't think she can open that portal. I think she needs a lock on my location, and then she needs to keep that portal open until my energy is fully drained and my body has died."

I nodded, a plan forming, even if it was risky. And possibly crazy.

"Well, I guess we'll find out if your theory is correct," I said.

"What are we going to do?" Jackson asked.

I smiled. "We're going to take her with us."

Magda's head snapped up, and her eyes grew wide.

"That was not part of the deal," she said. "Gladys probably knows by now I've betrayed them. She'll kill me if I go with you."

"Not if she doesn't know you're there," I said. "Come on. We need to talk through our plan, change clothes, and make sure everyone else is okay up there. I'm also tired of being in this dungeon."

"For a dungeon, it's not that bad," she said. "I've seen worse."

I rolled my eyes and motioned for her to follow me.

"Don't try anything, please. I don't think I can convince Jackson not to kill you a third time today," I said.

Jackson lowered his head and hid a laugh.

We led the ruby priestess up the stairs, but just as we neared the top, I turned on her.

"From this moment forward, you're my friend Molly," I said. "You're a human refugee from the Underground, and you stick by my side, no matter what."

I connected to my power, breathing into the flow of energy deep within me. It wouldn't be easy to keep up with a glamour for hours on end, but if I could get by with very small changes, I didn't think anyone would recognize her. We were going to need to get her some new clothes, though. There was no need to waste energy on glamouring her clothing, too.

I imagined the ruby priestess younger. My age, maybe. With brown hair and a slightly larger nose. Higher cheekbones. Brown eyes.

When I opened my eyes, she was transformed. Nothing too hard to keep up with, but enough no one would recognize her.

I passed a hand in front of her body, and her long, red dress transformed into a pair of dark jeans and a black t-shirt.

"Once we get upstairs, I'll have you change for real," I said.

Magda groaned. "This is not my style at all," she said. "I haven't worn a pair of jeans in my life. And black? Are you serious?"

"I'm trying to glamour you. Not your style is the whole point."

She made a clicking sound with her tongue. "Fine," she said, twirling her finger around a strand of brown hair. "I am so glad I can't see my face right now."

"Let's go," I said.

I led her up the rest of the stairs, glad to see that most of the debris from the bombs had been cleared and the throne room was mostly empty for now.

We'd put our bags in a room on the opposite side of the castle near where the guards slept, so I headed that way with Jackson and my new friend, "Molly", following closely behind.

A few people stopped us, asking for instructions about repairs to the building and rooms for the refugees, but most conversations were short, and no one spoke to Magda.

When we finally got into the room, I let out a sigh of relief and locked the door behind us.

Knowing it was possible one of our own Council members here in the Southern Kingdom had ratted us out to the High Priestess had me completely on edge.

Who would do that?

I went through the list of everyone who had been there when we'd discussed the ruby priestess.

Mordecai, Joost, Erick, and Cristo had been members of the Resistance, along with Lea, for a very long time. They had traveled with her to the human world and joined in the fight against the Order of Shadows long before I was even born.

My sister, Angela, had acted as queen in my absence. She had given so much of herself to this war, and she loved me. She wouldn't betray me.

Mary Anne and Essex were practically family, too, by now. Mary Anne had sacrificed her own family ties in order to save my life years ago.

The idea of Jackson betraying me wasn't even on the table, and I didn't believe Illana would, either. She'd joined our fight late, but she left behind everything she knew back in the King's City to stand at Jackson's side.

And then there was Brooke.

Brooke might have been an enemy a long time ago, but I never would have escaped the Evers Institute without her Still, she was a wild card, and probably the most likely person to have betrayed us, if anyone.

I would have to keep my eye on Brooke.

"What has you so lost in thought?" Jackson asked. "Hopefully our plan for how to survive this next part?"

I smiled. "Nothing that pleasant," I said.

"If I could just say something for a—"

Magda started talking, but I waved my hand in front of her face, blocking her sight and hearing. She stomped her foot like a child, and I laughed, guiding her to a nearby chair where she could sit and pout all she wanted.

Jackson and I sat on the bed in the small guard's room, facing each other as we talked through every possibility we could think of until we had what we felt like was our best shot.

"Is this plan going to work?" I asked.

"The timing has to be perfect," he said. "One thing out of place, and we're screwed."

I bit my lower lip. I wanted some kind of assurance that I was doing the right thing, but something I'd learned a lot time ago was that it was easy to see your enemy when they were out in the open, doing enemy things right in your face.

But the enemy who pretended to be your friend was much more dangerous and harder to spot.

Magda was an enemy who I wanted to trust. I couldn't explain why. Only that my gut told me she was truly trying to help.

But my gut also told me everyone on our Council was trustworthy.

Both of those things couldn't be true.

Still, I just had a feeling I was doing the right thing, trusting Magda.

"It's going to work out," I said, smiling and taking his hand. "Are you ready?"

"Not yet."

He took in a deep breath and let it go very slowly.

"Has it really only been a couple of days since you got home?" he asked. "I thought we'd have weeks to focus on the emerald gates and relax here at the castle. Maybe start rebuilding Brighton Manor. We haven't had a moment to rest or just be together since that first night."

He moved closer, pulling me into his arms. I lay my head against his strong chest and listened to the beating of his heart. Ran my fingers along every ridge of muscle.

"It's such a weird thing to be terrified and in constant danger, but also to be happier than I've ever been," he said. "I was so lost without you, Harper. You are a part of me now, and I don't want to live without you ever again."

"You know, the whole time I was there at Evers Institute, they kept feeding me this story about how I'd burned my own house down and killed my family," I said. "They told me I'd done terrible things, trying to brainwash me."

I leaned back, studying him. Memorizing his face all over again.

"But no matter what they did to me—the injections, the torture, the memory-stealing spells—they couldn't take you away from me," I said. I placed his hand on my heart. "Even when I couldn't remember your name, my heart knew your face. It knew the way you moved and the way your skin felt against my own. You and I are so much a part of each other, all the magic in the world couldn't make me forget that we belong together. Nothing is ever going to change that. Not even death."

Jackson placed his hand gently on the back of my neck, his eyes searching mine before he leaned down and kissed me. God, how I had missed the feel of his lips against mine. The way his hands felt on my skin.

I moved, wrapping my legs around his body and pulling myself closer.

He smiled against my mouth as his hands disappeared under the back of my shirt to press flat against my skin.

"I love you," he said softly, nuzzling my neck.

"I love you, too," I said.

We held each other like that for as long as we could.

And it was never long enough.

"Are you ready now?" I asked, when I knew we couldn't afford to wait any longer.

There was still a lot of work to do, and Andros needed us.

Jackson pulled away slowly and nodded. He pulled a ruby communication stone from his pocket.

"I'm ready," he said.

He placed a finger over the top and the stone began to glow.

Our plan had been set in motion.

STANDING WHERE WE STAND

LEA

I opened my eyes to find Aerden reading. Our hands were clasped, and I wondered if I'd reached for him in my sleep.

I didn't really want to let go.

My dreams had been full of nightmares. Storms. A woman in a white cloak, always watching me.

I shuddered and moved to sit up.

Aerden's eyes widened. "You're awake," he said. "How are you feeling?"

He set his book aside and grabbed a cool cloth to place on my forehead. Had he been here all night?

"Better, I think. What happened?"

"You got pulled into a vision in the abandoned wing," he said. "You've been resting since then."

I smiled. "Have we already had this conversation once? Or am I still dreaming?"

Aerden laughed and pushed a strand of my hair to the side.

"You woke up once before and asked similar questions," he said.

"I thought so."

I tried to sit up, and instead of telling me to rest more, Aerden helped me up. That was a good sign.

He helped to prop a few pillows behind my back and brought me a glass of water. He was patient, but when I met his eyes, I could see that he wanted to talk. He'd found something.

"What is it?" I asked. I glanced at the books that littered the desk nearby.

"Are you sure you're up for talking?" he asked, but his eyes swirled with eagerness.

"Tell me," I said, sitting up straighter and pulling my legs toward me on the bed.

"Trention was right. There is a continent across the Sea of Glass," he said. "Most of these books aren't dated, but I would say around a thousand years ago, during the Age of Stone, someone conjured that storm that separates us from each other. From the writings in these books, we used to be all one world. Different kingdoms, but demons traveled freely between them."

I shook my head. "But only a thousand years ago? My father was alive a thousand years ago. He doesn't remember that continent. He said he only remembers the Storm."

"I don't have all the answers," Aerden said. "But what if something about the Storm also blocked our memories of that place?"

I frowned. "Why would someone go to all that trouble?"

I thought of my vision. The woman on the ship.

"One of the books I found describes that kingdom as a land rich with diamonds, Lea. Maybe the demons over there have something to do with the High Priestess," he said. "What if all of her diamonds come from that kingdom, and she's keeping us from it so that we don't have access to them? What if she conjured a storm to keep all of us separate so that we can't work together?"

I shook my head.

"I don't think the woman who conjured that storm was the High Priestess," I said, thinking of the woman in the white cloak who'd destroyed her with fire. "I think she was running from something."

He studied me. "Where is this coming from?" he asked. He placed a hand on the diamond key that dangles from the chain around my neck. "Did you see something in that vision? Something important?"

"I don't know," I said, putting a hand on my forehead. "It was different from other visions. Instead of one continuous scene, it was like flashes of memory. Bits and pieces of the story that were broken or torn. It's hard to describe."

"Just tell me what you saw," he said.

I explained it all as best as I could. The ship and the woman who seemed to conjure the storm. She'd been wearing the diamond key, much like I wore it now. She'd come to the King's City. Maybe to hide?

"I think she kept the key hidden under the floorboards in that room," I said.

Part of me wanted to go back there and see if I could locate the hidden cubby. To see if it was real.

But part of me was terrified to ever go back into that room. I didn't want to get sucked into a vision like that ever again. It had left the taste of sulfur in the back of my throat.

"I think maybe she had kept that key from the woman in the white cloak," I said, unsure if I was remembering it right. "Maybe she stole it from her? I can't be sure. It was all so disconnected."

"Who was the woman in the white cloak?" Aerden asked.

I looked into his eyes. "I think it was the High Priestess."

"But that can't be right," he said. "You said you thought this happened a thousand years ago. The Order of Shadows is less than two hundred years ago. None of the witches are that old."

"There's something else happening here, Aerden. Something I can't explain," I said, my body shivering. "I got the feeling she was watching me as I slept. That she could somehow see me in my dreams. She knows I saw her in that vision. That I have the key."

I closed my eyes and placed my head against my knees as I drew them up close to my body.

All I could see was the fire that filled the room when the white-cloaked woman raised her hands. It had been almost effortless for her, and yet that spell had been so powerful, it had damaged stone beyond repair for a thousand years. Tainted it with evil that the builder could still feel.

If that was truly the High Priestess, we were messing with something here none of us were fully prepared for.

"We have to talk to your mother," I said.

"But we decided not to talk to her about this," Aerden said, shaking his head. "If she made some kind of deal like your father, talking to her is only going to make things worse."

"I saw her in my vision. Time kept leaping forward, but near the end, she was there. She was in the garden, crying. I think the woman in the white cloak came to her and offered her that key," I said. "I want to know what your mother agreed to give her in return."

Aerden closed his eyes.

"I can't believe she's somehow mixed up in all of this," he said. "It's all my fault."

He stood and paced the floor.

"If I had never left, none of this would have happened," he said. "I should have just told you how I felt, and if you still decided to marry my brother, I should have stood by your side and taken my place on the King's Guard. Instead, I pulled us all into danger."

I climbed off the bed and walked over to him, placing my hand on his arm.

"We could spend the rest of our days climbing mountains of regrets, blaming ourselves for the way things are," I said. "Or we can decide right now that we're going to put things right. For our families. For ourselves."

He turned and looked into my eyes, searching.

I turned away and walked over to get my bag. I pulled a strip of cloth from inside and showed him the diamond amulet I had gotten from the hunter the night the domed city was attacked.

It felt like ages ago now, even though it had only been a few months since that attack.

"I got this diamond off a hunter who attacked the Southern Kingdom," I said. "In my vision, the woman in the white cloak was wearing an amulet that looked like this, Aerden. It may have been the same exact one, but I can't be sure. If that vision was a thousand years old, then so is the High Priestess. It's all connected, somehow. We have to find the truth."

He shook his head. "But the priestesses are human," he said. "It doesn't make sense."

I brought the diamond over to him. "The five priestesses we've been hunting are human, but what if the High Priestess is something else? What if she's a demon?" I asked, chills running across my skin. "What if she's been here in this castle, standing where we stand? Watching us this whole time? What if your mother knows who she is?"

"Lea, this is madness," he said, fear flashing in his eyes. "Why would a demon create the Order of Shadows? Why would they destroy their own lands and give our power to human witches?"

"I don't have those answers, Aerden, but I think we're finally starting to ask the right questions," I said. "I can feel it. We're closer than ever to finding out who she is. We have to talk to your mother, Aerden. Tonight."

He closed his eyes and turned away.

After a long moment, he finally nodded.

"Okay," he said. "But if we take this risk, we promise to protect her. We take her away from here, maybe. Send her to the Southern Kingdom. She won't want to leave the King's City, but she might not have a choice."

I put the diamond amulet back in my bag, but as I moved to close it, a red light emanated from deep inside.

The communication stone.

I quickly pulled the stone from my bag and placed my hand over the top of it.

"Jackson?" I asked, my heart beating frantically. "What's going on? Is there news about Andros?"

"We're leaving soon to get him," he said. "And we need your help."

"Anything," Aerden said. "What can we do?"

"You can meet us here in the Southern Kingdom," he said. "And bring an army."

Aerden and I exchanged looks. As much as I was dying to question his mother and see what she knew, Tatiana and the High Priestess would have to wait.

We had work to do.

THE ELEMENT OF SURPRISE

HARPER

My nerves were completely on edge as I stood in front of the small group gathered in the war room. Last time we gathered, just a few short days ago, I would have trusted each one of them with my life.

But now, as I searched the faces of each person—humans and demons I had fought beside and risked my life to save—I wondered which one of them was our betrayer. Which one had the High Priestess gotten to?

Had they turned because of some threat? Were they sitting here with regret and pain in their hearts? Or were they more like Lark? Someone who had always been loyal to the other side, happy to betray me or watch me fall?

The Order should have learned by now that no matter how many people they turned against me, whether by force or by choice, it would not be easy to break me.

All they did was make me stronger.

Jackson's eyes met mine, and he nodded. It was now or never.

If there truly was a betrayer in our midst, we were going to use them to our advantage.

"Thank you all for coming on such short notice," I said. "I know there are other things going on right now that made it difficult for you to be here. Rend and Franki are facing a threat right now that I know some of you are helping with. I'm hopeful that after this, I can help him more, too. But right now, we have another friend to save."

"Are we going after Andros?" Mordecai asked.

"We are," I said. "Tomorrow night, the amethyst priestess is planning a mass initiation ritual. From what Magda Thorn has told me, there have only been a handful of these rituals performed in the history of the Order of Shadows. Timing with these rituals is everything, which is going to be both an advantage and a disadvantage for us."

All eyes were locked on me.

"We haven't been able to find where the amethyst hunters are holding Andros here in the Shadow World, but the ruby priestess has given us the location of her sister's home where the ritual will be performed," I said. "Tomorrow, we will gather a massive army and lead a direct assault on the amethyst priestess's house. Our goal is to bring her down before the ritual begins. If we can infiltrate her castle and stop that ritual, we can save Andros tonight and possibly have a shot at taking down the amethyst priestess, as well."

"This sounds risky," Mary Anne said. "We're just going to take it by force? Just try to walk straight through the front door?"

"That's exactly what we're going to do," I said. "We'll attack in waves. The first wave will be a smaller group of guards and fighters from the Southern Kingdom. Jackson will lead this attack and those of you on the Council will join him there, if you're willing. You'll attack at a distance, draw their attention and then retreat. This is a diversion, pulling their forces away and leaving their entrance vulnerable to the surprise second wave of our attack."

"Who's leading the second wave?" Angela asked.

"I'll be leading the second wave," I said. "It will be made up of an army of witches and demons from our domed city. Our job will be to surround the fortress—a mansion in Wyoming called Blackwood—and attack from every side. This should scatter and split whatever forces they have left guarding the entrance."

"Wow," Mary Anne said. "We've never done anything this organized or complicated before. It's a lot to take in."

"The Order has never been this organized before, either," I said. "They're working together now, so we need to work together, too."

"You said there were more waves?" Illana asked. "Who else is coming?"

"If they can put together a small force of soldiers from what's left of the Resistance, Lea and Aerden will be joining us in Wyoming," I said. "They'll travel here to the domed city first and then go through the same rose-portal at Brighton Lake, following us to Wyoming shortly after our first attack. While we're drawing the attention of the amethyst priestess's forces and scattering them throughout the woods, this third wave will focus on entering the house, going to the dungeons, and putting an end to the ritual and to Priestess Black."

"But how will we get to Andros, if he's stuck on the other side in the Shadow World?" Mordecai asked.

"The only way we'll be able to get to him is if we allow the ritual to begin," I said. "That's why I said timing is everything on this. The ritual itself will take considerably longer than a normal initiation ritual. Possibly around thirty minutes. During that time, the portal to the Shadow World will open, allowing both humans and demons to pass through. Our plan is to time our surprise attack for right at three in the morning when the ritual is set to begin. That means we'll have thirty minutes or less to storm the fortress, get inside, rescue Andros from the other side, and kill the amethyst priestess."

Essex whistled and sat back in his chair.

No one else spoke.

"We have numbers on our side," I said. "And the element of surprise. No one here mentioned anything to Ezrah or anyone else about knowing where Andros was being held, right? Or that the ruby priestess is here?"

Everyone around the table shook their heads, but someone was lying.

"Then the Order will have no idea we're coming," I said, infusing my words with excitement and hope, as if I truly believed we were going to own the night because no one had a clue we were on our way. "The priestesses are very confident that no one knows where they are or how to get to them. Priestess Black might have some increased security on her home that night just because of the ritual, but she'll never be expecting a full army. Most of her defenses will be the hunters in the Shadow World, but the hunter can't come through the portal to help her here. She'll be defenseless against our attack."

"We thought we had a jump on them in the Underground, too, but they showed up early with twice the forces," Mary Anne said, shaking her head.

"We knew going into it that someone inside the Resistance was going to betray them," I said. "If Ezrah hadn't been there when you arrived, it could have been very different, but he must have triggered the attack early and called for reinforcements. This time, though, there's no one to betray us. Priestess Black will have no warning that we're coming. As long as we wait until the right time to attack, there won't be anything she can do to stop us."

Erick nodded and stood up. "This is one of the craziest plans you've ever had, and I like it," he said. "I wish we could just show up at every priestess's house and go in, spells blazing. Maybe we could have put an end to the Order a long time ago with tactics like that."

I laughed. "Well, if the ruby priestess really is telling the truth about where to go and what we'll find when we get there, maybe we will show up at the citrine priestess's house next," I said. "I'll let you ring the doorbell."

Everyone laughed, but I had a growing ball of nerves in my stomach.

Was this going to work? Or was I trusting the wrong person and leading my people to slaughter?

Jackson took over the meeting, showing everyone a crude mockup of the amethyst priestess's estate. He marked the anticipated location of the guards, the place where the first wave would attack and then retreat to, and noted where Lea and Aerden would be waiting to initiate the final surprise wave.

Everyone studied the map intently, listening as he went over the plan several times.

Over the next few hours, someone in this room would most likely pass that plan over to the High Priestess, word-for-word.

There would be no element of surprise for us. At least not at Blackwood.

Jackson and I knew that going in.

We would take losses tomorrow. There was almost no way around that if we wanted to save Andros and have a shot at killing the amethyst priestess in the process.

But the plan we'd laid out here was only a piece of the real plan.

The real plan was much more intricate. Much more dangerous.

And I hoped to God it was going to work.

HOPE

AERDEN

After we listened to Jackson's plan, we said goodbye and just stared at each other.

"Do you think we can really pull all of this together in a day?" Lea asked. "It's a lot."

"But it could be our best chance to hit the Order hard so soon after the death of the emerald priestess," I said. "Just think of how things look for us if amethyst falls tonight. Three priestesses dead out of five. Three full gates released in just a matter of a month or two from now. The ruby priestess on our side with some hope of being able to free her gates soon, too. All we'd have left would be citrine, and if ruby is really helping us, citrine should be easy to get to. It could all be over by the end of the year."

Lea stood and started throwing supplies into her backpack.

"You're forgetting about the High Priestess," she said. "If the white-cloaked woman from my vision is really the High Priestess, she's incredibly powerful."

"Yes, but she's just one person," I said. "Or demon. Or

whatever she is. Without the rest of the Order, she's nothing compared to our entire army."

Lea shook her head. "I hope you're right about that," she said. "But let's not get ahead of ourselves here. There are no guarantees we're going to be able to take the amethyst priestess down tonight."

"No. There are never any guarantees, but there's a chance," I said, smiling. "There's hope."

Lea stopped and nodded, finally relaxing enough to let the smallest smile touch her lips.

"I have to admit, after months of being trapped in this castle, forced to wear a dress every day and walk around talking about the weather, it's exciting to be back in the middle of it all, fighting for what we believe in," she said. She slung her bag over her shoulder. "Are you ready?"

"I just have to stop by my room and grab my weapons," I said. "Meet you in the throne room?"

"Get there as soon as you can," she said.

I shifted and flew toward my suite of rooms, packing as fast as I could and reaching for my axe when a figure appeared in the doorway.

"Mom?" I asked, stepping forward.

Her eyes dipped to the packed bag on my bed and the axe in my hand. "Going somewhere?" she asked.

I itched to tell her what was going on, but if she was really in some kind of debt to the High Priestess, I couldn't afford for her to know what we had planned.

I wish we'd had time to talk with her before this happened, but it would simply have to wait until we got home.

"I have to go," I said. "But I won't be gone long, I hope. Did you need something?"

She walked closer, and I found that I saw her in a totally new light now. Maybe she had been a victim in all this, too. Maybe she really had sacrificed a lot to try to keep me safe.

I wanted to find a way to tell her that I would do whatever I could to repay her and to make up for my mistakes, but there wasn't time for that now.

"I just wanted to see you," she said, running a hand along the edge of my backpack. "To talk to you for a few minutes. Can't you sit down with me for a little while? I really have missed you so much."

I glanced at the door and sighed. "I'm sorry. I can't," I said. "But as soon as I get back, we should sit down and talk. There are so many things I want to say to you. I just want you to know that I realize I haven't always appreciated the things you've done for me. I haven't always made the right choices. But I love you, Mom. I hope that when things are quieter, we can really talk about these things more openly."

I tried to choose my words carefully, not knowing if the High Priestess was listening. Was my mother wearing a diamond somewhere, the way the king and queen had been?

My mother blinked back tears, then quickly cleared her throat.

"I don't know what to say. I love you, too, son. I always have."

I pulled her into a hug, and she slowly wrapped her arms around me. I couldn't remember the last time we had even touched, but it felt good. It felt like old wounds healing, and I suddenly remembered Trention's words to me one day during our talks in the dungeons.

Where there is life, there is hope.

If there was one lesson I had learned through all my pain,

it was to never give up on hope, no matter how dark or impossible things seemed.

Just a few short years ago, I was sure I would be a slave to the Order of Shadows forever.

Now, I was free, on my way to possibly witness the death of the third priestess of the Order, freeing thousands more just like me.

I smiled, enjoying this rare moment with a mother I thought I'd lost in so many ways.

Maybe soon, we would all be free.

INTO THE DARKNESS

LEA

I had an army to assemble, and I needed them on the move within the next twenty-four hours. It seemed so impossible, but hadn't everything we'd accomplished so far?

We weren't about to give up yet.

I flew toward the abandoned wing, searching for Ourelia. After asking for her in several rooms, I finally found her on the third hallway, sitting on the floor surrounded by shadowlings who played a game I hadn't played in over a century.

I watched them for a moment, remembering simpler days.

Ourelia noticed me watching and came to stand near the door.

I nodded toward the little ones. "They're so resilient," I said. "Laughing here and playing like they weren't just attacked and forced from their own home. I admire that."

"That is what we fight for," she said. "To give them a future free of terror. It's worth dying for, if that's what it comes to, and I know my Andros feels the same way. Is there news? Is that why you've come?"

"The ritual to enslave Andros and the others happens tomorrow night," I said.

Ourelia closed her eyes, but she kept it together better than I probably would have if it were my mate.

"What can we do?" she asked.

"We're going to save him," I said, giving her a smile.

I explained the plan, only telling her the version Jackson asked me to share. Not the real one. I hated to keep anything from Ourelia, since it was her mate we were saving, but Jackson had been adamant about keeping the actual plan just between the four of us.

No one else could be trusted, he'd said. And after the things we'd all been through, I understood his concern.

I asked her to gather as many of the Resistance forces as she could.

"I know it's a lot to ask after what they've been through, but anyone who can carry a sword and cast needs to be with us," I said. "Let them rest tonight, but tomorrow, I want them training and gearing up. We leave at sunset."

"Many are too injured to fight. But those who are able will come," she said.

"How many?" I asked.

"Tomorrow? Maybe four hundred," she said. "Maybe less."

My heart sank. Four hundred soldiers on the brink of exhaustion. But it would have to be enough.

She glanced at her daughter, Sasha, playing on the floor with her friends. "Promise me that if Andros and I don't return, you'll take care of her for me."

"It's not going to come to that," I said. "But you know I will also make sure Sasha is taken care of. You have my word on that."

Ourelia went to sit by her daughter and say goodbye, while I shifted and flew toward the throne room.

The Resistance fighters wouldn't be enough to do what we needed to do tomorrow. Not in the time we had to accomplish it. I would have to ask my father for his help, once again, and hope that he would keep his word.

I took a deep breath before knocking on the door to his study.

He called me inside and stood the moment he saw my weapon strapped to my back.

"What are you doing? Last time I saw you, you were unconscious in bed, recovering from taking yourself to the edge of exhaustion," he said. "You can't be leaving again so soon. You're in no shape—"

"I'm leaving tomorrow, and I don't have time to argue about it."

The worry and anger in my father's eyes left me wondering for a moment if he was considering just throwing me in the dungeons again to keep me safe.

"I need soldiers," I said. "We're going to save the leader of the Resistance, and there isn't enough left of his army who can fight to do what we need to do. I need your help and your support, and I need it fast."

"How fast?" he asked. "And how many?"

"Immediately," I said. "We need to leave by sunset tomorrow night. How many soldiers can you spare without compromising the safety of the city?"

Father turned, running a hand along his jaw and shaking his head.

"Is this what your life has been like for the past seventy years or more? Constant danger? Battling for your life on a daily basis? Never getting enough rest or taking time to just enjoy your life?" he asked. "Is this really the life you want, Lazalea?"

I smiled and really took a second to consider his question. I'd put my happiness on a shelf for so long, convinced what I truly wanted was not available to me, anymore. Convinced I'd sacrificed the life I wanted and would never get it back.

But I had changed. I realized that now.

I didn't want a leisurely life here in the castle, wearing fancy dresses and tending to the flowers. I wanted a life filled with adventure. Risk.

But it was more than that.

I wanted a life that meant something. Not just to me, but to the world.

"It hasn't always been this hectic," I said. "But yes, life has been one great, beautiful, dangerous adventure for a long time now, and I truly wouldn't have it any other way. What I'm doing is making a real difference, Father. It means a lot to me. So, yes, this is the life I want. I followed Jackson into this war, because I felt that loving him was my duty. My destiny. But maybe this war was my destiny."

He studied my face as I spoke.

"We make our own destiny, Lazalea," he said. "And if you feel that this war—and saving our kingdom from the Order—is yours, then I'm going to do what I can to help you win. I can only spare a hundred soldiers on such short notice, though. The soldiers who went with you earlier are injured and recovering, so they'll be no good to either of us tonight. I've taken precautions to have the sapphires in the basement moved outside of the city, but until we can destroy the Stone Guardians, I have to keep the majority of my soldiers here to protect those inside the walls. Especially now that you have brought more to us in need."

A hundred soldiers.

My heart tightened, but I kept my head held high.

"I was hoping for more like five hundred," I said. "At least."

Father's eyes widened. "That's nearly a quarter of my army," he said. "You would put them at risk to save the lives of one demon?"

"Forty demons," I said. "But it's more than that. We have a chance tonight to take down another priestess. It would be a huge victory."

"I would need to hear the entire plan to commit that much of my force," he said. "We would need weeks to put together that kind of assault."

"We don't have weeks," I said. "The opportunity is tomorrow night. And with the Order of Shadows, an opportunity like this may never come along again."

"It's reckless."

"You said that you would trust me. That you would respect my decisions as a leader," I said. "I know that we need to keep the demons here in the city safe. Maybe that means we start training more soldiers for the future. But I also know that until the Order of Shadows is defeated, none of us are safe. Give me at least three hundred soldiers. I need that just to have a chance tonight. A chance to end another priestess. A chance to free a thousand or more demons from the human world. Yes, it's a risk. Yes, it's difficult. But I believe in what I'm doing. In what we can do, if we are willing to take these risks. Give me that chance, Father."

He shook his head and walked slowly around to the other side of his desk, and I resigned myself to the hundred soldiers. Things had changed here in the castle, but they hadn't changed enough. We would have to make it work.

"I have to go," I said. "We're running out of time, and I cannot be late to this battle, or we will lose everything. I have a lot to do tonight to prepare. The Southern Kingdom is counting on us. I need your answer."

My father sat down behind his desk, his eyes lowered in thought for a long time before he finally looked up at me, his eyes clear and sure.

"I would never commit so much of my force to some haphazard plan, put together at a moment's notice," he said. "But I also am the king responsible for the abandoned villages out there. I have hidden myself in this city for so long, I think I forgot what it was like to be passionate about anything the way you are. To believe in something the way you believe in this war and your ability to win it."

He wrote something out on a piece of paper on his desk and placed his hand over the top, a shimmering light embossing his official seal as his signature.

"Take these orders to Mazrock in the barracks," he said. "Tell him to choose three of his best Lieutenants to lead the troops. You may have your three hundred soldiers. I can't spare more than that without compromising the safety of this city, but I will give you that chance, Princess."

He stood and handed the paper to me, and I threw my arms around him.

"Thank you," I said.

"May the light shine on you and bring you victory," he said. "And may the dawn bring you home safely."

I planted a kiss on his cheek and shifted, flying as fast as I could toward the barracks.

By sunset the next evening, the gates of the King's City were opened once again, and I led an army of soldiers into the darkness, our shadows racing toward the borderlands and the unknown outcome of the battle beyond.

THE DEAD OF NIGHT

JACKSON

As we gathered our soldiers on the steps of the castle and in the streets of the domed city, Harper's eyes met mine.

A private moment just between the two of us, and without a word spoken, I knew exactly what she was thinking. What she was feeling.

Hope. Determination. A connection that only grew stronger as our own allies betrayed us.

No matter what, we had each other.

No matter what, we would give our all.

So much depended on what happened in the next few hours.

We'd fought many battles before, but our enemy was more spread out. Less organized.

They had always underestimated us, thinking we were weak or powerless against such a vast and mighty organization. For a long time, they believed they were invincible, so they didn't protect themselves as fiercely or take us quite so seriously.

But now, they knew better.

The sisters had gotten smart and started working together, but more importantly, the High Priestess herself had gotten involved. She was pulling the strings now, commanding her troops. And with the High Priestess, sometimes that meant troops in unexpected places.

Right now, everything was turned upside down.

We were trusting the word of our enemy and counting on the betrayal of a friend.

A very dangerous game. I couldn't help but shake the feeling we were playing on a whole new level. One I wasn't certain we were ready for.

But there was no turning back now.

Lea and Aerden would already be on their way now, their soldiers expecting to head here to the domed city where they would pass through to the human world and attack the amethyst priestess's home—a fortress in Wyoming called Blackwood—in the final wave of the night.

Only, there would be no final wave. Not like the Order thought, anyway.

The pieces were falling into place, and now it was a matter of timing and luck.

Magda Thorn stood close to Harper, dressed in her jeans and t-shirt like any normal witch who had joined forces with the Resistance, rather than a priestess. So far, no one had questioned her, and as far as we had told the others, the ruby priestess was still locked away in the dungeons below.

Willow, one of the witches in charge of creating and maintaining the shield here in the domed city, had spent some time with Magda Thorn this morning. After a lot of heavy experimentation, she was able to create an invisible shield around the ruby priestess that prevented her from casting magic of her own and also kept her safe from any spells that might come near her.

The shield was maintained by a diamond kept in Harper's pocket.

One of the diamonds she had taken from the bodies of the dead hunters in the Underground.

It had taken some work to clear the spells and curses from those diamonds, but they were so rare and valuable, it had been worth the effort.

Magda hadn't been too happy about giving up her own magic for the night, insisting she could be helpful in the fight, but she had eventually agreed to it. We couldn't take any chances of her turning on Harper in the middle of the attack.

Besides, we were hoping the shield would also keep the High Priestess from being able to locate her and pull her back to that strange ritual room we'd seen earlier.

We needed Magda for this plan to work. If she was the one betraying us tonight, it would all be over.

I sighed, wishing I had not had to give up my visions to Sabine. Without those visions, I had no idea whether to expect victory tonight, or ruin.

"You ready?" Harper asked.

"I'm ready if you are," I said.

I took her hand in mine and brought it to my lips.

"You have the stones?" I asked.

She patted her pocket and nodded. "Everything is in place," she said. "Let's just hope our plan made it to the intended audience."

The knots in my stomach tightened, but one look from Harper, and they eased a little.

Despite everything, she was smiling, a confident look in her eyes.

"I bet Priestess Black is shaking in her boots right now." Harper said in a whisper, winking.

The corners of my lips turned up in a slow smile. "If she's not, she damn well should be."

Harper threw her arms around me, holding on tightly.

"Be careful," I whispered in her ear. "I love you."

"I love you, too," she said.

We didn't dare say anything more. Not out here.

But I hated the fact that we were splitting up tonight. I wanted to keep her close to me. We'd only had a few days back together, and it was nowhere near enough. Not by a long shot.

Harper addressed the large group gathered in the streets of the domed city.

"Tonight, we will face one of the founding members of the Order of Shadows," she said. "I never dreamed we would get a chance like this so soon after defeating the emerald priestess, but we are not going to let this opportunity slip through our fingers."

We had gathered nearly five hundred soldiers for tonight's assault on Blackwood. I would lead the first wave, a group of a hundred that was a mix of witches and demons of different abilities. I had hand-picked my group, and they all stood off to one side, near the entrance to the gardens.

We would be the first to go through, and it was almost time.

"I wish I could promise you that we would all return from this battle, unharmed," she said. 'But that's not a promise I can make. What I can promise you is that your life matters. The fact that you are standing here, prepared to fight a powerful enemy to save the lives of others who are oppressed, matters. It matters a great deal, and no matter what else happens tonight, I can promise you that we will never give up. We will not stop fighting until the last priestess is dead and all our demons are free."

A cheer rose from the crowd. A battle cry for the ages as we prepared to make our first real assault on one of the Order's leaders in their own home.

Tonight was evidence of just how far we had come.

This war was no longer just about defending ourselves. It was about taking back our freedom. Going after it instead of simply trying to stay alive.

"It's time," she said, turning to me.

I gathered my small group of one hundred and walked toward the portal of white roses.

We were banking on the Order planting all their defenses around Blackwood, but we knew there was a chance some would be waiting for us at Brighton Lake.

When we'd first started using the roses more often, we'd put up traps and detection magic to make sure no one could use the portals but us. So far, none of those traps had gone off.

Still, I took a deep breath and connected to my power, ready to cast if anything happened the moment I arrived in the human world.

I stepped through the portal, barely taking a breath as I listened for any sign of movement in the forest surrounding the lake.

It was the dead of night here in Georgia, and even though the moon was full, the forest was filled with shadows. I could see clearly in the dark, though, and I turned in a slow circle, watching.

The other members of our Council followed me through in quick succession. Then came the other witches and demons I had wanted by my side tonight. People with special abilities that might come in handy.

Since we would travel by flying, each human had already been paired with a demon who would carry them through the night toward Blackwood.

I waited until all of my people were here, and then gave the signal.

Brooke grabbed my hand tightly.

"I'm so nervous," she whispered.

Was she the one who had betrayed us? I searched her eyes for any sign, but all I saw there was fear.

"Let's go," I said.

I pulled just enough power from the trees surrounding the lake to shift into demon form and fly into the night. It was a good thing we didn't actually have as many demons taking off from this location as we had said we would, or Brighton Lake would have been a wasteland come morning.

Once we were up in the sky and soaring fast, it was easy to draw power from the living things below without taking too much from any one source. Luckily, the amethyst priestess had chosen a location for her home that was heavily forested. It would make things a lot easier for us in our attack, since the majority of our forces were demons.

Now, that place was going to take a serious hit. Shadow demons needed to draw power from living things here in the human world in order to cast, so we would all be pulling from the trees and surrounding nature, destroying large swaths of forest.

A small price to pay for killing a priestess and rescuing a friend, but I had no doubt we would return as soon as possible to heal the earth we damaged tonight. Just thinking of it made me miss Zara. She was so good at growing things and healing the earth after a demon had pulled power from it.

Maybe she would wake soon and help us heal the Black Hills.

When Magda had told us her sister, Priestess Black, actually lived in the Black Hills, I had laughed at the irony. How long had we been searching for the homes of the priestesses? And we had never once considered something that would seem way too obvious or coincidental.

And yet, here we were.

It took over an hour for us to fly to our staging ground near a place called Devil's Tower, and the whole way there, I dreamed of life beyond the Order of Shadows. It fueled me for the battle to come, remembering just what I was fighting for.

Our group of one hundred landed in a wooded section near some hiking trails. We spread out, securing the area and making sure no one was waiting for us.

And no one was.

Of course, I hadn't shared the exact location of our staging ground in the Council meeting. I had only shown people where to go tonight just before we took off.

So far, everything was going our way. Why did that just make me more nervous, though?

There was no way this night was going to be easy, so at this point, I think I was just waiting for things to go wrong. This was the calm before the storm, but the storm itself would be brutal.

"All clear," Mordecai said, joining me. "It's eerie as hell out here, man. Can you feel that? It's too quiet."

His words put me on high alert, and I looked around again, listening more carefully this time.

I had learned over the years not to ignore someone's intuition. When someone said they had a bad feeling, there was usually something very bad about to happen.

"I want everyone here to be on your toes. Keep an eye out for anything suspicious in the area. Any movement. Pay attention to your instincts," I said. I glanced at the time, nervous tension building inside me.

We had twenty minutes. Then we were going in.

UNDER HIS COMMAND

HARPER

Jackson disappeared through the portal with the members of the Council, and I took a deep breath.

As far as they were concerned, everything was going exactly according to the plan I had set out for them at the meeting. Now, though, things would begin to take a turn. At first, in subtle ways. Later, in much bigger ways.

I could only hope that by the time the Order realized we were not doing what we said we would do, it would be too late for them to do a darn thing about it.

I paced the stone steps, glancing toward the dome's entrance every few minutes.

Everything tonight would depend on perfect timing.

Come on. Where are you?

I tried to keep my hands occupied by running my thumb along the sapphire embedded in my father's sword. A piece of his power was there inside it, always with me in battle. There had been a time not that long ago when I'd been hesitant to carry this sword, unsure I was really worthy of it or the sacrifice he'd made to save my life the day we faced Priestess Winter.

But now, instead of feeling unworthy every time I touched this sword, I felt proud. Grateful.

And I knew that if my father were here with me today, he would have been proud of what we were trying to do tonight.

I touched the sapphire again and glanced toward the dome's entrance.

Movement just outside in the forest caught my eye, and I stopped cold, not taking a breath as I watched.

There were so many variables tonight, and we had based our entire plan around our best guesses of what the Order would do in reaction to what they thought was happening. But there were no guarantees we had guessed right.

What if the Order sent hunters here to attack the dome, trying to keep us from heading out to Wyoming?

But the thought only flashed inside my mind for a moment before the shadow in the woods took solid form and nodded to my guards. I could just barely make him out at this distance, but I could feel his presence.

Aerden smiled at me as he walked toward the castle.

"Nice night for killing a priestess, huh?" he asked.

I put my arms around him. "I'm so glad you're here," I said "Jackson's already gone through. He should be well on his way to Devil's Tower by now. Lea?"

"She's on her way to the staging point." He looked over the crowd gathered in the streets. "Is this my crew?"

"Yep," I said. "Right now, they still think they're heading to Blackwood to fight witches, but I think they're going to be pretty excited when they hear what they'll really be doing."

"It's a risky plan, Harper. Are you really sure someone

here is betraying you to the High Priestess? Who would do that?" he asked.

"After tonight, we'll know one way or another," I said. "And I'm not sure who it is. Brooke, maybe. She helped me get through my time at Evers, though, which is hard for me to reconcile. I don't know why she would have helped me there just to betray me once I got home. It's also possible the High Priestess got to one of the demons in Mordecai's group."

Aerden shook his head. "No way. I just can't believe that," he said. "They've been with Lea for a very long time. They're loyal."

"What about Illana?" I asked.

I hadn't brought her up to Jackson before this, because I didn't want him to get upset, but I didn't know his sister very well. She'd only joined our group the night I was taken by the emerald priestess, and though she'd been here for Jackson when I was missing, I didn't know her well enough to trust her.

To my surprise, Aerden hesitated to answer.

I had expected him to come to his sister's defense right away.

"What?" I asked. "Do you think it's possible?"

Aerden turned around so that he was facing away from anyone in the crowd who might be able to hear him. "There are some things that might give us a reason to question her loyalty," he said. "For one, I made a good friend in the dungeons who used to be a scholar. I told you about him before. Trention?"

"I remember. The one who could read books in any language?"

"Right. Well, when I told him I'd heard Illana left the King's City to come to be with us in the Southern Kingdom, he was surprised by that," he said. "When I asked why, he told me that he'd once overheard Illana saying she was actually glad her brothers were gone. That it gave her a chance to be closer to our mother."

I shook my head. "That's not proof of anything, though. Trention had been in the dungeons for years, right? When Illana said that, she probably didn't think there was any chance of you ever going free," I said. "She was young. She could have been saying that just to hide the fact that she was hurting. And when she found out you were free, it might have seriously affected her."

"There's more," Aerden said, frowning. "I told you about the diamond key my mother gave me before I left the city all those years ago. Well, yesterday, Lea had a vision where she saw a woman in a white cloak hand my mother that key. The vision was pretty damaged and the whole thing wasn't as clear as she normally sees, but it's possible my mother did make a deal with the High Priestess to keep me safe."

"And if your mother made a deal, you think that might have also carried over to Illana?" I asked.

I kind of felt sick to my stomach.

"I think it's possible," he said. "If you get a chance to talk to Jackson, tell him to keep an eye out for her. I don't think she'd ever do anything to directly hurt him, but I wouldn't trust her. Just in case. I hope I'm wrong, but right now, no one is immune from suspicion."

"Thank you for telling me," I said.

I glanced down at the watch I'd put on earlier tonight. I had set it to mountain time so that I'd always know exactly what time it was at Blackwood. The mass initiation ritual would need to begin exactly at three in the morning there, and it was vital we had all our forces in position by then.

"It's time for you to go," I said. "Fight well, my friend."

He nodded and reached for my hand. "You, too," he said. "Come back with that amethyst heart in your hands."

"Hey, if you guys get there before me, don't feel like you have to wait," I said with a smile. "You might like the feeling of ripping a priestess's heart out. Might not make up for a century lost, but it's a start. Could be good therapy."

Aerden laughed and shook his head. "I'll keep that in mind."

I raised my hand to gather the attention of my troops. Here is where things took a detour, so from here on out, we were off-plan. At least as far as the Order was concerned.

"There's been a slight shift, and you're no longer going to be following me to the human world," I said. "Your true target is here in the Shadow World."

There was a murmur of surprised voices and questions from the crowd, but they kept their eyes on me.

"Many of you know Aerden, Jackson's twin brother," I said. "You are now under his command."

I nodded to Aerden, and he stepped forward.

As he began giving the soldiers their new mission, I met the eye of the glamoured witch standing near the entrance to the rose garden. From here on out, it would just be the two of us.

What the hell was I thinking?

With a sigh, I led her through the portal and stepped into the forest by the lake.

"This is so exciting," she whispered. "I never knew how much fun it could be to fight with the good guys."

I held my hand out to her. We would see how much fun she found shifting for the first time. I nearly threw up the first time Jackson had shifted with me, back before I had any idea I'd be able to do it on my own.

"Just don't get me killed," I mumbled.

Magda laughed and placed her hand in mine.

"I won't if you won't," she said.

I took a deep breath as I connected to my power and shifted to demon smoke, carrying us both off into the night.

THE LIFE I WAS BORN FOR

LEA

I t felt strange leading such a large group toward an attack and knowing they were mine to command. I was born to be a leader, but when I was a shadowling being trained to take over the kingdom, it was mostly talk of managing resources, keeping up relations with the villages outside the city, and balancing budgets.

It was the twins who had been taken to the training grounds and taught to fight.

Aerden was the one who had been groomed to lead my army, and he was the one who had spent countless hours with me after our schooling was done, showing me everything he'd learned.

We used to sneak away to the library and pull out maps of the kingdom. He taught me what he'd learned about strategy and using terrain to your advantage. And when we would leave the city to play, Jackson and Aerden both would spar with me, showing me what they'd learned in training.

It wasn't that women weren't allowed to fight. There were

plenty of women in the King's Guard who knew how to hold their own in battle.

It was simply that no one thought to teach a princess.

I was never meant to be a fierce warrior. I was meant to be a queen. A beautiful leader who rallied our people and pulled them together in times of peace. People didn't believe you could be both.

And yet, here I was, soaring ahead of an army of seven hundred demons, leading them into battle against one of the greatest foes demonkind had ever known.

I had never been more grateful for those days of our youth when the three of us had trained together.

Tonight, I hoped to make them both proud. I hoped to make myself proud.

My father had asked me if this was really the life I wanted, and as I led the army into the mountains toward our staging ground, there was no doubt in my mind. This was the life I was born for.

I think I had somehow always known it.

I waited for the army to assemble in a valley cloaked in darkness. The men and women at my command expected to continue on to the Southern Kingdom, but this is where we deviated from that plan and hoped for the best.

As far as the Order of Shadows knew, our only attack would come at the entrance to Blackwood, because that was the location we knew.

But Magda Thorn had given us more than just the location of Blackwood.

She had also given us the location of the portal entrance here in the Shadow World that matched up to that demon gate.

In order to enslave a demon inside the body of a witch, that demon had to be brought through a specific gate. The stone at that gate would bind the demon to that witch until the day she died. That witch, in turn, was also bound to that demon gate and its Prima.

It was part of the hierarchy and structure of the Order of Shadows. A way for them to give their witches more power while controlling them at the same time.

A mass initiation like this one, where the Order wanted to bind dozens of new witches to a gate on a single evening, could only be done at one of the original demon gates. Places like Winterhaven and Blackwood, where the Prima of that gate was the priestess who ruled all the gates for that color of stone.

Tonight, Priestess Black would be initiating forty-one witches into her coven. Witches who had once been bound to a sapphire or emerald gate before those priestesses were killed. Witches who wanted a second chance to get back into the Order.

In order to perform this ritual, though, there was only one demon gate she could possibly use. Her own gate at Blackwood.

And like all demon gates, the gate at Blackwood had a corresponding portal entrance here in the Shadow World. An entrance framed with black roses that would appear when the portal was activated, helping to pull the demons through to the other side.

We didn't know where the hunters were keeping Andros and the rest of his squad all this time, but we knew where they were going to be tonight.

We were all taking a huge chance on what Magda Thorn had said, but if Harper trusted her, I was behind her.

"There has been a change of plans," I announced to the army settled in front of me. "Soon, demons from the Southern Kingdom will join us here. Together, instead of continuing on to their domed city and the human world, we will head west. In a field not too far from here, the amethyst priestess will soon open a portal to her home in Blackwood. That portal will be guarded by an army of her own hunters. And those hunters will be guarding Ancros and other members of the Resistance army captured by the Order."

The army was silent as they listened.

"Instead of attacking Priestess Black in the human world as she likely suspects, we are going to attack here in our own world," I said. "We'll be facing hunters, instead of witches, but our objective is the same. Rescue the demons before they can be pulled through the portal to the human world."

Someone pointed toward the sky, and I smiled as a white cloud of demon smoke soared toward us. Soldiers from the Southern Kingdom, led by a demon who had been trained from birth to fight wars for his queen.

Aerden reformed on a rocky ledge on the side of the mountain, his axe already in hand and his eyes locked on mine.

Across the distance, our hearts met in silence.

I think deep down, we'd been waiting our whole lives for a night like this, and there was no one in the world I would have rather had by my side.

NO TURNING BACK

HARPER

Magda and I landed in the backyard of a quiet little house on the edge of the small town.

Somewhere in the distance, a coyote howled.

The grass here had grown all the way up to my knees, and it made a zipping sound against my jeans as I walked through it.

"It's muddy out here," Magda said, lifting onto her toes, as if that would help. "Would you be a dear and release my magic for a second, so I can please walk through here without getting mud all over my shoes?"

I snorted. "No. You can use the doormat to clean them off," I said. "Just like a regular human."

Magda made a grunting sound as she tiptoed through the grass.

I kept my eye on the house, making sure no one was inside.

This house was far enough out in the country to not have many neighbors around to keep an eye on the place, especially now that the owners had left town. That was part of what made it a great use to us in the Demon Liberation Movement when we needed a place to access the Hall of Doorways without being seen.

I hadn't been here in a long time. Not since last summer when we'd been actively working to release the sapphire demon gates.

In the woods near this house, there was a sapphire demon gate similar to the one in Peachville. This had been the Prima's home for the past seventy years. A more modest home than a lot of the Primas chose to keep.

When we had released this demon gate, the Prima and her most devoted followers had fought like hell. It had taken everything we had just to restrain her long enough to free the demon inside her. She didn't stop fighting when it was done, though, and Mary Anne had put a ritual dagger through the woman's heart to stop her from sending a poisonous arrow into my back.

Ever since then, we had claimed this house for ourselves when we needed a quick place to hide or an entrance to the Hall of Doorways.

I wasn't sure when anyone from our group had used it last, though, and there was always a chance some squatters may have moved in.

Magda mumbled as she scraped the mud off her shoes by the back door, and when I waved a hand over my own and lifted the mud with a single gesture, she scowled at me.

"Now you're just being rude," she said.

I laughed and waved the mud from her own shoes, carrying it off into the grass and letting it fall to the ground with a thud.

She lifted her chin. "Thank you."

"You're welcome," I said. "Follow me."

I used my magic to open the locked door and walked inside. It was dark and there was no electricity turned on in this house, anymore, so I quickly conjured an orb of light and let it lead us through the first floor and up the creaking steps.

"Such a life of adventure," Magda said. "Before I came to your domed city, I'd hardly left my own house in years except to visit Hazel or the occasional trip to check on one of the gates. I made a lovely trip into the city recently to meet a little girl by the name of Rayla who is believed to be a seeress. We haven't had a true seeress in the Order in years. She was a sweet girl, though her older sister glared at me the entire time I was there."

I wondered if Magda intended to talk about random stuff all night, and I laughed as I thought about the horrified look on Gregory's face when I had threatened to put him back in the dungeon beside her all night.

"Well, you're going to get your fill of adventure tonight," I said, heading up the narrow staircase that led to the third floor and its five-sided room. I threw an extra look back at her. "If you survive it, that is."

She sighed. "I am beginning to think you like toying with me."

"I thought you said you enjoyed a good challenge."

I stepped into the Hall of Doorways and shuddered. Some distant memory of being dragged through this hallway reared its ugly head. Probably because I was standing next to the sister of the woman who'd done the dragging.

"I do, actually," she said. "Do you have any idea how boring it can be when everyone around you is terrified of upsetting you? No one is ever sarcastic or funny, unless they feel like they need to be, in which case it just comes out forced, anyway. And no one ever feels comfortable just being themselves. It gets lonely."

"Well, there's always the option of starting your own doll collection," I said.

A terrible joke, but at least Priestess Evers' dolls were finally free. It was hard to imagine just sitting back and watching your sister do something like that to a bunch of girls and doing nothing at all to stop her.

"Distasteful, Harper, really," she said. "Here, let me lead the way. If we walk this slowly the whole way there, we'll never arrive in time."

Magda moved out ahead of me, walking so fast, I almost had to jog to keep up with her. She seemed to know exactly where she was going, though, which kind of amazed me since there were so many doors in the seemingly endless hallway.

A few minutes later, she stopped in front of a door with a panther carved into its surface. The panther had two amethysts in place of eyes.

"Here we are," she said, lifting her hand toward the panther.

"Wait," I said, grabbing her wrist. "Let's go over this one more time."

She sighed and pulled her hand away, taking a moment to straighten her shirt. "We go inside, and you use magic to hold all the doors shut as we check for guards and traps inside the room," she said. "Though, I really don't think Gladys will have anyone guarding this door. No one can get inside except her daughters and sisters."

"Yes, and she knows her sister Magda is in the custody of

her enemy, giving out information like Halloween candy," I said.

Magda made a face. "Yes, you have a point. I guess in that case, we might as well be ready for the door to explode in our faces the moment we open it."

My eyes widened. "Do you really think that's a possibility?"

She shrugged. "Could be," she said. "Gladys is militant, sometimes. She tends to overdo it, if you ask me."

"Okay, so new plan. You unlock the door for us but don't open it right away. I will put up a magical shield first. Then we open it and hope for the best," I said. "If it doesn't blow up, I lock all the doors in this room and secure it from anyone getting in or out while I use my astral projection to explore the inside of the house."

My stomach swirled with nerves as I said this last part.

Using astral projection meant leaving my body completely defenseless. All Magda would have to do is strangle me or put a knife through my back while my mind was roaming around the house, and I would be gone forever.

Jackson had begged me to take someone along who could watch Magda while I left, and when I said we couldn't risk it, he'd asked me to promise to bind her, instead.

I kind of led him to believe I would, but the truth was that I needed Magda to protect me.

I closed my eyes and shook my head.

I could hardly believe I was really counting on her.

"You know, this whole thing would be a lot easier if you would just release my magic and let me cast," she said. "If we get attacked or you are restrained in any way, I'll be powerless to help you."

"No," I said for about the fiftieth time since I'd bound her magic in the first place. "Unlock the door please."

I cleared my mind, picturing a rose in the darkness. I focused all of my attention on that one point and then dipped into that well of power surging inside me. With each slow breath, I went deeper, sending the power throughout my entire body.

As Magda reached out to place her palm over the panther's eyes, I lifted a magical shield like Zara had taught me so long ago and kicked the door open.

Nothing exploded, but five witches jumped up from a black lacquered table in the center of the room. A spell immediately slammed into the shield I'd put up, and I could taste the dark magic on my tongue.

With my free hand, I conjured a rope of white smoke and sent it around the waist of a witch who'd been heading for the door.

I couldn't afford to have anyone sound the alarm downstairs, which meant I was about to put my powers of multitasking to the test.

"Get down," I shouted at Magda, and she dropped to the floor.

I blocked another wave of attacks with a shield I controlled with my left hand, and then used my pure mind power to lift the heavy black table and turn it on its side. With a surge of energy, I sent the table straight back to the wall. It slammed into two witches, and they both fell unconscious onto the floor.

I cried out as the witch I'd held with the white smoke did something to burn me where my power had made contact with her skin. I jumped backward as if she'd just pressed a hot knife to my palm.

She threw the door open, but I shifted to demon form and slipped between her and the exit, pushing her backwards and slamming the door behind me. I hadn't had a chance to see if there were more witches outside this door, but I had to deal with these before I could worry about anyone else.

"Dagger," Magda shouted, and I managed to shift just as a silver dagger embedded itself in the door where my head had just been.

"Thank you," I said, honestly shocked she'd warned me.

"If you'd—"

"No," I shouted, grabbing the wrist of the witch who had thrown the dagger and twisting it around until it was behind her back. I held her in front of me like a shield against the other two witches who were still awake.

I needed to get these witches down in the next couple of minutes, or our timeline was about to go right out the window.

But how?

There wasn't enough room in this small space to make any good use of my sword, and I couldn't risk accidentally hitting Magda with a misplaced spell.

My mind worked fast as I made a few timing calculations in my mind and spun into action.

I kicked the witch in front of me, sending her stumbling into a second witch who had some kind of thick black spell gathered in her hands. The magic splattered onto the chest of the stumbling witch, and she screamed as an acid-like substance ate into her skin.

At the same time, I grabbed the hilt of the dagger in the door behind me with my mind and crouched as I pulled it loose and sent it flying toward the head of the third witch.

I winced as the blade hit its mark, right between her eyes and she fell to the ground with a thud.

The only witch left standing already had another spell recharged, and she reared back to unleash it. I sent a rope of pure white smoke toward her ankles and yanked hard, pulling her feet out from under her.

The spell in her hands exploded into the ceiling in a shower of sparks that singed my clothing and left tiny burns on my already-scarred arms. I pulled my sword from its sheath and quickly buried it in her chest.

I checked to make sure all the other witches in the room were down and not getting up any time soon. Three of them were dead, and the other two were knocked out cold and trapped under the table. They were still breathing, though, and I considered killing them to just keep us safe, but every witch I killed took her demon with her.

There would be some losses, no matter what, but I couldn't bring myself to kill those enslaved demons if I didn't have to.

I hurried to the door that led downstairs to the main part of the house and put my ear against the wood, listening for any sound of voices or footsteps. When I didn't hear anything, I sheathed my sword and waved a hand in front of me, clearing the floor in front of that door so that I could sit comfortably.

"Magda?"

The ruby priestess was sitting with her back pressed against one door and her knees drawn up to her chest. Her eyes were wide, and her hands were fidgeting with a string on the hem of her jeans.

It surprised me to see her looking so vulnerable and scared. She was the ruby priestess. She had eaten the souls of her own daughters, for crying out loud. Now, all of a sudden, she couldn't handle the sight of violence?

"I don't have time for you to be freaking out right now," I said. "Pull yourself together and tell me you're ready to protect me and bring me back to my body if anything happens in this room."

"I'm not freaking out," she said, lifting her chin defiantly. "I'm just realizing for the first time that you really are as powerful as they say you are. I saw five witches at once, and I considered running back into that hallway and going straight to my house in L.A. I didn't think you'd survive it."

"You live in L.A.?" I asked.

She smiled. "Not right in the city, of course. I have a gorgeous house by the beach. The best money can buy," she said. "It's beautiful there. Have you ever been? You'll have to come visit me sometime."

"Yeah, we'll plan a dinner party. Invite the High Priestess and everything," I said, rolling my eyes. "Now, are you going to help me do this, or what?"

She stood and walked over to stand near the door to downstairs. "Astral projection," she said softly. "I wish I could do that."

"Magda."

"Okay, yes, I'm ready," she said.

"If one of these two witches under the table wakes up or anyone tries to get into these doors, you shake me until I wake up," I said. "I can jump back to my body pretty quickly if I know something's wrong. Slap me if you have to."

I glanced back at the witch with the dagger still embedded between her eyes and shuddered.

This was one of the biggest risks I'd ever taken in my life, but if I was ever going to be a true leader, I was going to have to learn to trust myself above all.

And my gut told me Magda was not going to hurt me.

"Timing, child. Go," she said.

I let out a long breath.

From this point forward, there was no turning back. I closed my eyes, and moments later, I had left my body behind

MAGICAL SHIELDS

JACKSON

I closed my eyes and sent up a silent prayer.

Keep them safe.

Without my ability to see visions of the future, I had no idea what might come of this night. No flashes. Not even cryptic messages to decipher. I was blind, and I was scared.

But we were strong. We had faced the impossible before and come out on top, and I knew that as long as we kept believing, we could do it again.

Over and over until the High Priestess herself was nothing but a pile of dust on the floor at our feet.

"It's time," Mary Anne said, touching my arm.

"Thank you for being here, even with all the stuff going on with the crows. It means a lot."

"I still say Rend and Franki are going to be furious when they find out we kept all of this from them, but you know I'll always be here for you when you need me," she said.

We weren't supposed to trust anyone tonight but our own closest group of four, but there was no part of me that believed

Mary Anne could be capable of betraying us. She was my family just as much as Aerden was at this point.

"Here we go, guys," I said, walking to the front of the pack. "Blackwood is straight through these trees about five miles ahead. You all have your instructions, but I want to remind you to stay close together at first. Don't advance on the fortress. Our sole job is to draw them out."

I gave them the signal, and we all grabbed hands with any humans we needed to transport with us and shifted to demon smoke. It only took a minute to get into position just inside the tree line, and we all got our first good look at the amethyst priestess's home.

I understood now what Mordecai had meant about the place being too quiet. There were no animals rustling in the woods, no coyotes in the distance. Not a single thing around us moved.

Was that because some spell kept them away?

Or could they sense the evil that lived in this house?

Blackwood was more like a castle than a mansion. It was nestled in a wooded valley backed up against the mountains. There were no roads leading up to it, and no neighbors in sight.

We were on the edge of the Black Hills National Forest, just shy of the border into South Dakota. It wasn't exactly legal for her to have a home here, of course, but since when did the Order of Shadows follow anyone else's rules?

Magda said her sister had sacrificed at least fifteen witches in order to create a permanent glamour on the place that made it impossible to see from the air or the nearby hills and mountains.

Lucky for us, though, as long as you knew where to go.

once you made it past the barrier glamours, you could see the house clearly.

It was a large home made out of some kind of thick, yellow stone that blended in easily with the surrounding landscape. A set of broad, stone steps led up to a flat porch that seemed to wrap around the entire house.

From here, I could see a row of ten witches stretching across the front of the porch. The witches were dressed all in black with a hint of amethysts gleaming in the moonlight from the collars around their necks.

I let my eyes travel over the row of witches and out from there, checking for what other defenses Priestess Black had in place tonight. If she really was expecting us to attack with the force of an army, she would have a lot more to defend herself than ten witches.

For a moment, I hoped she didn't know we were coming. Yes, we'd based our real plan on someone ratting us out, but what if the ruby priestess had been wrong? What if no one on our Council had been giving away our plans?

We would crush the Order tonight with the numbers we had brought.

And we'd return home, knowing we could trust the people we loved.

The best of both worlds.

I'd never wanted to be wrong about something so badly in my life.

"Do you think it's only those few witches guarding the place?" Mary Anne asked. "If so, we're going to be inside in minutes. Have you heard from Harper? Is the second wave almost here?"

"Harper should be here soon," I said, leaving it at that.

"And I only see that one row of witches for now, but I have a feeling we're going to face more than that. I doubt Priestess Black is planning such an important ritual with such low defense. Keep your eyes open."

I moved back to the front line and motioned for the builders to get into place. They nodded and separated, standing about ten feet apart from each other.

I'd brought five builders with me—demons who were more like architects, able to weave and build things with ease out of a variety of materials.

The builders quietly began pulling magic from deep inside the earth. They were careful to pull from trees and wildlife far enough away from the house so not to attract attention. Not yet, anyway.

As they worked to gather power, I motioned for the human witches in the group to step forward, forming a line in front of the builders. They would be our first line of attack, and I had a feeling as soon as they started casting, we would get a better look at whoever was hiding over there near the house.

The rest of the group stayed behind. Our plan was to cast and retreat, switching places so that we would have different types of magic bombarding the fortress, giving the impression that there were a hell of a lot more of us than there really were.

I glanced at my watch. One minute.

It was time for the ritual to begin. I prayed everyone else was in place, because all hell was about to break loose.

I stepped forward, catching the eyes of the witches on the front line, but just as I was about to signal for them to start, a violet light lit up the sky from behind.

I turned as twenty witches dressed in black blocked my group off from behind, but just as soon as they cast the first spell toward us, their bodies dropped to the ground, trembling as if they'd been electrocuted.

Apparently, Willow's idea to put a reactive shield around our group from behind and to the sides was a good one. The minute those witches cast something that hit that shield, they were down.

"Bind them," I shouted.

I gave the signal to the witches at the front. No point in trying to hide the fact we were here now. They already knew.

Arrows made of light flew through the sky like fireworks. Hundreds of arrows, despite the fact that it was only a handful of witches who were casting. It was a trick Lea had once shown them, and it was a good way to make your enemy think you had a lot more people than you did.

By the time the first arrows hit, the second round was already in the air.

I gritted my teeth, though, as their magic dispersed about twenty feet before hitting their marks.

Looked like Priestess Black had some shields of her own.

"More," I shouted, motioning to the group of demons waiting in the back. "Hit them with more. Bring those shields down."

As they started blasting the shield with magic of every different type—fire, poison, wind, ice, and more—I moved to the front to look for any witch who might be maintaining that active shield.

I sucked in a breath as the true defenses of this fortress finally showed themselves.

Instead of a single line of ten witches like before, there was now a row of witches pouring out of the front door like ants. Hundreds of witches.

And that wasn't the worst of it. I had no idea how she'd gotten them here from the Shadow World, but ten rock golems rolled off the hills surrounding the house and positioned themselves at equal distances around the perimeter.

If they turned all their forces on our small group, thinking we were all that was coming, we were screwed. With this many to fight, I wasn't even sure we could shift and fly away fast enough to escape.

But if the High Priestess had gotten hold of our plans and she believed we had an army of a thousand currently sneaking up to circle that castle, those forces would hold their ground, no matter what. They wouldn't dare leave the entrance undefended just to come after us.

So, what would it be? Had we been betrayed?

We would need to actually hit them and do some damage to find out, but no matter what my team was throwing at that shield, nothing was going through. I also couldn't see any witch casting or focusing hard enough to be maintaining. It was possible she was inside the house.

I've got to do something.

My mind searched for a solution, panic rising as the witches who had now surrounded the entire house prepared to retaliate. We needed to do some damage and back the hell up.

Suddenly, my mind locked on a moment sometime after the fall of the sapphire gates. We were training in the cheerleader's room at Peachville High, all of us sending every spell we could think of flying toward Zara, who floated peacefully in the air, totally protected.

Aerden, who normally sulked in the corner, simply stood and tossed a pebble at her, hitting her square in the nose.

I smiled and looked around, an idea forming.

Magical shields were very useful when it came to deflecting magic. But what about things that weren't magic?

"Uproot the trees," I shouted, running down the line, my heart racing. "Grab chunks of rock from the mountains. Throw anything at that house that actually has substance. Let's go."

At first, some of the witches looked at me like I was crazy, but Mary Anne laughed.

She turned and focused her energy on a nearby spruce. "Essex, pull power from the root system of that tree," she said.

Essex closed his eyes, his body suddenly surrounded by a soft green aura.

Mary Anne lifted her arms and the spruce ripped out of the ground and hovered in the air. She reared back and with all the force of her magic, hurled the tree toward the house.

I held my breath, fingers crossed as the tree flew through the air.

It sailed through the magical shield and crashed into a group of witches, also taking out a support beam that held up part of the overhang. Stone crashed to the ground and witches scrambled out of the way, temporarily distracted.

"Go," I yelled, and the witches on my line followed Mary Anne's lead, working together with the demons behind them to draw power from the deep root systems, weakening the trees, and then rip them from the ground.

I ran to the builders. "Trebuchets," I said. "Can you make trebuchets?"

They nodded and got to work immediately, using a beautiful form of spellweaving to build giant catapults out of materials they pulled from the forest floor around us.

In minutes, we had two working trebuchets and twenty demons ripping huge chunks of rock from the nearby hills.

With each rock that hit the house, the witches worked harder to figure out a way to defend against it. The few spells they sent flying toward us missed their marks as we moved back and to the sides, giving the impression that we had a large force out here, rather than just a single team of fifty.

"Retreat further back," I said. "Draw them away from the house."

We moved back twenty feet, continuing our assault from a further distance.

I waited, my nerves on edge.

"They aren't following us," Brooke shouted. "They're not coming. We have to draw them back. Jackson, what do we do? We have to get them away from the house?"

"Where's Harper?" Illana shouted. "She should be here by now."

We tried again, executing our plan with precision. If those defenders thought we were the only ones they had to contend with, they would have already been out here, fighting us directly.

My heart sank as I looked out at my group of friends, all seeming to fight together as a team. But the ruby priestess had been right.

"Why aren't they following us?" Angela asked, her hands gathering into fists.

I shook my head. "Because they knew we were coming," I said. "They aren't going to leave their posts."

That meant we were safe out here as long as we kept our distance, but also meant that someone here had betrayed us again.

AN AMETHYST SUNRISE

AERDEN

Soldiers from the North and South waited silently in demon form, lost in the shadows of the night as they waited for our orders.

Lea and I lay flat to the ground at the top of the hill, looking out over the field to the west where the hunters would gather. It was almost time, and my heart raced as I waited for any sign of them.

The only way we knew where to go was because the ruby priestess had told Harper. If she was lying, we just moved the majority of our army out into the middle of nowhere. Andros would be enslaved, and it would be a miracle if any of our friends survived.

Even my brother.

I couldn't believe we had placed so much trust in the ruby priestess, but I trusted Harper.

As the minutes ticked by, though, anxiety buzzed through my veins with a slight hum that made it hard for me to stay still.

"They should be here by now," Lea said, glancing around. "We never should have trusted a priestess. What was Harper thinking? She's going to get us all killed."

Surprisingly, there wasn't quite as much hatred in her voice as usual when it came to Harper. Was it possible they could someday learn to get along? They were going to end up ruling the two kingdoms on this continent, so it would probably be a good idea for them to at least play nice.

"You didn't have to say you'd follow their plan," I reminded her. "You could have flat-out refused and taken your army to Blackwood. Or just left them all in the King's City."

Lea narrowed her eyes at me, but she knew I was right.

"I'm not saying she made a mistake. Yet. I'm just saying it's possible she did."

"Besides, if the hunters don't show up here, it's not our group that will be in danger," I said. "I'm more worried about Jackson and the others. They only have a small group over there on the human side. If this plan doesn't work and we bet on the wrong set of information, it's not going to be pretty for them."

"Or for Andros," Lea said, shaking her head and scanning the area again. "Come on. Where are they?"

I watched the time closely, and I already had a backup plan in mind if those hunters didn't show up in the next few minutes.

I was about to tell Lea we should notify the army of the alternate plan, just in case, when she gasped, her shoulders tensing.

"Look," she whispered so softly, I hardly heard.

I followed her gaze, and every muscle in my body tightened.

Movement just over the next hill near a stream. Too far to tell exactly what it was yet, but it was definitely a group of some kind, hovering like shadows.

Lea reached over to grab my hand. She didn't look at me, but she squeezed so hard, and I knew her thoughts. I knew exactly what she was feeling.

Hope. Fear. Anticipation.

The hunters had come.

And there, in the center of their group, a group of demons connected by silver chains that caught the light when someone turned.

"Seventy," Lea whispered. "Maybe a handful more. Seventy-five?"

I squeezed her hand back. More than we'd hoped, but not so bad that we couldn't bring them down.

The question was whether we could do it fast enough to save Andros.

"We can do this," I whispered, lowering even closer to the ground as the hunters approached.

They were still about a hundred yards away when they stopped and spread out, creating a circular barrier around the prisoners. One of the demons in the group shouted something I couldn't quite hear, and the others cheered.

Lea smiled and glanced at me.

Andros.

He was a fighter until the end.

We just couldn't let this be his end. We needed him in the war to come. Lea needed him.

She hadn't mentioned it to me yet, but I knew her father planned to ask her to take over the kingdom. I could see it in his eyes when he looked at her in the Council meeting, like he was sizing her up. Seeing if the crown would fit.

He wanted her to have it, and politically, it was the right move for the kingdom. The demons in the city needed a leader they could trust, and even though the king had kept them safe, they had still been scared.

They needed someone who could inspire them.

I had no doubt she was up for the job, but did she really want it?

I wasn't sure, but I knew if the time came that she felt it was what her people needed, she would step up as queen and rule them. And I knew that even though I was technically the one who had been groomed for taking over as her Guard Captain, it was Andros she would trust with that job.

They had fought together for a very long time, and Andros would be good at it.

The truth was, I was still holding out hope for another position.

Not that I'd ever really dreamed of being king. I just wanted to be hers.

"Can you do me a favor?" I asked softly. "Don't purposely try to get yourself killed tonight just to force my powers. I mean it, Lea."

She shrugged, barely glancing at me.

I wanted to wring her neck. She was going to get herself hurt.

I vowed that as soon as we got back to the city, I would train tirelessly until I could learn to control this power inside me, whatever it was. I wouldn't have her throwing herself in front of danger every time she needed me to step up.

"Watch," she said, nodding toward the hunters.

One of the hunters in the middle of the group held her hands out, palms lifted toward the sky as she began to chant. Dark vines sprung from the ground at her feet, growing up in a wide circle before the hunter.

"We need to move," she said. "Get them ready, but be as still and quiet as you can until you see that portal open."

I nodded, and she turned to me, suddenly breathless.

Her lips parted, and she almost said more, but finally, she shook her head, changing her mind.

"Go," she whispered.

I shifted and crept silently back down the side of the hill toward my soldiers. They were waiting, a mass of swirling shadows in the darkness.

They followed me around to the north side of the hill while Lea's forces took the south side. We were to attack first, drawing the hunters toward us while Lea's soldiers came up behind them.

She said the hunters had used a similar tactic to capture Andros. She wanted to give them a dose of their own medicine.

With the soldiers of the Southern Kingdom at my back, I flew to the top of the hill and waited, watching as the vines grew tight black buds that slowly opened to the darkness, their petals giving off a dark mist that rose upward.

I held my breath. Just a minute more. We had to hold our position. As long as they did not know we were here, there was a chance we could win the night and save our friend.

The dark mist swirled, taking the form of a large oval above the roses.

Just a second more.

The hunter lifted her arms higher, her voice carrying across the night.

I hung in the air, my life completely suspended as I waited for the first hint of light to appear.

Almost there.

My eyes locked on that oval mist. Waiting.

A pinprick of light appeared in the corner of the darkness and began to spread across the mist like an amethyst sunrise.

The warrior inside me roared, and I signaled the troops, leading them over the top of the hill and down to the field below toward glory.

The battle to save Andros and free the amethyst gates had begun.

THE AMETHYST DEMON GATE

HARPER

I walked through Blackwood with a body that was there, yet not there.

When I was in this non-physical state, I could explore other places, but my vision wasn't exactly the same. Colors weren't as bright. Details weren't as crisp.

Still, it was one of my more useful skills. Especially at a time like this when I wanted to get a better idea of how many guards and witches were stationed inside the house without actually having to fight them all.

I could also sense energy, like the energy coming from other witches here in the house.

And there were a ton of them.

Not exactly what I'd been hoping to find, but I forced myself to move forward, following the path Magda had given me toward the basement where I would find the original amethyst portal.

And, hopefully, the amethyst priestess.

I made a mental note of any witches I passed who seemed to be stationed in a permanent location.

So far, there were two who seemed to roam the halls near the secret staircase up to the third floor. The two witches, dressed in black catsuits, paced the floors back and forth, crossing each other every few minutes.

I couldn't sense anyone in the bedrooms up here, but there were so many people in and around this house right now, it was difficult to pinpoint the energy exactly.

I turned left and floated down to the end of this hallway where the second-floor landing opened up to a grand entryway with a huge oval chandelier made of teardrop-shaped amethysts hung over the white marble floor below. In the center of the marble tile was a gemstone inlay in the shape of a panther.

A double staircase descended on either side of the entryway, the steps covered in a ridiculously plush purple carpet.

Magda had said her sister was militant, but she hadn't said anything about her being tacky.

I made my way down the nearest staircase, making note of the witches stationed at the top of each one. They were facing downstairs, though, rather than watching for anyone who might intrude from upstairs.

This place was gaudy central with floor-to-ceiling purple curtains in every single room on the first floor made of thick velvet that pooled on the white floor. It was like an amethyst monster threw up all over this place.

And, I guess, if you thought about it, one kind of did.

I was pretty sure Priestess Black counted as a monster.

But I needed to stay focused. I finished my sweep of the first floor and made my way to the basement doorway. It

wouldn't be far from here, but as I passed through the doorway, chills broke out all over my skin.

All the energy of this house was coming from somewhere
down here.

With a racing heart, I pushed my energy forward, through
the next door, which Magda had said was a gathering room. A
meeting place for the coven.

When she'd first told me that, I had pictured a room full of
chairs, kind of like a PTA meeting or something. Maybe there
would be a table along the outside wall with stale donuts and
old coffee.

But this...

This room was wall-to-wall witches, all dressed in identical
black catsuits, amethyst collars glittering at their neckline. I
gasped, then slapped a hand over my mouth before I even realized they couldn't hear or see me.

Still, I needed to be more careful. One witch toward the
back of the crowd had turned to look when I gasped. She must
have sensed me here, and if she decided to act on that hunch
and send out a search party for intruders, Magda and I would
be toast.

I inched forward, avoiding the sensitive kitty near the back,
and counted the rows.

Twenty-five rows of ten. No one talking. Hardly anyone
moving. They were just waiting.

Waiting for Jackson.

I knew it with absolute certainty. This was part of the
army called together solely because they knew we were
coming.

Which meant our plan might actually work. No one was
expecting an attack at the portal on the Shadow World side,

and during the ritual, they would have no way of getting any troops over to attack them. It would take too long for them to send witches to another portal and out to the Shadow World.

These witches couldn't fast-travel the way demons could, which would be a major disadvantage in the Shadow World.

Lea and Aerden would have the amethyst hunters to deal with, which was no small feat, but the concentrated force would be here at Blackwood.

Hope rose in my heart.

Everything was going exactly as we'd hoped so far, and I needed to get to the portal room to see just what I'd have to contend with in there. I needed to hurry. Jackson's group would attack at any moment, and I intended to be ready when he did.

I left the room full of witches and continued straight down the hallway, past four more guards in black, and finally, I was there.

The founding ritual room of the amethyst gates, and there, standing near the table by the giant portal stone, was Priestess Black herself.

She was dressed like her minions, except she got the good leather, while they wore something that looked more pleather. Only the best for the leader. Which seemed to be true for her collar, too.

While most of her witches had a black collar with small amethysts along the front, the priestess wore a tight collar around her neck that had large amethysts all the way around. An amethyst panther charm dangled from the front.

She was a beautiful woman with smooth, pale skin and long black hair that fell down her back in one long sheet.

This ritual room was larger than the ones at most gates,

and the stone in the center—the amethyst demon gate—was just as big as the one we'd seen at Winterhaven.

Like all gates, though, it was in the center of a pentagram carved into the floor.

Witches in black robes lined with purple ribbon stood at each point of the star, waiting, while no less than forty witches in matching purple dresses lined the walls. There were no guards in this room at all, which seemed odd considering they knew an army was on their way.

Maybe they figured if the army got all the way down here, they were dead, anyway.

No one spoke as the priestess examined the ritual items. She picked the chalice off the table and studied it as if she'd never seen it before, pulling it close to her face and then holding it up to the light.

She called one of the women over to her, and they shared a look before one of them rushed over, bowing her head toward the priestess.

I winced as Priestess Black slapped the woman across the face, hard enough to leave a huge red welt on the woman's cheek.

"There is a smudge here on the chalice," she said. "This is the most important night of our coven's recent history, and I will not have it ruined by this kind of filth. You have one minute to fix it, or I'll suck your soul from your body and find someone to replace you. Now, go."

My eyes widened at the cold way she delivered her threat. This woman truly was a monster.

I took one final survey of the room before turning back toward the doorway when something seemed to nearly knock me off my feet. At first, I thought maybe Jackson had started the assault, but when I looked around, no one in the room had reacted at all.

The jolt came again, and I realized with a start that Magda was trying to wake me up. To bring me back to my body.

I blinked, focusing my energy back to my body in an instant, and my eyes snapped open to find Magda standing over me, the amethyst dagger in her hand.

For a split second, I thought for sure she was going to kill me, but when she thrust the dagger forward, it was not me she aimed to kill.

One of the witches who'd been knocked unconscious must have woken up, but thanks to Magda, she would never wake again.

"You scared me to death," I said, clutching my heart.

Magda fell back against the door. "Me? I tried to wake you up. You said you'd come straight back," she said. "I'm absolutely going to need my magic back. We'll never make it down there without us both."

I was about to tell her no for the millionth time when something slammed against the house, shaking the third floor as if a freaking tree had fallen on top of us. Jackson's attacks must have finally begun, and from the sound of it, he was doing a darn fine job of causing a disturbance.

Something else hit the house with a loud boom, and I wondered if he actually remembered I was in here.

I shook my head and stood up, retrieving the dagger from the dead body of the witch behind me.

I handed it to Magda. "You can have this," I said.

She opened her mouth to speak, but I held my hand up and gave her a sideways look that made her shut it with a snap and straighten her shoulders.

As the battle raged outside, I took Magda's hand and pulled her into my glamour until we both appeared invisible. The color of air.

Together, we stepped through the doorway and descended the narrow staircase into the heart of Blackwood.

A CHORUS OF SCREAMS

LEA

J ust as the amethyst portal opened, Aerden led his
army over the hill. A small ring of eight hunters
guarded the prisoners on the other side of the portal,
while the rest of them spread out in a line, defending
the portal against Aerden's assault.

I watched, waiting until the hunters were fully engaged
before sneaking across the field with my own soldiers in almost
perfect silence. We stayed close to the ground, moving as one
like a mist rolling through the field.

When we were just a few feet away from the throng of
hunters, we quickly spread out into several rows, taking a
formation we had only practiced once as we attacked the
hunters from behind.

They never saw us coming.

We downed six before they even had a chance to retaliate,
and from what I could tell, Aerden's group had already
successfully killed a handful, as well. But the element of

surprise was gone. Now, it was all about blocking them in and keeping them under our control.

Sometimes, if a hunter was strong, it could take five or six fighting to bring them down.

We didn't have those kinds of numbers today, but we had them surrounded. All we had to do was keep them in the center and pick them off one at a time.

I wanted so badly to break away and free the members of the Resistance from the eight hunters guarding them, but I knew that our best advantage right now was that we were working together as one large army. If we started breaking off into smaller groups, the hunters would start to have the advantage.

The eight guarding Andros couldn't afford to leave their post, either, so they were useless for now, watching as we killed their fellow hunters.

But time was ticking now. The ritual had begun, and when I glanced toward the amethyst light pouring from the portal, I could just make out parts of the ritual room on the other side. I couldn't see Priestess Black from here, but I could see a few of the other black-robed witches standing on the pentagram carved into the floor.

They couldn't move, their bodies locked into the ritual now. They wouldn't be able to move or cast until the ritual was complete. Or until someone put an end to it by force.

The witches standing behind them, however, women in purple robes that fell all the way to the floor, were clutching each other's hands and pointing toward the portal, shouting words I couldn't hear.

Probably something along the lines of, *"Oh my God, demons are attacking. We're all gonna die."*

Or at least that's what I hoped they were shouting.

The women in those robes were the ones who were the intended initiates in tonight's special edition of the ritual. From what Magda had said, they were all witches who'd been freed from the sapphire and emerald gates, but who wanted to be reinstated as members of the Order.

It disgusted me so much, I wanted the chance to kill them twice.

I definitely didn't want any of them enslaving Andros inside their bodies, and I fought with all my heart, hoping to keep that very thing from happening tonight.

I itched to fly through that portal and rip the priestess's heart from her chest. So far, Harper was the only one who'd had that privilege, but there were only three left, and I intended to kill at least one of them myself.

Of course, it was Harper who was sneaking around in that house right now, not me, and if she got to Priestess Black first, I wasn't going to complain.

I just wanted the witch dead.

A hunter spewed acid onto my pants, and I jumped back, cursing as the bile ate its way through the leather and started working on my skin. It burned like hell, but the most it would do was leave a few welts.

I nocked an arrow made of poison and aimed it right for the hunter's throat.

Let her choke on that for a while.

I loosed the arrow, and it hit its mark with absolute precision. The hunter gripped the arrow with both hands, but it was too late for her. Thick black and green blood oozed across her lips as she fell to her knees, her body already failing her.

I moved to the next, holding slightly back from the main part of the army so I could have room to aim.

Twenty-five or so of the hunters were already down in just a few minutes, and I let out an excited cry. We were actually doing it. We might get these down with time to spare.

The plan had worked, and I swear, if we saved my friends and killed Priestess Black tonight, I was going to be tempted to kiss Harper and the ruby priestess flat on the mouth.

I nocked another poison arrow and took aim, but just before I let the arrow fly, the hunters grew still, their eyes widening as sickening smiles stretched across their skeletal faces.

Those smiles unsettled me to my core, and I flipped around, looking to see whatever these hunters had seen.

I nearly dropped to my knees as a chorus of screams ripped through the night. I winced in pain and drew my hands up to my ears, my heart tightening in my chest.

I shook my head and blinked, wanting to just blink them away. Praying this was all in my imagination. We were winning. Everything was going exactly like we planned.

But when I looked again, I realized this was no dream. No illusion.

While we'd been fighting, pulling in tighter to the amethyst hunters, another, larger group of hunters had been surrounding us.

Not again.

I realized my fatal mistake too late. I had seen them use this trick before. Hell, I'd just used it on them.

But now, we were surrounded with no way out, our forces split down the middle by a row of hunters. I shifted, hoping to rally the soldiers to fly up to the hills and join me there, but the hunters had expected we would try to shift and fly. It was our only chance to escape.

My demon form hit a barrier about ten feet above the ground, and I was forced back to my body as a series of shocks pulsed through me like lightning.

Trembling, I forced myself to stand and conjure another arrow.

The only way out of this was to fight, but now we were outnumbered with no way to shift and fly more than a few feet into the air.

What the hell were we going to do?

And where the hell had all these extra hunters come from? There had to be another two hundred on the field now, and there was no way the amethyst priestess had that many hunters.

But then I saw a glittering necklace shining as it bounced against the chest of one approaching hunter. The stone was pure and white, a sparkling diamond as big as a quarter.

It was just like what happened at the Underground. Diamond hunters sent to aid in the attack.

So, who had betrayed us this time?

I suddenly wished for Aerden at my side. I needed him now. I needed that golem.

"Shift and stay low to the ground," I shouted, amplifying my voice with magic the way my father had taught me to do when he addressed a crowd. "Get out of the circle. Now."

We were sitting ducks. If we didn't move now, we'd all be killed.

But just as I shifted and tried to fly toward a crack between hunters, aiming for the hills beyond, a huge ring of fire erupted all around us, locking us into the center. No way around. No way up or over.

How had this happened? How did the High Priestess know we would be here?

It didn't make sense.

Fellow soldiers battled for their lives all around me as the hunters inched forward. I conjured sets of arrows as fast as I could, and took aim, letting them fly faster than I ever had before.

But it wasn't enough. There were too many.

I cried out for Aerden, but at first, I didn't see him anywhere.

He'd asked me not to step into danger on purpose, but this was real. No games. I needed him now. That golem could save us all.

I loosed another set of arrows, finally taking down two hunters as they approached.

Someone behind me screamed, and I turned to find an amethyst hunter reaching for my throat, her fingertips dripping with glowing green acid.

I reached for the scimitar at my side and turned with all my force, slicing the top half of her head off in one swift movement. I dodged her falling body and quickly put up a magical shield to absorb an attack from a diamond hunter to my left.

All around me, members of the Resistance and the King's Guard fell, and I wanted to scream.

This could not be happening. Where the hell was he?

But then, over the roar of the battle, I heard my name on the wind.

Aerden?

Something in the sound of his voice—a level of desperation I'd never heard before—rattled me to the core.

I turned, praying to see the golem towering over the battle-field, but instead, what I saw nearly ripped my heart in two.

Four hunters glided toward the hills beyond us carrying a crystal cage made of shifting colors, like a prism being held up to the sunlight. Inside the cage, Aerden beat his fists against the bars as he screamed my name.

I had never seen anything like it, but I knew exactly what it was.

It was the end of any advantage we might have had.

TO TRUST MY OWN HEART

HARPER

What the heck was Jackson doing out there? Trying to bring the whole house down?

The entire house trembled every time a boulder hit the house. Or at least, I assumed it was boulders, as evidenced by the giant one that came flying through the window just before Magda and I walked right past it.

I was tempted to shift instead of walking through the house invisible, hoping no one would notice a white mist traveling across the white marble floors, but it was too risky. We needed to get down to the ritual room as soon as possible so we'd have a shot at killing Priestess Black while she was vulnerable from the ritual.

During a regular initiation ritual, the Prima would exert some energy, sure, but it was nothing compared to a mass initiation. Pulling forty demons through at once and binding them in the bodies of forty different witches took extreme power. The power only a priestess had.

No normal Prima could have survived it.

For the twenty or more minutes that the ritual went on, Priestess Black would be unable to cast at all, even to defend herself, without completely breaking the ritual. And apparently breaking the ritual could have severe consequences for her power.

Magda said once when they'd tried this with Hazel, the ritual had been cut short by an attack from the Resistance on the Shadow World side. Hazel had survived it, of course, but she'd been completely incapacitated for nearly six months, and the only reason she'd recovered that fast was because she'd consumed the power of twenty witches through the use of soul stones.

Priestess Black would not be quick to stop the ritual, which meant she would be vulnerable for the next twenty minutes and counting.

I had to get down to her, and the only way to do that fast enough to have a shot at her was to bypass as many of these witches on the first and second floors as possible.

Luckily, the two-hundred and fifty who had been downstairs in the gathering room seemed to have gone outside to deal with the giant trees and rocks being thrown at the house. I couldn't help but laugh at the thought of a giant pine tree flying straight toward the head of a witch dressed like a cat.

At least they seemed to be keeping the focus on the defenses outside. They just needed to keep it going for a little while longer.

I wondered how things were going on the Shadow World side now that the portal had surely been opened. Lea hadn't been able to gather as many soldiers as she'd wanted, but the combined forces of North and South should have been enough to take out whatever hunters the amethyst priestess had guarding the portal.

They weren't expecting anyone to be fighting on that side, so she wouldn't have prepared for it.

I hope not, anyway.

I was dying to reach into my pocket to see if any of them had tried to contact me through the ruby com stones, but I couldn't risk the light being seen. Inside my pocket, it was covered by the glamour, but if I brought it out into the open, it might be something that could catch the attention of a nearby witch. I couldn't take the risk.

As soon as I was downstairs, I would step into a side room and check the stones, just to make sure everything was going according to plan.

So far, I had high hopes. Everything Magda had told us had been true, and I had done the right thing by trusting her.

Hell, she'd even saved my life back there. She wouldn't do that and then turn around and betray me five minutes later.

Tonight, we were going to kill another priestess. I could feel it.

Magda and I moved together, my hand tight on her wrist so that my glamour would easily include her body, as well as mine.

We passed by the two guards pacing the floors on the second level, just barely squeezing tight enough against the wall for one of them to miss us as she passed. When we got to the landing that separated into two grand staircases, we tiptoed past the guards stationed there, too.

Even though we were invisible to the eye, we weren't silent. There was so much noise going on from the attacks outside, though, that we didn't have to worry about it too much unless we were literally standing right next to one of the guards.

The biggest scare we had was when two cat-like women came running out of the basement, practically smacking right into us. I did shift that time, knowing there was no way we were going to get out of their way fast enough if I didn't.

Thankfully, the women were moving too fast to notice the wisp of white smoke that flew toward the floor as they passed.

I waited for my heart to stop beating before I led us into the butler's pantry in the kitchen so that I could shift back to human form and glamour us back to our invisible state. I probably could have pulled it off without needing to step away, but it was tricky making the transition with two people.

We disappeared just as three more guards rushed through the kitchen. I had no idea where they were coming from or where they were going in that much of a hurry, but I didn't particularly care. All that mattered to me was that they had no idea we were here.

When we finally made it to the door leading down to the basement, I breathed a sigh of relief and stepped onto the stairs.

We were alone for the moment, so I released the glamour and placed my hand on the door we'd just come through, magically nailing it shut so that no one could come through without a great deal of force. It wouldn't hold forever without me here to maintain the spell, but all we needed was about ten minutes.

In ten minutes, I could end it all.

I motioned for Magda to lead the way. "You first, my dear."

She straightened and nodded. "Here we go," she said. "Stay as close as you can."

I shifted to demon smoke and practically plastered myself to Magda's back, sticking as close to her as I possibly could.

Priestess Black liked to put traps in her dungeons. Traps I wouldn't have seen or triggered in my astral form, but which would go off and possibly snap me in two as a human.

Lucky for all of us, Magda was immune to her sister's traps. It was one of the agreements they'd all made early on as sisters. They would all have access to each other's homes and doorways, and they could not harm one another directly.

Which meant immunity to traps.

It was a kind of magical contract they had signed with each other decades ago, and even if one sister thought another had betrayed her, as Magda had done, the agreement could not be altered.

I just prayed my presence didn't somehow confuse the traps and cause them to go off, anyway.

Magda had been down here before, many times, and she knew that her sister Gladys only had traps from the stairway to the gathering room, so as long as we could make it that far, we'd be in the clear.

I don't think I took a breath the entire time we walked down that narrow hallway. It was literally only fifty steps to the gathering room, but every single one of them seemed to take an eternity.

My heart jumped every time something slammed against the side of the house, because I was sure it was one of those traps.

And Gladys's traps were apparently horror show quality. Blades that lifted straight up from the floor. Acid that fell from the ceiling in waves. A trap door that dropped you straight down to a pit full of actual panthers, trained to rip the flesh from your bones.

To be honest, I wasn't sure I believed that last one, but Magda had seemed to think it was clever.

Either way, thanks to Magda, none of the traps seemed to go off, and when we stepped into the gathering room, I finally drew my first breath in what felt like forever.

We took a peek inside the room to be sure there were no rows of witches standing there, and when we were sure it was empty, we stepped inside and hid behind the door.

"I just want to check the communication stones, really quick," I said. "As long as things are going well with Lea on the other side, I think we're clear to head into the ritual room and put a dagger through your sister's heart."

Magda sighed. "I never have liked Gladys," she said. "Now, Hazel was a different story, even if she was crazy rest her soul. But Gladys? She's cruel."

I cut my eyes toward the ruby priestess, curious exactly where she drew the line on that one.

I didn't ask, though, and focused on finding the right stone.

Each ruby stone connected with one that had been linked to it as a mate. The problem with the stones, however, was that there were no marks on them to tell which ones were linked to which ones.

I'd gotten in the habit of placing different people's stones in different pockets, just to keep them straight.

Lea was always in my shoe.

I quickly fished it out and rubbed my finger over the top of it, casting a quick sound-dampening spell on the doorway so that no one in the hallway could hear us talking in here.

It took a while for her to answer. Too long.

My stomach tightened into knots as I waited, staring at that stone and begging it to light up with the sound of her voice, telling me everything was great.

Except that when she did finally come through, she was frantic. The sounds of battle and the screams of hunters nearly drowned out her voice, entirely.

I charged up the sound-dampening spell, just in case and asked her what was happening.

"An ambush," she screamed. "Diamond hunters. Hundreds of them, Harper. They knew we were coming here, too. Ruby betrayed us all. Get out of there."

"What?" I asked, looking to Magda and grabbing her wrist so hard, tears sprung to her eyes.

"We're fighting for our lives here, Harper," she said, her words breaking my heart in two. "Even if we can survive this, we'll never make it to Andros in time."

Without warning, tears slid down my cheeks. I had to help her.

"I'll come through," I said. "I'm close to the open portal. I'll push my way through and help you."

"No, it's over," she said, grunting as her weapon made contact with something near the communication stone. "Aerden's gone. Taken by hunters in some kind of cage made of colors. Tell Jackson. Get out of there, if you can. Find Aerden."

She choked on her own words, but through it all, she kept fighting.

I wanted nothing more than to be there by her side right now. I stared at Magda's face as Lea spoke, searching for answers. Reasons.

"Lea, I'm sorry," I said, tears streaming down my face. "I'm sorry, I failed you. I won't just leave you there. I'm coming."

But my last words were cut off as the stone's light cut out. Lea's connection had been severed, and my heart was broken.

"Was this you?" I asked, taking Magda by the shoulders and sending a swirling rope of white smoke around her body over and over again. "Did you tell the High Priestess our plan? Did I just lose this war and all our lives by trusting you?"

Magda shook her head, a ruby-colored tear falling down her cheek.

"Harper, I did not do this," she said.

The dagger she'd been holding this whole time dropped to the floor as my ropes of smoke squeezed her tighter.

Every piece of logic in my mind said that I should take her heart now and never look back. Take her heart and then walk in the next room and take her sister's, too.

Trusting a priestess was stupid and reckless and everyone knew it but me.

But deep in my heart, I saw something different in her eyes.

Those tears were not fake. And she was not crying them just because she was afraid to die.

Magda Thorn wanted us to win.

I couldn't explain why or how I knew, but I looked inside her soul and I knew. She hated the Order of Shadows just as much as I did. She wanted all of it to end.

"It wasn't me, Harper," she said again. "But I can help you. You have to trust me. I can't give you any reason why you should, other than I think you're the kind of person who can see things other people can't. That's why I came to you when I knew I couldn't go to anyone else for help. There's been no one else all these years. I can help them. I can help Lea, but you have to let me go. You have to trust me, and you have to let me go."

It was the kind of moment that defined an entire lifetime.

A fork in the road that asked you to choose between logic and instinct. Between what you knew was right because it made sense and what you felt was right because your heart told you it was so.

I stared into the eyes of an enemy, and I saw something familiar.

The need to truly be seen. To not be judged by what things looked like from the outside, but to have someone finally look inside and see what was real.

I'd felt that way most of my life before I came to Peachville.

Everyone judged me by the strange things that happened around me, and no one saw my heart. No one saw how much I wanted to be good. How much I wanted to be loved.

Jackson did that for me, and my life was changed forever. He saw something in me when no one else did, and with that kind of unconditional love and understanding, I had already changed the world.

What could someone like Magda Thorn do if she were given that kind of grace?

My entire body was trembling in fear, because I already knew what I wanted to do. And I knew just how stupid and risky it was.

This was life or death for the people I loved more than anything.

But the only way forward for me was to follow my heart. Anything else, and I would lose this war. I had to learn to trust myself. To trust my own heart.

And deep down, I believed the ruby priestess was telling the truth.

I dropped the ropes that held her and stepped back, my hands shaking uncontrollably.

Magda's breath hitched twice as she stared at me, mouth open in surprise.

I reached inside my pocket and took out the small diamond stone that bound her magic. "Can you save them?" I asked. "Do you promise me?"

She nodded, not looking away from my eyes. "I promise," she said.

I lifted the diamond to my lips and blew over the top of it, releasing the magical bindings that kept the ruby priestess from connecting to her power.

I half expected her to kill me right there, but instead, she smiled and put a hand to her heart.

"Thank you," she said. "I'll be back, Harper. I promise."

With that, she ran from the room. To go where, I had no idea.

I took a deep breath, trying to still the shaking of my hands. I needed to pull it together. What was done was done now. I needed to figure out my next move.

I leaned over to grab the dagger that had fallen on the floor. I tucked it into my belt, next to my father's sword.

I would go to the ritual room and face Priestess Black. That was the only move there was, really. If my friends died tonight, I had to at least do this for them.

I would not run away, no matter how bad things got.

I closed my eyes and gathered my power into my body, charging it up until it buzzed through me like electricity. And when I was ready, I started for the door, nearly running into someone on my way out.

On instinct, I sent my ropes of smoke out to grab them, but before I could get the spell off, pain sliced through the lower half of my body in so many places, I couldn't count.

I tried to take a step, but my legs gave out. Blood pooled on the floor beneath me, and I fell, my head slamming against the hard, marble floor with a force that knocked the breath from my lungs and sent me toward oblivion.

But not before I'd gotten a look at my attacker's face.

An enemy disguised as a friend.

My betrayer had finally made herself known.

WE JUST HAD TO HOLD ON

JACKSON

T he barrage of spells was never ending. Rows of
witches blasted the woods around us with lightning
and poison, spells that lit the trees on fire and
pushed us farther back into the woods.

We'd spread out slightly to draw their attacks in multiple
directions, but we kept having to push back to stay under the
forest's protection. So far, the witches and rock golems
stationed around the house had not moved from their posts,
except to dodge the things we threw at them.

It was obvious they had been told to hold their positions in
expectation of a much larger army arriving at any moment. As
long as that ritual was still in progress in the basement, they
couldn't leave their fortress entrance undefended.

But one glance at my watch told me that we only had
about ten more minutes before the ritual would end. At that
point, Priestess Black would no longer be quite so vulnerable.
And what was worse, if they succeeded, some witch downstairs would have Andros's power at her command.

Actually, forty witches would have access to the power of the Resistance members they had kidnapped.

Add that to the force already battling us out here, and we would be in serious trouble if they left their stations in front of the house and charged into the woods.

I kept an eye on the time, anxious to hear some kind of word from the others about how their battles were going. I'd briefly heard from Aerden at the beginning of their assault, and he'd sounded elated. Sure they would win the night and save the Resistance leader.

But as time ticked on and I didn't hear anyone confirming victory at stopping the ritual, I grew more and more concerned.

Nothing from Harper, either. She was somewhere inside that house right now, making her way down to the amethyst priestess, ready to kill her if the opportunity arose.

But I also knew that Harper had a backup plan if everything seemed to go to hell.

I ran a hand through my hair and stared up at the fortress that seemed to simply emerge from the rock, as if it had grown there, rather than being built.

If Lea and Aerden couldn't save Andros on the Shadow World side of the portal, Harper was carrying something in her pocket that could level this entire place and stop the ritual in an instant.

I had told her a thousand times I didn't think it was a good idea. That it was a huge risk to blow up the original amethyst demon gate, but after the damage those tiny bombs had done to Harper's castle, she thought a few well-placed bombs inside Priestess Black's house might be a good failsafe to stop the ritual and potentially kill Priestess Black if all else seemed lost.

It had been Magda who had off-handedly remarked that a diamond infused with one of her detonating spells would do significantly more damage to a much larger area. And of course, Harper just happened to have an entire pouch full of Shadow World diamonds now that she'd taken off the bodies of the hunters.

Magda had apparently created many bombs like the ones she'd planted in our house. She seemed to enjoy blowing things up, which was a surprise considering the woman loved to wear dresses and go to the Opera.

My biggest concern about the bombs was that Harper would have to be inside the house to plant them, and after what happened at the castle, we couldn't necessarily control when they went off. If she wasn't able to get out before they went off, I would lose her.

I didn't want to take that risk.

Magda tried to explain what had gone wrong there, apologizing from the bottom of her heart that someone had lost their life. To her credit, she did genuinely seem sorry about Tuli's death, but that hadn't stopped me from wanting to wrap my hands around her neck and choke the life out of her for what she had done.

The detonation spell Magda had placed on the two rubies planted in our castle was timed to go off at exactly the right time, just before dawn on the night we had gone to the Underground.

When our plans had changed and we decided to leave, Magda said that whoever betrayed us inside the castle must have changed the detonation spell so that they could manually set them off. I didn't know how this was possible, but Magda said it was relatively easy if you knew the exact spell that had been used to set it. Which the High Priestess apparently did, because she was the one who had taught Magda the spell in the first place.

The idea of some saboteur inside the castle—one of our friends—actually changing the bombs to a manual setting and detonating them when they thought they had a decent chance of killing Harper as she stood under the balcony overhang was a little far-fetched for me.

Until tonight.

Now that I could see with my own eyes clear evidence that someone had definitely relayed our plan to the Order of Shadows, it seemed more real than I had ever imagined.

I wished more than ever that I still had my ability to see visions. Even if they had often been no more than flashes of scenes that didn't always make sense, knowing at least a few details of what was to come had given me power. It had allowed me to be ready for what was coming and to look for the signs.

Without those visions, I was blind with no way of knowing whether we were supposed to win or lose. If this night ended with the blood of our enemies on our hands or the blood of our allies pooled on the ground.

But it was no use wishing for something that was gone. I had made the only decision I could make at the time to get Harper home.

I wondered if Sabine had seen any visions of this night? Did she know how this all would end?

I kept my eye on the witches standing in a cluster on the front porch, gesturing toward the woods on both sides.

They were on to us. I was sure of it.

They'd been told to expect a large army to secretly circle

the castle while we drew them away from the entrance, but our siege of the fortress had started nearly half an hour ago, and there was still no secret army out there ready to close in on Blackwood.

If they believed the threat was not real, or if somehow, they'd already heard news that the army attacked on the Shadow World side, they might take the risk of sending half their forces out into the woods to attack us directly.

I couldn't let that happen.

We didn't have enough people out here to fight off over a hundred witches and a handful of rock golems.

I'd fought those nasty things a few times in the caves when I'd been hunting the hunters, and they were not easy to kill. You had to find the witch controlling them in order to kill them permanently, and out here, that was going to be impossible.

If they decided to come into the woods after us, we would have no choice but to retreat.

I really didn't want to do that without knowing for sure we'd saved Andros and the others.

And that Harper was safely out of that house.

The witches arguing on the porch concerned me, though. One of them was definitely telling the others that they should at least send out a scouting team to see if there was an army of demons hiding in the woods, just waiting for them to leave an entrance open.

I glanced at my small crew of witches and demons, still working hard to send boulders and trees flying toward the house, along with poisonous arrows and blasts of fire. What could we do from here that would convince those witches to stay at their posts?

I wished Lea was here with her ability to conjure targets or illusions, but no one in my current group could do that.

We needed it to seem that our group of fighters had suddenly grown in size. Like they would be putting the entire ritual, and their priestess, in danger to step away from those entrances and leave their defenses weakened.

I moved to the back of the group and gathered up the fastest demons in the group. Mordecai, Joost, Cristo, Erick, and five others. I wanted Illana on this, too, but I couldn't find her anywhere.

"Has anyone seen my sister?" I asked, frantically searching through the darkness. I couldn't afford to stop and look for her right now, but maybe she had gone back with the builders who'd retreated a few yards back to get more distance.

I asked the demons I'd pulled together to spread through the woods around the house. If each demon took a small section and flew back and forth inside it, casting spells and sending flaming arrows and whatever else they could conjure toward the house as quickly as possible, it might seem that a new army had shown up, ready to attack.

"Don't stop moving," I said. "The spells you cast and the things you conjure don't actually have to be damaging. Don't put so much of your power and magic into them that you'll end up exhausted in two minutes. All we have to do is make them think the reinforcements just arrived."

I glanced at my watch again.

Eight minutes, max. We just had to hold on for eight more minutes.

After that, the battle would be over, one way or another, and it would be time to get the hell out of here.

As the new attacks appeared to shoot out of the woods

from all directions, the witches on the porch scattered, taking up their posts again and firing back at the woods, shouting orders for everyone to hold their positions.

I breathed a sigh of relief and continued my own assault on the castle. A few more minutes.

We just had to keep them occupied for a few more minutes, then it would all be over.

A sharp pain seemed to flash through my mind, and I saw my brother's face, twisted in agony. I doubled-over, sensing his distress, even though he was distant, separated from me now by the distance between the two worlds.

I tried to see him again, to reach out to whatever that flash of vision had been, but when I searched for our connection, it was gone.

I closed my eyes and took several deep breaths, forcing myself to focus on him, despite the battle that raged around me.

No, our connection wasn't gone. He was still there. He was just...

Dangit, I couldn't quite figure out what had happened to him. He was dim. I had no other way to describe it.

Why didn't anyone check in? What was going on?

I rubbed my finger over the top of Aerden's communication stone, but there was no answer. There was no answer from anyone.

Come on. Where are you guys? What's happening?

But for now, I was on my own.

I glanced around, remembering again that my sister had also seemed to go missing. I checked with the builders in the back, but no one had seen her.

"Illana," I shouted into the woods, but there was no

response.

Where the hell had everyone gone?

Decaying bodies fell to the ground at our feet, turning to dust and sludge. With every swing of my axe, another hunter screamed, and the fury of battle swelled inside me, urging me forward.

Our surprise attack had worked. These hunters had no idea we were coming, and now they had no chance to escape. Unlike demons, they couldn't shift and fly between the spaces in our army, and we had them surrounded.

My troops from the Southern Kingdom had curved around to meet up with Lea's larger force from the Northern Kingdom on both sides, so that now we had the amethyst hunters completely pinned inside.

As soon as this group was down to just a few, I would turn my sights on the portal and free Andros and the others.

I glanced over to check the state of the ritual and noticed that a purple mist filled with light had snaked out of the portal and curled around the bodies of several of the demons standing there in chains.

Each tendril of mist meant that a connection to one of the witches on the other side had been made.

Once every witch had connected with her intended demon, the final words of the spell would be recited and the initiation for all forty witches in that room would complete in a matter of seconds.

We couldn't let all of those connections be made. We had to get these hunters down in time to stop that ritual, one way or another.

But there would be time.

I swung my double-headed axe, enjoying the weight of it in my hand as the blade sunk into the torso of another hunter, slicing her through.

Everything was going according to plan. I'd checked in with Jackson just seconds ago to hear that the assault on Blackwood was right on time and Harper was safely inside the house with Magda. I never would have dreamed a priestess would come through like this, but Harper had been right.

Magda's help had turned the tide for us. With her, we could possible hope to end it all in a matter of months, rather than decades.

But just as I lifted my axe to slice the hand from a hunter who'd been reaching for her magic, something seemed to steal my breath completely, and I froze.

I struggled against whatever strange magic held me in its grasp and searched for the hunter who'd cast it.

Only, the hunters in front of me were fighting for their lives. None of them were even looking at me as I stood there, frozen in my movements.

My axe was suddenly ripped out of my hands, and some

invisible force pulled me backward so rapidly, I couldn't even comprehend what was happening until it was done.

My body flew straight back into a cage made of something shimmering in the moonlight. Something I'd never seen before in my life. I regained control of my legs and ran forward, attempting to shift, but feeling the source of my power cut off in a way I'd experienced too many times before for it not to drive me insane with rage and sorrow that flowed through me like lava.

"No," I shouted, ramming straight into a doorway that seemed to appear instantly and lock me inside.

I gripped the shimmering glass with both hands and shouted out warnings to my army, but when they turned, their eyes widened in terror at the sight of more hunters pouring out of the darkness of the woods just beyond the stream.

A hundred. Maybe more.

I kicked and clawed at the cage as the four hunters who'd captured me glided back through the hills, taking me away from the battle.

"Lea."

I shouted her name, over and over.

She'd been fighting on the other side of the amethyst hunters, and I didn't catch sight of her until her head lifted from the crowd and sought me out, fear and hopelessness in her eyes as I disappeared over the hill and out into the darkness.

Where had all these hunters come from?

And what in the hell was this cage?

I struggled against it, throwing my body against the bars and kicking at them, as if I could tear them apart with sheer force of will. When it was obvious there was no forcing my way out, I closed my eyes and reached for my magic. Even a spark might set me free.

But after all this time of fighting to regain control of magic and feeling that it had abandoned me, the feeling of being cut off from it completely nearly took me to my knees.

"What are you doing to me?" I asked, moving to the edge of the cage near one of the hunters who carried it. "Where are you taking me?"

The hunter cut her eyes toward me without moving her head, but she gave no answer other than a slight tilting of her lips.

"Damn you, let me out of here," I said, the truth of the situation dawning on me. I was trapped, and Lea was being ambushed.

A hundred extra hunters? How would they survive? And even if they did manage to hold on, was there any hope they could do it in time to stop the ritual?

Our army would still have numbers on our side for now, but fighting a hunter was not an even match. It could take several skilled demons just to kill one. I needed to get back out there.

I gripped the bars of the strange cage and screamed again, pulling at them with every ounce of my strength.

The strange, multi-colored material didn't budge. It was cool to the touch like glass, but hard as demon steel.

I reached in my pocket, feeling for the communication stones. I wasn't sure who could come to my aid, but I had another charge on my stone that linked with Jackson. Maybe he could get word to the Southern Kingdom. Have them send reinforcements.

But when I placed my finger over the top of the stone to

call for help, nothing happened. No hum of energy or dim light inside. Nothing magical could happen inside this cage.

I didn't care about me, but I couldn't bear to think of Lea out there, fighting more than twice as many hunters as we'd expected.

How had those hunters even known we were there?

Had the amethyst ones somehow called for help? Or had the hunters been there waiting in the shadows, all along?

I was powerless and furious, being led away from a battle I needed to fight. I felt as though I had so much anger and fear inside my body that I should have been able to tear this cage apart and kill each of these four hunters with nothing more than a glance, but the feelings inside me were useless without any connection to the source of my power.

Whatever this material was, it seemed to act like the shackles the guards placed on my wrists each day before we'd gone out to the mines. It cut off my access to that well of power within me, just like turning off a light switch.

I could still feel it there, swirling and calling to me, but I had no way to dip into it and use it.

My arms shook as I pulled on the bars of the cage, willing them to budge just a little, but it was no use.

The hunters who carried me, changed direction suddenly and flew up the side of a nearby mountain, disappearing finally into a dark cave that lit up as the cage entered it.

Light made up of a thousand different colors and shades reflected off the jagged onyx walls, and I searched for any sign of hope. Anything that I could get my hands on to help break this cage or kill a hunter.

"Let me go," I shouted, watching in horror as the hunters glided toward the open door, as if to just leave me here. "Your amethyst priestess will die tonight, and my armies will hunt you all down and put an end to all of you."

The hunter toward the back turned on me and laughed, unable to resist the chance to taunt me.

"Amethyst?" she asked. "You're a fool. The amethyst priestess is nothing compared to my mistress."

That's when I noticed the diamond ring that slid back and forth on one bony finger as the hunter spoke.

"Diamonds, then?" I asked. I wanted to keep her talking. Get her to tell me something useful or to let me go so that she could prove to me just how powerful she really was. I had to get out of this cage.

The three hunters who had come with her also turned at the sound of my voice.

They slithered back into the room like snakes, gliding effortlessly over the top of the floor.

"You think your diamond priestess is any better? She's just some human with a god-complex, thinking she can steal the souls and power of demons to make herself immortal. She's nothing, your diamond priestess."

I was trying to anger this hunter. To make her so mad, she just had to prove her own power.

But instead, she threw her head back and laughed, the sound echoing off the brittle onyx walls.

"You really don't know, do you?" she asked, moving forward until the stench of her was heavy in my nose. "The High Priestess is no human, filth. Unlike me, she has never been human. She is all-powerful, and someday, worlds will bow to her."

The hunter turned, but the moment she did, a flash of brilliant, blinding white light pulsed through the room.

All four hunters fell to the ground, reduced to nothing more than a pile of rags. As if they had simply been vaporized.

I trembled as I clutched the bars of my cage, unsure if I should be grateful or terrified as a small woman seemed to step out of the light. Her long hair fell in white waves down her back and shoulder. Her pale skin seemed to almost glow from within.

A pair of wings fluttered against her back, their colors shifting just as the colors of my cage shifted.

I backed away, awed by the raw power that seemed to radiate from her.

"I have wanted to meet you for a very long time, Aerden," she said, her voice almost like two voices at once. Almost like a song. "But there is no time to talk."

"Who are you?" I asked in a whisper.

I could not draw my eyes away from her.

The corners of her lips lifted slightly, almost in a smile, but not exactly.

"My name is Sabine," she said, not offering more than that.

She lifted a delicate fingertip to the door of my cage and in an instant, the bars holding me in disappeared on that side.

I wasn't sure whether to back away or walk out. Whether to thank her by falling to my knees in gratitude or to beg for my life.

"Come," she said, beckoning with a slight motion of her fingers. "You have work to do, and time is running thin. For all of us."

Time. I have to get back to Lea.

I stepped out of the cage, desperate to get back to the fight but filled with confusion and questions.

"I have to go," I said. "I owe you my life, Sabine. I don't know how to repay you."

She did smile at that. A knowing smile.

"For now, you have a battle to fight," she said. "An important battle in a war you haven't even begun to understand."

Her words held me to the spot. More questions. And this woman—this fae—had answers we'd been seeking for lifetimes. I could feel the depth of her knowledge. See it in her ancient eyes.

"What does that mean?" I asked. "What don't we understand? Do you know who the High Priestess is or why those hunters pulled me away from battle? How did you even find me here, Sabine?"

She shook her head. "This is not a time for answers," she said. "Your answers will come as long as you continue to seek them."

She reached toward me, and I had to force my feet to stay on the ground, rather than back away. I think she knew how much will it took to let her move closer, and admiration shone in her eyes.

As I stared into them, I realized they, too shifted colors. A prism of light, glowing with the knowledge of centuries. Possibly longer.

Her pale palm hovered in the air in front of me, as if she were trying to feel my power. Connect to it somehow.

"You are so much more powerful than you allow yourself to be," she said. "Stop fighting it. Embrace who you are, and it will flow from you like water."

She touched a single fingertip to the center of my forehead, and an energy so great, I felt it might consume me flowed from that spot and down through my body like an avalanche. It lit me up from the inside, and I gasped, drawing one massive breath as the power seemed to spill out of me.

Just beyond the doorway to the cave, the light of my golem shone brighter than ever before, and I could feel my connection to him strengthen. My control of him tighten.

"There are worlds of power inside you," she said in a whisper, looking at the golem with such admiration in her eyes. "And your twin."

My mouth fell open at the mention of Jackson.

"Can he—"

"You must go," Sabine said. "Now."

She pressed a slip of paper into my hand and held my eyes for a moment.

"For Jackson," she said. "Tell no one I was here but those you must tell. It is time for you to see. For all of you to see."

She spoke in riddles, twisting my mind into more questions.

"I don't under—"

But she was already gone, and there was a battle still to fight.

I tucked the paper into my pocket and shifted to black smoke, flying through the night toward battle with the light of a thousand suns at my back and the fate of two worlds on my shoulders.

UNTIL THE END

LEA

I stood in the blood of hunters and heroes, my two scimitars slicing through any hunter who dared to come close to me.

My arrows were useless this close, but I kept an eye on the portal several yards away, watching as each new amethyst tendril connected to another demon and our time slipped by like sand through our fingertips.

If it came to it, I would use my arrows on the hunters who surrounded the portal, even if it meant letting the hunters near me slice me to shreds in the process. I couldn't let that ritual complete.

"Keep pushing through," I shouted to the soldiers who surrounded me.

We'd managed to systematically take down all the remaining amethyst hunters except the eight who guarded the portal, and we had shifted our attention to the ring of diamond hunters that now surrounded us.

If we could just manage to push through their line, we'd be free of this invisible ceiling they'd placed above us. We'd be free to shift and regroup, attack the portal before they had a chance to kill us all.

We'd suffered staggering losses, but I would not let that stop us now. I would let it fuel my fury.

Fury at a ruby witch who had betrayed us all to her High Priestess. There was no other explanation for how these hunters had known where to find us. Other than Harper and Jackson, no other soul knew where we were going until the time had come.

If Harper hadn't killed that witch by the time this night was over, I would do it myself.

I didn't care if I had to come back from the Afterworld to get it done.

"There," I shouted, waving soldiers toward a break in the chain of diamond hunters as another fell. "Focus your attacks on this row."

I wasn't even sure how many of the soldiers could hear my commands. It was a problem leading this kind of battle, and I wished for a way that I could communicate my order to everyone on the field, no matter how far away they were.

But for now, all I could do was shout and lead by example.

I rushed forward, slicing my way through another hunter's neck as several soldiers joined me, downing the next hunter in the row. If we could take several of them down at once and split their force, we could usher everyone out of this circle of death they'd formed around us.

We could retreat and gather together as one united front.

It was our only chance.

"Everything you've got," I shouted, throwing the force of my body and my will at the next hunter in the line.

A mist of green poison formed on the tip of my blades, as I combined my magic and my blades.

For so long, demons had focused mainly on the magical attacks in battle, but watching Aerden on the battlefield of the arena and during our training sessions, I had learned that a combination of forces, using shifting and magic and physical weapons in harmony, could be more brutal than any one thing on its own.

I was still learning, but with Aerden, it had become a dance, shifting easily and reforming as his axe sliced through the air.

I held his form and balance and strength in my mind as my example as I forced my way through the line of hunters.

But just as we pushed through, a new throng flew in from another location, blocking us off before we could split their forces.

Were there still more hunters coming to join the fight? How many could one priestess possibly have?

We were holding our own, despite our losses, but if a new wave of hunters arrived, we would have to find a way to force our retreat, or we would all die tonight.

I glanced toward the portal. More than half of the demons there had now been connected to a witch on the other side. We had minutes left, if we were lucky.

We weren't going to make it on time.

Andros, I'm trying.

At least my friend knew I was here. Knew I was fighting with everything I had to save his life.

A blast of cold energy slammed into my side, and I fell

back against a fellow soldier, cursing as the ice seemed to spread up my torso. I shivered and pushed back against the pain of the blast. It had hit me straight on, and it hurt like the devil, but it wasn't going to kill me.

Not quickly, anyway.

I gritted my teeth and blocked the pain from my mind as best I could as I rushed back toward the line of hunters, trying once again to puncture a hole in their defenses so we could push through.

But as I lifted my scimitar and went to strike again, the sight of more hunters pouring over the hills made my knees buckle and my heart nearly stop.

A tear slid down my cheek like a traitor.

The soldiers around me must have seen them, too, because they paused for a moment, and I knew we were all feeling the same thing.

Utter exhaustion. The weight of it all coming down on us.

But we could not give up, no matter how hopeless it seemed.

We would fight until the end.

"Don't lose hope," I shouted. "Pull in tighter. They will not break us."

All around me, the soldiers rallied, seeming to come out of their shock as the new wave of hunters approached. We braced ourselves for impact.

But as the hunters approached, their spells glowing in their rotting hands, they did not aim for me or the soldiers in the center of the circle.

Instead, their spells hit targets that screamed in confusion and pain as they turned away from us.

Hunters turned on hunters as screams shook the air

around us, the sound nearly a tangible thing as it vibrated in my skull.

At first, I thought surely it had been some mistake. Some miscalculation.

But my mouth fell open, and my breath hitched in my chest as a hunter with a ruby amulet around her neck moved past me to grab the head of a diamond hunter between her bony fingertips. She growled low in her throat as a pulsing red energy rattled the skull of the diamond hunter until it broke into a thousand pieces in her hand.

The ruby hunter turned to me, and I lifted my scimitar in defense, ready to strike, but she shook her head and bowed to me, slightly.

I stumbled backward, spinning on the battlefield as I took in the scene.

Ruby hunters now outnumbered the rest, and the tide was turning.

"Kill the diamonds," I shouted. "Ruby is our ally."

Cheers and shouts of surprise and elation rang through the hills as I set my sights on the portal fifty yards away.

"No," I whispered, watching as another tendril of purple mist snapped into place. There were only three demons left to connect.

The ritual was almost complete, and there were still eight amethyst hunters guarding the portal and the demons.

There wasn't enough time.

But I had to try.

I ran toward a group of soldiers and thrust my weapon toward the portal. "Take out those hunters," I cried. "The ritual is almost complete."

Another amethyst tendril snapped into place, and only two free demons remained.

I shifted and flew toward the hunters.

We needed to take them down and destroy the black roses holding that portal open. It was our only chance, but a handful of us against eight was too dangerous. I didn't know if we could make it.

I had almost reached the hunters when a bright light emerged from the darkness behind me. I turned to see the golem rise over the hills, led by a streak of dark smoke as Aerden flew toward us.

I had no idea where he'd been taken or how he'd gotten free, but I had never been so happy to see someone in my life.

"The portal," I shouted, hoping somehow, he could hear me. "We have to close the portal."

The golem shifted direction and aimed for the hunters surrounding Andros and the others.

The hunters' faces showed fear in the light of the strange being, and they moved together, pilling on to him, attacking the golem with fire and poison and ice, focusing their attacks in a way I'd never seen from a group of hunters.

With each attack, the light of the golem seemed to dim, black spots appearing throughout its body as it absorbed all the attacks.

Aerden took solid form and charged at the hunters, but as the attacks landed on the golem, they seemed to also land on Aerden.

He stumbled, doubling over. He forced himself upright only to stumble again.

I shifted and flew to his side, but he pushed a hand out toward me and met my eyes.

"Stop that ritual," he said. "I'll hold them off as long as I can."

I backed away, seeing the determination in his eyes and knowing he was right. Another tendril had snapped into place, and we had run out of time.

A single demon remained. Seconds until Andros was trapped inside the body of a witch and the portal closed to our advances.

I gripped both my scimitar and flew toward the now-unguarded portal as the battle raged around me. Light flashed across the sky as I reared back and sliced through the stems of the black roses that created the portal to the human world.

A swirling darkness spread across part of the portal, blocking its light.

The darkness spread with each of my wild slashes, as I desperately swung my weapons at the roses.

Two more soldiers joined me, their swords seeking out what-ever roses were still left intact, and the portal closed a little more.

"Hurry," I shouted, tears of exhaustion and need flowing down my cheeks.

I gave that moment everything I had, thinking of the lives that had been lost and those who could still be saved.

A small tendril of purple mist snaked through the edge of the portal, seeking the final demon to complete the ritual.

But I would not let this happen. I would never give up until there was nothing of me left to give.

I sliced through the final cluster of black roses just as the mist snapped toward the final demon. The portal closed in an instant, severing each strand of purple mist and setting the forty demons free.

More soldiers from the battlefield rushed to the demons, breaking their silver chains and handing them weapons to join the fight.

I fell to my knees, my weapons falling to the ground at my side. I cried out through my pain and exhaustion as Andros, one of my dearest friends, stepped forward, and took one fallen weapon in his hand.

"I knew you would come," he said, placing a hand on the back of my head and pressing his forehead to mine. "You are a true warrior. A true queen. Let's finish this, my friend."

He stood with the scimitar raised to the sky as I took my bow from its holster and found the strength to stand, despite the pain.

Andros and his elite squad raised their voices in a battle cry of freedom and then shifted, soaring across the battlefield to face the diamond hunters who remained.

I conjured a set of deadly arrows and turned my aim on the two hunters who still worked to take down Aerden's golem. Both my arrows met their mark, and the hunters screamed, clawing at their throats as the poison spread through their system.

Aerden shifted and flew to my side as we pushed forward, exhausted but alive.

Injured but victorious.

We fought until there was no one left to fight, the battlefield littered with the bodies of fallen soldiers and hunters, their blood mingling in the dirt.

Fifty ruby hunters remained, and Andros tensed as they turned toward the five hundred of us who had survived. I grabbed his arm and shook my head.

"Thank you," I said to the hunters, lowering my head in an acknowledgement of what they had done for us.

The battlefield was silent as the hunters all turned and bowed their heads in unison before turning to fade off into the darkness.

For the first time ever, I saw in them the faces of those women they used to be. Women who had wanted something better for their lives and had been pulled into an organization they did not understand until it was too late.

Women who had dared to speak up for themselves or their families.

Women who had refused to obey when their conscience would not allow it.

They had been punished for their fight against the Order. Turned into these rotting, immortal beings, doomed to seek out demons as prey and deliver them to their Primas.

But today, I honored them for who they used to be.

For who they might have been.

I had no idea how she'd called them to our aid or why she'd joined our fight, but the ruby priestess had saved our lives tonight. Her actions would not erase the sins of her past, but it would be something this world would never forget.

Andros put his arm around my shoulders and pulled me close. His wife, Ourelia, stood at his side, her arm around his waist.

In all the years I'd known him, I had never seen him cry. He was one of the strongest, most defiant demons I'd ever known, and as we watched the souls of the fallen rise toward their journey into the Afterworld, tears of gratitude slid down his war-weathered face.

"You honor me," he whispered, and the words were

repeated on the lips of all those who stood as witnesses to this moment.

And when the last of the fallen had parted from this world, we gathered our injured and our weapons and began our own journey back to the domed city, our thoughts turned toward those whose battle still raged on.

WE DESERVED THAT LIFE

HARPER

I pushed against the wave of darkness that tried to pull me under.

If I lost consciousness completely, I would most likely never wake up.

"Jackson's going to kill you," I said, fighting against the unbearable pain. Deep gashes ran down my legs. I needed to find a way to stop this bleeding. "How could you do this to your own brother?"

Illana cut her eyes toward me, a malicious smile on her face. "Jackson will be a blubbering mess," she said. "He'll need a shoulder to cry on, just like when you disappeared before. Harper taken from Winterhaven and miraculously rescued, only to disappear from Blackwood, never to be seen again."

What was she doing over there?

Illana had shut the door to the gathering room, using some kind of shield to block it. Now, she was standing in the center of the room, setting stones on the floor. I couldn't focus enough to tell exactly what she was doing.

Making a pentagram?

What the hell?

I closed my eyes against the pain and a wave of dizziness nearly knocked me to the floor again.

I can't pass out. I have to hold on.

If I could just reach the communication stones in my pocket, I could call for help. Or at the very least, tell him what happened. Make sure he doesn't let Illana back into my damn castle.

Say goodbye to him before it's too late.

"All this time, you've been working for her? For the High Priestess?" I asked. "Just like your mother?"

Her eyes widened, and she stood. "How do you know about my mother's relationship with the High Priestess?"

She had a diamond ritual dagger in her hand—something I unfortunately had not noticed before I started taunting her— and she pointed the tip down at me.

"It's that stupid key, isn't it?" she asked, bringing the point of that dagger closer than I was comfortable with, considering I already had cuts that were deep enough to end my life if they weren't dealt with soon. "I told Mother that key would be the end to us all, but no, she just had to give it to Aerden. She just had to try to save his life. Then, he went and gave it to the princess. All that sacrifice for nothing. He wasn't supposed to spend eternity in a witch's body, but what could the High Priestess do once he'd been taken? Tell me that. It wasn't like she could just release one of her own gates. Not even for us."

Us? Who else in her family was working for the High Priestess? From the sound of it, they had some kind of relationship that went beyond just a key.

What was going on with them? Just how far had Jackson's family gone down this path? And why?

I needed to keep her talking. If, by some miracle, I did manage to survive this, I wanted to know how she was tied to the High Priestess.

I also needed to find the strength to get to the stones in my pockets.

Jackson's stone. Which pocket was that in again? Right or left?

I couldn't seem to remember through my daze.

God, my legs hurt. I'd never seen a spell that could slash through a person like that. Had she poisoned me, too? Was I dying?

"Why would you guys work for the High Priestess? Demons working for a witch who kills demons? It doesn't make any sense," I said. "You're all crazy."

Illana moved something across the room and crouched low to study it. She seemed to change her mind and moved the item again.

"The High Priestess is not a witch," she said, laughing. "Everyone assumes she is. Even the lesser priestesses, I think. Just because she uses witches does not mean she is one."

My stomach rolled with nausea, but I held on, taking slow breaths and trying to focus.

"The priestesses don't know who the High Priestess is?" I asked. That came as a surprise. How did you join a cult where you didn't even know whether the leader was a witch or a demon? And why would a demon do this to her kingdom? To her people?

"Of course they don't," Illana said. "She's been very good at keeping her identity secret. I've learned so much from her, really. Once you learn how to properly manipulate people, you can let them do most of the dirty work for you."

She glanced at me, pointing the dagger my way again.

"I'm hoping you're my ticket to being done with the grunt work," she said. "Once she has you, she'll reward me for sure. No more spying and pretending to be something I'm not. You're a major prize, and I can't wait until she sees what I've done."

She turned away, and I slowly reached into my pocket and grabbed the stones inside.

I pulled them out as slowly as I could, praying she wouldn't notice me. She was so wrapped up in whatever it was she was building over there, she didn't seem to be at all concerned about what I might try to do.

She hadn't even bothered to take away my sword. Not that I could do much with it lying on the floor.

Three stones in this pocket. One a small ruby communication stone. Jackson's, I was almost certain.

Two others were diamonds. Small bombs that I could set with a timer, but Magda hadn't told me yet the spell to set them. The only way to use them now would be to detonate them instantly with the right spell word and die at the same time.

I wasn't quite ready to give up.

If I could separate myself from the pain, I might still have some hope of shifting to my shadow form and flying out of this place.

I had a feeling I very much needed to be gone before she was done setting up whatever little altar or makeshift ritual she had going on there.

I glanced at the stones in my hand. If I contacted Jackson,

Illana would just take the stone the second he answered. I wouldn't have time to tell him anything significant before she shut us off.

There had to be something I could do, though. This couldn't be the end. Not yet.

"When you came to stay with us at Brighton Manor, you were captured by the emerald priestess," I said. "Why would your High Priestess let that happen to you. Do you really think she's watching out for you? Is that really the kind of demon you want to place your loyalty with?"

Illana laughed, a low sound that vibrated in her chest.

She placed something on the floor and stood. The satisfied look in her eye as she studied the stones on the floor put terror in my heart. If she was done fooling with those things, that meant she was going to use them.

For what?

"I never said the High Priestess was a demon, either," she said, her eyes practically sparkling with the thought. "And she arranged for the emerald priestess to have me. It was a trap to lure you all in. She needed my ability to reach out to you in dreams so that you'd come for me. It wasn't too hard, but unfortunately, that night did not at all end as planned."

"No, it didn't," I said sadly, thinking of all the heartache we'd been through since that night.

And all the heartache to come.

My head dipped as I struggled to stay awake. To stay alive.

I had to do something. I wasn't sure how much longer I could hold on.

"Of course, tonight might rival that one for devastation when it comes to your little Demon Liberation Movement," she said with a laugh that made me want to find the strength to get up and punch her in her stupid face. "From the sound of it, things weren't going too well for Lea and Aerden, either. Such a pity, too, when you guys must have gone to so much trouble to tell me the wrong plan."

"We didn't know it was you," I said. "We didn't know anyone had betrayed us for sure. Not until tonight. We had to be sure."

"And now, they'll all assume it was poor Magda who betrayed them all," Illana said. "She was always one of the weakest of the five. I don't think her sisters will be that devastated to see her go."

I shook my head. "Another priestess dead is still a victory," I said. "And if Lea can get through that portal tonight, maybe she'll put an end to Priestess Black. Then what will you and your High Priestess have? Citrine? That's all?"

"You are so human, Harper." Illana shook her head, frowning at me. "Your mind is too small to grasp the big picture. But you'll understand soon enough."

I dragged myself backward on the floor, just needing to get away from that sudden look in her eye that said she was about to do very bad things.

My heart tightened in my chest, and I pushed through the pain to reach for my power. If I could just connect to it for a moment, I could silence the incoming sound on that stone. Jackson could hear me, even if I couldn't hear him.

I couldn't die tonight and leave him alone, never knowing what happened.

Never knowing his own sister was working for the High Priestess.

And his mother.

I closed my eyes and tried to draw energy from my source.

The well of power that lived deep inside me. I could feel it there, still flowing. But when I reached for it, the pain blocked me.

And I'd lost so much blood.

My vision blurred, but I fought so hard against it. Deep breaths.

I felt like I had been here before.

Visions of Priestess Winter dragging me down the hallway, my blood streaking down the hallway, swirled through my mind.

I would not go through that again.

I couldn't.

As Illana turned to move one stone on the floor to another location, I surrendered to the thought of death. I let go of all the fight and the tension. I submitted to the pain, just letting it be a part of me. I stopped pushing against it and just felt it.

Tear rolled down my cheeks as I reached for my power again, releasing all the barriers and tapping into the essence of who I truly was, deep down.

A trickle of energy flowed through me. I tried to shift, but there was not enough left in me to escape. I could try to fight with this tiny bit of hope, or I could use what little power I had left to warn the ones I loved.

I focused on covering the ruby stone with a one-way sound barrier, careful to make sure that no sound could escape into this room, but that everything that happened here could be heard on the other side.

When the spell was in place, I placed my trembling finger over the stone, praying for the red light within to form.

I lowered the stone to my side and placed it under my leg to try to shield the light.

Please, Jackson. I just need you to know. There's still so much I need to say.

The light clicked on inside the stone, and I pressed my lips together, holding back a sob. I would have given anything to hear his voice right now, but it was enough just to know he was there.

"Illana, I don't understand how you could do this to me," I said. "You're crazy if you think Jackson and Aerden won't find out. You can't kill me and get away with this."

"Hush, now," she said, stepping over to me and running the tip of the ritual dagger across my forehead, just soft enough not to draw blood. "I never said anything about killing you, Harper. After what you've done to the Order of Shadows, the High Priestess has plans that will have you begging for death before it's all over. Now, hush. I don't want you dying on me before the ritual is complete."

Her words chilled me to the core.

I'd survived so much torture at the hands of the emerald priestess. I knew I was strong, but how strong would I have to be to survive the next thing? And the next?

Part of me wanted to give up right there, but I thought of the demon I loved on the other side of that stone, listening. He would want me to fight, no matter what.

"What ritual?" I asked. "We're in the basement of Blackwood, Illana, just steps away from the priestess's ritual room. What do you think you're planning to do down here with a pile of rocks?"

I tried to give as much information to Jackson as I could without making Illana suspicious, and just knowing he was there kept me alert and awake.

"I'm almost there," she said. "It's always so tricky to get the angles just right, but I think I've almost got it."

She moved one of the stones—possibly an emerald, though it was hard to tell from here—a little to the left and laughed, turning in a circle.

"Here we go," she said, flashing an excited look toward me. "I can't wait for you to meet the High Priestess. I know she's going to be very excited to meet you."

My body started trembling, whether from fear or shock, I wasn't sure.

Illana stepped into the center of the pentagram she'd drawn on the floor with a series of stones and rocks. She lifted her arms on either side of her body and let her head fall back, eyes toward the ceiling.

She began to speak in a language I had never heard before. Nothing from the Latin phrases of the Order's rituals.

This was...ancient.

The power of the words vibrated through the room as a cool wind seemed to blow around us. Illana's dark hair lifted from her shoulders, and her breathing intensified as she spoke.

A shimmering light appeared in front of her body.

A light I recognized. It was exactly the same as the one Magda had been pulled through from my dungeons. Illana was taking me to the High Priestess and that strange onyx chamber.

That place is where the Order of Shadows was born.

I reached for any hope of power. I couldn't be handed over to this woman, whoever she was.

I may have been half human, but I was also half demon. That meant she could trap me inside the body of a witch, just like she'd done to Aerden and so many thousands of others.

I didn't want to live like that.

But I could not find my power. Maybe the smallest trickle, but whatever she'd done to my legs, she'd poisoned me or numbed my power in some way. Cut me off from the source of that energy.

I looked down at the ruby stone, trying to think of something I could tell Jackson. Something that might save me now, but the light of the stone went dark.

Either the magic that held it open was gone, or Jackson's stone had been broken.

I closed my eyes, fighting against the tears and hopelessness that threatened to fill me with darkness.

I should have married him when I had the chance. Why hadn't I just said yes? We could have been married in the throne room this morning.

Had he known something like this was going to happen?

I had to get back to him. I still wanted the chance to marry him. To have a life with him.

I had faced the impossible before and survived. As long as I was still alive and still fighting, there was hope. I would not give up.

I couldn't stand, and I couldn't shift. I had no access to my power, and I was alone here in the basement, separated from any allies by armies of witches and hunters on both sides.

There had to be something I could do, though. I just needed to think.

I moved to put the ruby communication stone in my pocket, wondering if I should try Aerden's or Mary Anne's when my finger brushed against the two small diamonds I'd placed there before we left the castle.

Chills ran across my skin, and I looked up at Illana.

She seemed to be locked in some kind of trance as the

portal formed in front of her. The onyx ritual room was beginning to take shape on the other side.

The room where the Order of Shadows was born.

The room where the High Priestess would come to meet me. To torture me.

My lips parted, and I clutched the stones in my hand as tears sprang to my eyes.

My heart ached, and I wanted to push away the thought. To pretend it had not come to me. To hope for something different.

But I knew what I had to do.

A calmness settled over me then.

I closed my eyes and pictured that beautiful little boy with the silver eyes playing on the grass in front of me. If I tried, I could almost hear the sound of his laughter and smell the scent of his hair. I could feel him in my arms.

And for a moment, I let myself be in that place. That future place where the war was over, and the Order of Shadows was destroyed. Where Jackson and I sat in the gardens with our son, our whole lives stretched out in front of us.

A peaceful life, surrounded by love.

We deserved that life.

Everyone did.

With one moment of sacrifice, I could give the gift of life to so many who had suffered.

I wanted to fight for my future, but if she took me through that portal, I would find the courage to end it all.

WITHERED

JACKSON

The light inside the ruby stone dimmed and blinked out.

Rage and fear warred inside me, and I threw the stone as far as I could.

My own sister had betrayed us all. I was heartbroken and sick, and I was not going to let her take Harper.

I had to get inside.

I turned to the builders and witches, who were winding down their attacks after Aerden's news that Andros had been saved. We'd been preparing to retreat, but I was waiting for final word from Harper that she'd either killed the priestess or gotten to safety.

Now, though, I needed them to hit that freaking house with everything they had.

"One final attack," I shouted. "Make this one the biggest yet. I have to get inside that house."

"What's happened?" Mary Anne asked, touching my arm.

"Illana betrayed us. She has Harper trapped inside," I said.

"She's trying to open a portal to take Harper to the High Priestess. I have to get inside now, if I have to fight my way through two hundred witches."

Essex shook his head.

"You will not have time to fight," he said. 'We will be getting you inside."

He shouted something to the builders, who nodded.

"We hit them with the hardest attack of all," he said. "You fly in the shadows of the largest boulder. We aim for second floor. No one will see you go."

I wanted to kiss him. "Essex, you're brilliant," I said. "Do it, now."

The entire team of witches and demons prepared for the largest attack yet. The ultimate diversion.

I climbed onto the back of the trebuchet, tensed and ready to shift.

The builder met my eyes. "Waiting for you," he said. "I'll aim for the second-floor windows."

I took a deep breath. This had to work.

"When I'm safely inside, I want you guys to retreat," I said. "You have to make it home. Promise me you won't risk your lives to go inside to get me."

"We'll go," Mary Anne said, but from the way she looked at Essex, I wasn't sure I believed her.

I looked forward, determination in my eyes. I would not let her be taken again.

"Now," I shouted.

The attack began, spells and arrows, trees and boulders, every bit of power we had left flew toward the fortress. As soon as the catapult took off, I shifted, pushing my speed to stay in the shadow of the huge boulder as it soared through the air.

The rock crashed into the second floor, widening an already-gaping hole we'd knocked through the wall.

Once inside, I flew through the hall, down the steps, and into the basement as fast as I could, not even caring at this point if any of the witches inside saw me. I would deal with them if it came to it.

The basement level was empty except for one woman.

Magda Thorn was throwing just about everything she had at a door in the main hallway. I shifted to solid form, and she jumped, grabbing a magical flame in her hand until she realized it was me.

"Harper's trapped inside," she said. "I can feel the energy shifting, Jackson. Something's happening."

"It's my sister," I said. "Illana's the one who's been telling the High Priestess all our plans. We have to get in there. She's planning to take Harper to that ritual room you were in before. With the onyx columns and the stones."

"No," she said, shaking her head and throwing more force at the doorway. "She'll never survive it. The High Priestess will have no mercy."

I rammed into the side of the door, but something was blocking it. A magical barrier unlike any I had felt before.

I would have given anything for a boulder to just bust through the wall itself right now, but there wasn't enough room in the small hallway to get any leverage.

I pressed a hand to the door, hoping to turn the entire area to ice and break it down. I'd used that trick before, but this time, the ice wouldn't stay. It seemed to melt instantly.

Fire wouldn't work, either.

Nothing seemed to be damaging that door, and we were running out of time.

"Stand back," I said.

I didn't even know what I intended to do, only that the woman I loved more than life itself was on the other side of that door, and I was not about to let her slip away again. I was not going to let anyone else hurt her.

I had spent a hundred years searching for my brother, losing myself in the process and nearly giving up all hope of ever truly living again.

But the moment Harper had come into my life, I had been reborn.

She had given me a reason to live and taught me that love is always worth fighting for, no matter how hopeless or dark it might seem.

She had also taught me that as long as you believe in something with all your heart, there is nothing that can stand in your way.

And I believed we were meant to be together forever.

That we were meant to survive this war together.

I did not have the promise of a vision to lean on, but I knew my love for her. And that was enough.

I stepped back, reaching deep within my soul.

Past all my fears. Past every doubt and every pain.

I reached down into that place where love is truly all there is. Where love is the only thing worth living for. Worth fighting for.

A power I'd never known filled my body, and I acted on instinct, stepping forward and punching my fist forward toward that door.

A bright, blue light formed around my fist, making it appear to be five times the size. It slammed against the door, crushing it into pieces that scattered across the floor of the gathering room.

"Jackson," Harper screamed as her body disappeared through a portal of shimmering light.

I reached out and wrapped the light around her, as if taking her in my own hands, and pulled her toward me.

Illana's head whipped around from inside the portal, anger flashing in her eyes as Harper was ripped from her magical grasp. She gathered a glowing light in her own hands and stepped forward, but as she moved, a huge gust of wind pushed her backward.

I looked over to see the ruby priestess with tornados dancing on her fingertips.

"The stones," she shouted. "Break the pentagram stones on the floor. Quickly."

I pulled back and sent the powerful blue light toward the portal, focusing the strength of my power on the stones Illana had used to summon the portal. Inside, she struggled against the wind, pushing back with a mighty power of her own.

The summoning stones resisted even the power of the light, but I'd hit them with enough force to send a few of them rolling across the room.

"It's closing," Harper shouted, leaning against me.

The shimmering light shrunk to almost nothing, with Illana still shouting and struggling on the other side.

At the last minute, just before the portal slimmed to nothing, Harper cried out and stepped forward, throwing a tiny diamond through the air.

The moment the stone hit Illana's chest, Harper's eyes locked forward, a determination inside that showed no fear. Only strength.

"Detonate," she said.

The bomb exploded just as the portal snapped closed, cutting off my sister's dying scream.

Harper collapsed against me. There was blood everywhere, and her legs were cut to pieces.

I gently lowered her to the floor. I wasn't sure I had enough power to heal her completely, but I could ease her pain.

She looked up at me, her brown eyes clear and full of love.

"You came for me," she whispered, lifting her hand to my cheek.

She winced as I placed a hand on the first gash and let my healing powers flow into her. She gasped and then relaxed when I moved onto the next. I didn't know if it was the strange, blue light or the tighter connection to my power, but my healing was stronger than ever.

When I was finished, there were still pink wounds on her legs, but the deep gashes were gone, and she could stand on her own.

To my surprise, Magda threw her arms around Harper's neck.

"Thank you for believing in me," she said. "It's been a very long time since anyone trusted me the way you did today."

Harper took her hand. "Lea?" she asked.

Magda looked to me, and I nodded.

"They saved Andros," I said. "Apparently, just when all hope seemed lost, a huge group of ruby hunters joined the fight."

"You really did help them," Harper said to Magda. "Thank you."

"I hate to break up the miniature celebration here, but we still have to get out of this house without losing our lives," I said, thinking about the hundreds of witches still guarding the door.

If my small group had left or the amethyst priestess had recovered from the loss of the ritual, they could be flooding back into the house any second now.

"We need to move," I said.

"I may have that covered, too," Magda said, peering out into the hallway.

She smiled as more than a dozen witches ran toward us, magic glowing on their fingertips.

"You ready to go?" A witch with ebony skin and dark eyes held her hand out toward Magda. "We've cleared a straight line out to the Hall of Doorways."

Magda took the woman's hand and squeezed. "Thank you, Issa," she said. "Come on. We need to get Harper out of here."

"Wait," Harper said, glancing toward the end of the hallway. "We have to kill the amethyst priestess. She'll be weakened after the ritual failed. We can't just leave without trying. She's right there."

I opened my mouth to protest when Mary Anne came rushing down the steps of the basement.

"Something's happened," she yelled.

"How did you get down here?" I asked.

Had the ruby witches killed all of the amethyst forces that quickly? How did Mary Anne get through their massive line of defense?

Her eyes were wide, but she paused, as if she wasn't sure how to explain it.

"They just all fell," Essex said. "As if they dried up."

"Who?" Harper asked.

"All the amethyst witches that were guarding the house,"

Mary Anne said. "One second we were fighting and the next, they all just seemed to stagger forward and fall. They look..."

"Withered?" Magda asked quietly.

Mary Anne nodded.

Magda shook her head. "You won't kill the amethyst priestess tonight."

"No," Harper shouted, running down the hall to the ritual room.

She threw open the door and gasped.

I stepped forward, bringing a hand to my mouth in shock.

The room was empty except for the bodies of forty women dressed in flowing purple robes.

Tonight, they had come here for glory and greed, hoping to get a second chance at joining the Order of Shadows.

Instead, they lay dead on the floor, their dry, withered skin tight against their bones, as if they had been mummified.

As if their life had been sucked out of them in an instant, fuel for a desperate witch determined to survive.

The amethyst priestess was gone.

THE SEA OF GLASS

LEA

At dawn, we gathered in the castle of the domed city. We had lost too many, but we had survived the night.

No, more than survived. We fought with our whole hearts. We dealt another huge blow to the Order of Shadows.

And as I got my first look at the ruby priestess, I realized we had gained a true ally.

I still wanted to know why she turned on the Order she had helped to create, but there would be time for questions later. For now, we vowed to do what we could to protect her.

There was no doubt the High Priestess would come for her again. Possibly for her entire coven.

While some in our group worked to keep freeing the emerald gates, others would now be tasked with protecting and hiding any ruby witch who chose to side with us. We were so close now to this dream of defeating the Order, but the closer we got to the truth, the more desperate and difficult this war would become.

We would suffer many more losses, and we would risk our lives again and again.

But there was hope now that someday, we would emerge from battle victorious, able to hang up our swords and bows for a while as we live in peace.

As we rebuild the lands that have been lost.

While our soldiers rested for the journey home, Jackson and Harper called Aerden and me into the war room to talk. There was still so much to sort through. So many questions left unanswered.

How had the High Priestess known to send diamond hunters to the portal in the Shadow World? Illana didn't know that part of the plan, so she couldn't have told her.

"I think it was our mother," Aerden said sadly. "I genuinely hoped she might be a victim in all this. That she'd just been trying to protect me the whole time, but after what Harper told me about Illana, I'm not so sure. My mother came to visit me just before we left the castle. We hugged, and I think it was the first time we'd touched in ages. Later, I found this on my clothing."

He brought a very small diamond out of the bag. A tracking stone.

"I got the feeling Illana and your mother had been working with the High Priestess for a long time," Harper said. "Maybe Orian, too."

"But why?" Jackson asked, running a hand through his hair. "What reason would they have to destroy our kingdom and support an organization that gives power to human witches? It makes no sense to me at all."

"Magda says the true purpose for the Order of Shadows goes much deeper than we ever thought," Harper said. "She's promised to tell me about it soon, but whatever it is, the truth of it scares her enough to want out."

"Maybe Tatiana can give us some of the answers," I said.

"She's going to be devastated Illana is gone," Jackson said.

Harper put her hand on Jackson's, and for the first time since I'd known her, the sight of them together didn't break my heart. It made me happy that they'd found each other.

It was a funny thing to learn the truth after all this time. As the days went on, I found it comforting. As if this great puzzle of my life had finally been solved. It didn't make it hurt any less. Not exactly.

But it made sense now, in a way it never had before.

Before I knew the truth, I saw Harper as someone who had stolen from me. Someone who had secretly given Jackson something I hadn't been able to give. I couldn't see past my resentment and my own feelings of not living up to whatever it was he wanted or needed in a mate.

But now, I realized she had stolen nothing.

I hadn't lost Jackson's love to her, because it was never mine to begin with.

It was a strangely liberating thought.

And there was no doubt in my mind now of Harper's strength and heart.

She had cuts and bruises all over her body, but she'd been ready to do whatever she had to do. She had risked so much to save us all.

I wasn't exactly ready to admit I liked her, but I admired her.

And I was glad she was home.

"I'm sorry," Harper said, squeezing Jackson's hand. "To be betrayed by your family like this is devastating, and I'm sorry I killed her. I didn't feel I had a choice. I still can't believe we didn't see it before."

"Do you think the bomb you threw destroyed that room, too?" Jackson asked.

He'd told us about the onyx ritual room, but I still didn't know exactly how it all fit in.

"I doubt it," Harper said. "I don't know that Illana could have survived it, but I have a feeling that room is pretty resilient. Magically reinforced the way most of the portal stones are."

"Except twice as much, I would guess," Aerden said. "The diamond you mentioned in the center of the room? It has to be important. I think we need to focus on figuring out what that diamond does. Where it came from."

My stomach tightened.

I knew what he was thinking, and I didn't want to admit just how much I didn't want him to go.

"Tell him about Sabine," I said, tilting my head toward Jackson.

Aerden hadn't wanted to mention the fae around anyone else, but now that it was just the four of us, it was something we needed to talk about before we left.

He told them about the strange cage with its shifting colors and ability to block off the source of his magic.

"I could still feel that my magic was there," he said. "But I just couldn't use it at all. It was very similar to being trapped inside a witch's body or left in any dungeon that has magical barriers. But it was just different in a way I can't quite put words to."

"How did you get out of there?" Harper asked. "You said four hunters were guarding you?"

"When those diamond hunters arrived, they came straight for me, before they even attacked the soldiers," he said. "I thought about it a lot on the way here from the battlefield. I think the High Priestess knew what I'd done to Kael and didn't want me to be able to do it again with her hunters. I think whatever that cage was it was meant to keep me from accessing that light."

"He was freed by a fairy named Sabine," I said.

I had never met the fae myself, but I had heard of her She was legend.

Jackson sucked in a surprised breath, and Harper straightened, her eyes wide.

"You know of her?" Aerden asked. "I had never heard of her at all, but she mentioned you."

Aerden pulled a piece of paper from his pocket and handed it to his brother.

"She said this was for you."

Jackson glanced nervously at Harper, his hands trembling just a little as he held the piece of paper.

"What?" Harper asked, tensing.

"I should have told you when you first got home, but you know that Sabine was the one who opened that portal for me," Jackson said to her. "The one I needed to bring you home."

Harper nodded. and I wondered what he was about to tell her that had him so afraid.

"Sabine's help almost always comes at a high price," Jackson said. "When I made it to her through the Swamp of Nightmares, she only asked for one thing."

"What?" Harper asked, her eyes dropping to the piece of paper.

"She wanted my ability to see visions of the future,"

Jackson said. "And with that, every vision I had ever seen would be no longer guaranteed to me. Including the one I gave you back in Peachville."

Harper's eyes closed briefly as she took a breath. Tears gathered in her eyes, but she did not let them fall.

I couldn't believe Jackson had given up such a rare ability, but if he hadn't done that, how would Harper have ever gotten home?

"Thank you," she said, finally leaning against him and putting her head on his shoulder. "Thank you for doing that for me, even though I know it must have been difficult."

"What's on the paper?" Jackson asked, looking to Aerden.

"Look for yourself," he said.

Of course, since Sabine had not told us we couldn't look at it, Aerden and I had already taken a peek of the drawing on the way here, so I already knew what had Jackson's eyes so wide now.

Harper and I shared a look, too.

On the paper was a ship heading toward The Storm. Aerden and Jackson stood on the ship, looking toward the darkness.

"What does this mean?" she asked.

"I think it means we're taking a trip across the sea," Aerden said. "But first, we need to get our soldiers home, and we need to talk to our mother. She has to know who the High Priestess is, and I intend to find out how she and Illana got roped into working for her."

"She'll probably just lie to you," Jackson said. "She's good at that."

"Then I'll keep asking," Aerden said. "Maybe we'll have the king throw her in the dungeons."

Maybe soon I'll have the authority to do it myself.

"We should really get going," I said. "It's a long journey home, and we have so much to do."

"What will you do about the Stone Guardians in the basement?" Harper asked. "Is there anything we can do to help with that?"

I thought about it for a minute. There was something I'd been wondering about, but I didn't know if it would work.

"The dome here works to keep people out," I said, "but do you think Willow and your shielders could build a similar barrier that might keep the Stone Guardians trapped inside? That way, if they do happen to wake up at some point, they would be stuck there, unable to use magic?"

Harper thought about it for a second and nodded. "We can certainly ask her," she said. "Willow knows a lot more about shielding magic than just about anyone I've ever known. If she can help you, I know she will."

"Thank you. I'll talk to my father about it, and if Willow thinks she can help, maybe we can have her come stay in the King's City for a while."

It was funny talking to Harper about kingdom business.

The summer we'd lived together at Brighton Manor, we'd all practically felt like kids, training and playing, freeing gates and having adventures.

But now, we were both queens.

Or close to it, anyway.

Soon, we would both be rulers, but I hoped that didn't mean our time for play and laughter and training was gone completely.

"You'll be back, then?" Jackson asked. "After you've talked to Mother?"

Aerden looked to me, and I nodded. We had already discussed the plan, even if I wasn't excited about it.

"Not back here," he said. "We'll meet at the docks in Jorna, just off the Black Cliffs. We'll arrange for one of the king's ships to take us to The Storm. And possibly beyond, if we can find our way."

Harper met my eyes again, and for a moment, we truly understood each other in a way I didn't think we ever would.

Neither of us wanted to be separated from the demon we loved.

And this time, it wasn't the same demon.

"When?" Jackson asked.

"A week?"

Jackson nodded. "I'll see you there, brother."

We said goodbye to them and to the rest of our friends in the Southern Kingdom, and we led our soldiers home. The journey was not too long, but I found myself thinking how cool it would be to see if Sabine might make us our own Hall of Doorways. A portal to use to travel between our two castles whenever we wanted.

Of course, according to Jackson, Sabine's price might be too steep to pay.

My father welcomed us back to the city, and I finally had the pleasure of introducing him to the future Captain of the Queen's Guard.

Andros bowed to my father—something I never thought I'd see my entire life—and my father invited him into his office to talk for a while.

Aerden and I excused ourselves and went straight to Tatiana's chambers. I wasn't sure how we would break the news to her of Illana's death, but I found myself reaching for my magic as we approached her door. I had no idea what she might do when she saw us or found out we knew about her involvement with the High Priestess.

When we reached her rooms, Aerden knocked several times, and I waited at his side, anxious to fit this next piece of the puzzle together.

We were definitely close to discovering something important. I could feel the truth just ahead of us, right around the next corner. Something that would change the entire war. Change everything we believed to be true about the Order of Shadows.

But at the same time, I could feel the High Priestess breathing down my neck, chasing me.

Chasing all of us.

We had to move quickly.

"Mother," Aerden said, leaning close to the door. "I need to talk to you. Are you in there?"

After a moment, he turned and shook his head.

"I don't think she's here. She should be in her chambers this late, but maybe—"

I gripped his arm, my eyes growing wide.

"What?" he asked. "Lea, what is it?"

I inhaled, the scent of sulfur strong here beside the door.

I remembered that smell from the vision I'd had in the abandoned wing. The one with the white-cloaked woman.

"We have to get inside," I said. I reached for the door handle and cried out as the metal burned my palm. It was so hot. "Knock it down. Aerden, we have to get in there."

"Back up," he shouted.

I moved out of the way, and Aerden took several steps back. A shimmering light appeared in front of him like a shield, and he ran forward, putting the force of all his magic behind the movement.

The door flew off its hinges and white-hot flames erupted from the room, knocking us both backward into the hallway.

"Mother," Aerden shouted, rushing toward the room.

I scrambled toward him, yanking him back, out of the flames.

"It's too late," I said, shaking my head.

I pulled him to me as he struggled to break free.

"We need answers," he said, throwing his arms around me. "I need to know why."

But when the flames subsided, it was exactly the same as the other room. The furniture, rugs, and curtains all looked completely untouched, but there was a long scar on the wall, like a wound that would never heal.

And there, on the floor in a pile, as if it had simply been discarded and forgotten, was a blue dress.

Tatiana was dead.

The High Priestess had gotten to her first.

Over the next few hours, we discovered Orian and Aerden's father had also been killed in similar fires. We might never know if she killed them as retribution for Illana's failure or as a way to protect her own identity, but it was difficult to watch Aerden struggle with the loss of almost his entire family.

"I already lost them once," he told us a week later, shaking his head as he loaded his bags onto the Wind Dancer—one of the finest ships in my father's fleet. "I guess part of me had really hoped we could be a true family again."

"We're your family now," Harper said, putting her arms around him.

And it was true.

Somewhere in the middle of all this, we had become a part of one another the way only families were.

I longed to tell him how I felt, but I still wasn't sure how much I had to offer him right now. He was leaving on a dangerous journey to look for a forgotten continent across the Sea of Glass, and I had a kingdom to rule.

What if we had already missed our chance long ago?

I didn't have the answers, but I knew that when he stepped onto that ship, I didn't want him to leave. I wanted to pull him into my arms and ask him to stay by my side.

Instead, I stepped back as the crewman prepared to cast off.

"Wait," someone shouted, and a figure appeared at the end of the dock, hiding something behind his back.

"Rend," Harper said, running to throw her arms around him. "We were so worried about you. We heard the news about Franki. I still can't believe it."

"I'm just glad you're both okay," Jackson said, stepping off the boat to shake hands with Rend. "What brings you all the way out here?"

"I'm glad I made it before you left," he said, his eyes turning toward Aerden as he smiled. "I heard you guys were leaving, and I knew you wouldn't want to go without this."

Tears formed in my eyes as Rend pulled Aerden's axe from behind his back.

Not the axe I'd had made for him in the city, but his real axe. The one he'd had since he was a shadowling who could barely wield it with both hands.

Aerden stepped down from the ship, gratitude and reverence in his eyes as he wrapped his fingers around the hilt.

"Where—"

"Turns out the Brotherhood of Darkness had it this whole time," Rend said. "They must have gotten it from the Order. Don't ask me how, but the moment I saw it, I knew it belonged to you."

"Thank you," Aerden said, throwing an arm around Rend's shoulders. "I can never repay you for this."

"Me, either," Jackson said. "I was the one who lost that axe in the first place. When Aerden disappeared, I kept it with me all the time until the witches in Peachville took it from me. If we can ever repay you for this, you know we'll be there."

"I think we're about even now," Rend said. "After everything."

"I hear you've got a dagger now that is enchanted with a truth spell," I said.

"Well, that would have come in handy a few weeks ago," Harper mumbled.

"It belonged to Franki's father," Rend said, a sad smile on his lips. "That's a story for another time. When you come home, you'll all have to visit Venom. We'll share stories and have some drinks. I also have some maps you might be interested in. We'll talk about it soon."

Rend said goodbye, and the brothers moved back to the ship.

Harper and Jackson stepped around the corner to have a moment of privacy, and I found myself fidgeting there on the docks, wanting to give Aerden a proper goodbye, but not wanting to make promises I couldn't keep.

Not ready to give my heart when our future was still so uncertain.

He stepped toward me, putting one foot up on the edge of

the ship and shaking his head as he propped the axe next to a barrel.

"Having this back reminds me of all those days when we used to train together," he said, lifting his eyes to mine. "Sometimes I miss those days, when things were so much simpler, and we had so much time to just be together. There was so much laughter in those years."

"I miss them, too," I said, a bit breathless.

My heart raced, and those butterflies swirled in my stomach. He was leaving, and I wanted more.

Why was I so scared?

"But sometimes, in the most unexpected moments, I turn and catch the light in your eyes and I'm struck by the fact that the years and the struggle, the days when things haven't been so simple, have made you even more beautiful than I ever could have imagined back then."

I wanted to look away, but I couldn't. I wanted to run, scared to allow myself to have something I might not be able to keep forever.

I did not want to love and lose again.

"You're the strongest, bravest person I've ever known," he said, "and even though I loved you with my whole heart all those years ago, I love you even more for who you've become. I didn't want to leave today without telling you that."

My heart told me to jump on that ship and tell him I loved him, too, but my feet would not move.

"I'll miss you," I said, knowing I was stupid for not saying more. For not telling him.

He smiled and looked away, a touch of sadness on his face that seemed to squeeze my heart.

"I will miss you, too," he said.

Our eyes met again, one long moment between us. I couldn't breathe. This was my chance, and if he sailed away and disappeared inside that Storm, it might be my last.

But before I could find the courage, Jackson appeared, announcing that it was time to leave and slapping his brother on the back.

"Our first true adventure together," he said, eyes sparkling.

Aerden smiled and moved into action, getting things secured and making sure all the supplies were loaded.

Whatever moment we'd shared—whatever chance I'd had—was gone.

Harper gave Jackson one long kiss, and I looked away, feeling like a fool.

A few minutes later, the ship cast off, bound for a destination filled with mystery and danger.

And hopefully, if we were lucky, answers.

Harper looped her arm with mine and lay her head on my shoulder.

"Love is terrifying and beautiful, but it's always a gift," she said. "Don't wait too long to tell him how you feel."

I tensed and started to protest, but Harper looked up at me and smiled, one eyebrow raised.

I closed my mouth and sighed. "I won't," I said. "I just need more time."

"You deserve to be happy, Lea," she said. "And so does he."

With that, she actually leaned over and kissed my cheek.

I gasped and stepped back, but Harper just laughed as she ran back up the dock toward the shore. I chased after her, and she turned around, mischief in her eyes.

"Just think, maybe someday we'll be sisters," she said. "You can borrow my clothes, and I can do your hair. It'll be fun."

"I might have to kill you," I grumbled. "Just so you know."

Harper laughed and flew up toward the Black Cliffs, and when I joined her, she reached out and took my hand, a more serious look in her brown eyes.

"They will come home to us," she said. "I promise."

We stood there together, hands clasped, and watched the demons we loved sail into the unknown across the Sea of Glass.

And when the Wind Dancer had finally faded from sight, we said our goodbyes, and I flew toward home, alone, my heart heavy with the words I'd failed to say.

EPILOGUE

THE HIGH PRIESTESS

The ship sailed across the ocean as the two princesses watched from the cliffs above.

Neither of them noticed me here, barely more than fifty steps away, my body cloaked from sight with a spell so simple, it hardly took any power at all.

And those girls called themselves leaders.

Warriors.

They had no idea what they were doing, messing with me.

I did not do all this work and wait this long just to be defeated by children.

They believed they'd been through so much. Fought so hard.

They knew nothing.

Oh, how I would enjoy showing them what it meant to fight.

To truly struggle.

They had taken more from me than I ever should have allowed, but I would not make the same mistakes again.

I looked out as the ship sailed toward The Storm, the two demon brothers looking for answers to questions they would soon wish they'd never asked.

I had protected them for as long as I could.

Now, it was time for them to die.

With a nod of my head, I teleported to the onyx ritual room. There were preparations to be made, after all.

Those children thought they were nearing the end of the battle, but soon, they would learn the truth.

The real battle had only just begun.

***

The End.

To find out what happens next and be notified for the release date of Book 11: Vengeful Darkness, sign up for my newsletter or join my Facebook group!

ABOUT THE AUTHOR

Sarra Cannon is the author of several series featuring young adult and college-aged characters, including the bestselling Shadow Demons Saga. Her novels often stem from her own experiences growing up in the small town of Hawkinsville, Georgia, where she learned that being popular always comes at a price and relationships are rarely as simple as they seem.

Sarra recently celebrated seven years in indie publishing and has sold over half a million copies of her books. She currently lives in Charleston, South Carolina with her programmer husband and adorable redheaded son.

Love Sarra's books? Join Sarra's Mailing List to be notified of new releases and giveaways!

Also, please come hang out with me in my Facebook Fan Group: Sarra Cannon's Coven. We have a lot of fun in there, and I often share exclusive short stories and teasers in the group. Join now.

Want more? Get insider information on my writing process, inspiration, and what it's like to be an author with weekly videos on my YouTube channel.

Connect With Sarra Online:

www.sarracannon.com